GAMMA RIFT

KALLI LANFORD

Entangled Publishing, LLC
2614 South Timberline Road
Suite 109
Fort Collins, CO 80525
Visit our website at www.entangledpublishing.com.

Embrace is an imprint of Entangled Publishing, LLC.

Edited by Robin Haseltine
Cover design by Louisa Maggio
Cover art from Shutterstock

Manufactured in the United States of America

First Edition August 2015

embrace

For my amazing husband and wonderful son

Chapter One

"I still don't think this is a good idea," I shouted ahead of me. "Let's go back."

Logan pushed a tree limb away from his face, knocking it with the flashlight and missing when he tried to catch it with his free hand. "Damn. Watch out," he called. The branch sprang back toward Atlanta, and she pushed it behind her. Kevin cut in front of me, grabbed the limb, and held it aside as I slipped behind my friend.

Damn, he was hot, but…

"Where's your sense of adventure, America? You were once a Girl Scout," said Attie.

Yeah, I was. I didn't like camping when I was nine, and I didn't like it now. Spending spring break sleeping in a tent and cooking on a camp stove was not my idea of fun, but Atlanta, Logan, and I were paying our own way through college. Camping was cheaper than going to Cabo, where I really wanted to go.

Kevin had been invited so he and I could possibly hook up. This was the third time Attie "conveniently" planned something where he and I would be together. After the last date, when I'd told Attie he just didn't do it for me, she had said, "What the fuck? He's totally into you. Can't you tell? On top of that, he's nice and blazing hot."

At six-feet-two and with an incredible build, there was no mistake that Kevin was an athlete. He was tan, his features rugged—strong jaw, high cheekbones, a nose perfectly proportioned to his face. Sounds great, right? There was only one problem; when he spoke, well, let's just say he wasn't a man of many words unless he was talking about the latest UFO sighting. I'd tried changing the subject, talking about different things, but then he'd switch to astronomy. His major. And then back to the possibility life existed elsewhere. So not interested in little green men.

Keeping to the dirt trail, we worked our way through the darkness. Occasionally the hoot of an owl or the crunch of dried leaves jerked Atlanta and me to a halt, and Kevin couldn't help but step on my heels and fall against my back, since we were walking so close to each other.

Just as we started hiking for the third time, a strange hum resonated through the trees and the limbs shook, their whisper adding to a mechanical whine, making me stop again.

"Hey, what's that noise?" I asked. The flashlight's beam bobbed ahead of us, revealing absolutely nothing.

"I didn't hear anything," said Attie. "But whatever it was, I hope it wasn't a mountain lion. There was an attack up here last summer."

"It wasn't an animal," I protested. "It was like a hum, not a person humming, but like something mechanical, something with a motor. Not a car or a truck, but like machinery."

We stood still and the hum came again, a purr that licked the leaves with sound and left them rattling. My heartbeat rose to my throat, and I reached behind me and grabbed Kevin's hand.

"That is definitely not the wind," said Kevin.

"Have you heard anything like that out here before?" Attie whispered to Logan.

The hum softened, and the vibration that came with it petered to a whine that thinned and disappeared.

"Well, that was creepy," I said and released Kevin's hand.

"How much farther, Logan? Are you sure we're not lost?" asked Attie.

"No, we are definitely not lost." He laughed. "It's at the end of this trail. In fact, it's right there," he said, pointing.

"There" was a clearing, consisting of tree logs lying end-to-end on the ground, forming a square around the remnants of many campfires, a pile of ash, and blackened wood bits.

Kevin and Logan reentered the woods to get some wood, and Attie pulled me down to sit next to her on one of the logs.

"You can thank me again," she said, knocking her knee against mine.

"For what?"

"What do you mean for what? For inviting Kevin to come with us. Don't even tell me that you don't think he's hot, because I know your type, and he's definitely your type."

"He's hot, but we don't have anything in common."

That was the most important thing to me when it came to relationships.

"You should at least give him a chance this time. You're the only virgin I know. Just fuck him and get it over with. Then you'll finally know what you've been missing out on all these years."

"All these years? Only two or three if I started having sex at seventeen like you did." Not that I wasn't anxious to have sex, just not with Kevin.

A large glowing object, its perimeter rimmed with lights, cut across the patch of visible sky. A chill fingered up my back and settled in my shoulders, making me tremble harder than I was shaking from the cold.

"What?" asked Atlanta as she tugged on her laces.

"Didn't you see that?"

"See what?"

"This thing in the sky. It was bright and—"

"Yeah, it's called the moon." Attie flipped her hair, bringing the long strands over her shoulders.

"It wasn't the moon. It moved, and there were lights."

"It was probably just a shooting star."

"No way. It was too big to be a star," I said, rubbing my arms. What the hell was it? There was something ominous about its unnatural, pallid glow, and fluid movement past the stars. "And it couldn't have been an airplane. It was shaped like a triangle." I stood and examined the sky, but there was no trace of what I had seen. "You don't think Kevin's pulling some E.T. gag on us…"

A beam of light shot through the trees and I jumped, the sole of my left flip-flop landing on a huge pinecone. Rolling under my weight, the cone sent me to one knee, and I landed on the dirt, bracing myself with my palms.

"Sorry, we didn't mean to scare you," said Kevin as he and Logan returned to the clearing with bundles of sticks under their arms. Logan flicked off the flashlight, and they built the campfire and got it going.

As the flames rose, a deep hum expanded over our heads, the same whirl of sound we heard earlier, and the light of the moon was snuffed by something above, something we couldn't see.

"Where did the moon go?" asked Attie.

"It didn't go anywhere," said Kevin. "It's being blocked by something."

There was no wind, but the flames of our campfire became erratic, flicking right and left, rising and falling, its crackle resounding through the woods.

Without looking down, Logan fumbled for the flashlight at his feet, caught it in his hand, and flicked its switch. He guided the yellow beam upward slowly while I squinted up at the night sky, straining to see the dim outline of something huge, something with enough bulk to cover the moon and quench its glow.

My heart pounded in my throat as the flashlight's beam settled on something dark and slick with three sides and three points, an enormous triangle.

"Oh my God! What the hell is that?" screamed Attie.

I shuddered. "That's what I saw earlier, but it was…" At that moment, the triangle's perimeter ignited with a row of tiny lights, lights that elongated to meet the forest floor and cast the belly of the shape bright white.

"I've never seen anything like that before," said Kevin.

"Let's get out of here!" yelled Logan.

I ran through the woods with Kevin pulling me along, my arm practically coming out from its socket. Atlanta screamed behind me. Logan yelled at someone or something to leave us alone. The sole of my left flip-flop folded at the toes, bringing me down face-first onto the dirt trail. Everything happened so fast. I couldn't think straight.

Attie, Logan, and Kevin barreled ahead of me on the trail, their heads toward the sky, and probably hadn't realized I'd fallen.

Me, all alone. A blinding light. Then everything turned black.

Chapter Two

GARRAN

"I know why Professor Glitch didn't show up to your class today." My servant, Lestra, sat in the sitting cube next to me in my room and scooted closer. "He was asked to communicate with one of your father's captives. It's from Earth."

"What?" I choked back my excitement, leaning forward. "Are you sure? Is it a male or a female?"

The shell plates on Lestra's forehead overlapped tightly. "I'm not sure, but I think its name is girl."

"Girl is not its name. Girl means that it is a female. A young, female human."

It wasn't like my father, King Meallian, rarely ordered alien abductions. He did it all the time. In order to keep the title as the most powerful beings in the Millennius, as my dad liked to put it, we had to explore not only our universe, but the three alien universes on our border, snatching living samples to study and prove that we, the Enestians, were indeed the most advanced life-forms in existence.

But taking a human from Earth was different.

Last year, when I began studying Earth customs and culture, I'd told Lestra I'd like to see a human in real life. But not like this, with it locked inside one of our labs, the subject of study, experimentation, and maybe worse…

Abductions had to stop. Once I became king, I'd make sure it never happened again.

It took me two years just to master course one of the English language, demonstrating their intellectual complexity. Many humans practiced the art of war and torture and abuse, but I also knew that the overwhelming majority of humans were passive and non-violent. Six months ago, I began studying British literature with its themes of love, passion, and respect, and I've spent the last year watching "American television" with its past and present programs.

"Do you know where it is?" I whispered. My father liked to keep his research a secret, even from his royal family. There was no point in asking *him* about his latest abductee.

"And whatever you do, don't tell my sister about the human," I said under my breath.

"I still don't understand why you want to see one so badly," Lestra announced, her eye sockets dilating. "They are hideous, barbaric creatures. I've seen the images."

Lestra pulled a ripe quip from a pouch on her tunic, something I'm sure she was saving for a mid-morning snack between chores. "Their faces are dimpled and squishy," she said, as she unwrapped the quip and displayed the crimson fruit in her opened palm, "like this." With a slight squeeze, the quip's casing erupted between her fingers. A trail of quip juice made its way from her wrist to her elbow, staining her shell. "And stuff grows from the top of their heads."

Lestra shuddered and rewrapped it in its protective package before returning the quip to her pocket.

"That stuff is called hair."

"It's disgusting."

I'd thought Lestra would understand. She was intelligent. I called up an image on my virtual generator, but she recoiled. "They're really not much different from us. Having two arms and two legs, and walking bipedally with an erect body carriage, their overall body figure is practically identical to ours."

"Except they're lumpy."

She was right about that. The Enestian silhouettes certainly were a thing of beauty with our smooth exteriors and overlapping shell plates. Human joints were knobby, and their exposed muscles and ligaments left their protective covering, which they called "skin," full of bumps and indentations.

Still, I had to see this girl. Not that I could help her, since my father had the ultimate authority until the day he died, but I could at least make her captivity easier. I just had to find her without being caught and punished.

As I was about to press Lestra for more information on the human's whereabouts, my door slid open.

"What do you want?" I shouted.

Chapter Three

AMERICA

Bare-ass naked, and with both hands flat against the smooth, cold walls, I managed to rise to my knees. "Attie?" I whispered across the dimly lit room.

No answer.

"Logan? Kevin? Is this some sort of stupid alien joke?"

No answer.

"Hello? Can anyone hear me?"

Still no answer.

Where was I? Where the hell were my clothes? My stomach turned. My head spun, and for a moment, I thought the beer I drank earlier would end up on the floor.

Three metal walls—the fourth wall being semi-clear— held me prisoner. The fourth wall's opaque, Zen-like quality enticed me to part its seemingly benign, milky curtain and make an escape, but my gut told me to do so would be lethal. Like liquid glass, the wall rippled to the floor, kicked into reverse, and undulated back toward the ceiling to hit and make another descent. This didn't seem like anything Kevin, or anyone else I knew, could have constructed. Then who did?

"Is anyone there?" I said, swallowing hard and licking my dry lips. My question was returned with an echo, my own words filling what must have been a dark, empty hall beyond the confines of this room. A chill lurched up my back. I hugged myself and shuddered, rubbing my cold arms.

As if alive, the wall continued its wave-like flow, and I yelled a little louder this time, "Is anyone there?" and held out my trembling hand, daring to touch it. An eerie reverberation of my words bounded through the room, and I jerked my hand away and leaned backward to dodge their muffled, unnatural echo.

Holding my forearm against my bare breasts, I set one foot firmly on the metallic floor. The muscles in my thigh contracted as I rose, but my foot, numb and beginning to tingle, buckled at the ankle, and I fell backward onto my rear.

"What's wrong with me? Please, someone tell me?" I shouted as I shook irrepressibly, and a fearful uncertainty filled my entire being.

After scooting to the corner of the room and pulling my knees into my chest, I sat in a little naked ball and screamed for help, hugging my shins, noticing for the first time that my ring was missing along with my watch, earrings, bracelets, and necklace — not that they were worth much — but still.

"What is this place? Give me back my clothes," I demanded, giving the wall to my right three hard smacks with the side of my hand. The loud thumps I expected to hear instantly dissolved into muffled twangs, weak and non-threatening, as if the wall, like a sponge, absorbed each sound wave, dispersing them through its interior where they dwindled and died, unheard and undetected.

The ceiling of this small room was one cloudy panel of dim light. There was no smell, but taking a deep breath filled my lungs with air that seemed foreign, thin, and artificial. Both of my feet continued to tingle, the sensation deep in my toes, but the numbness finally dissipated enough for me to try to stand again, and this time, I was steady enough to hobble to the far wall.

A nudist I wasn't, so baring all my parts, even in an empty room, was extremely uncomfortable, more so than walking on feet that felt like they were being pricked by a thousand pins. I kept one arm over my chest and covered my lower half with my other wrist and forearm.

"Stop screwing with me, and let me out of here."

Again no response, which creeped me out. The hairs on the back of my neck rose, and I took a deep breath, trying to calm myself.

The metallic walls were as naked as me and seemed solid and nonporous, void of any visible camera lenses or microphones. But even if the front wall hadn't been constructed from some sort of flowing, dense liquid, I felt like I was being watched.

Etched on the floor, three feet from the far wall, was a small circle. I touched its center with my big toe. Two rectangular sections of the seemingly seamless wall slowly and noiselessly extended in my direction, producing two thick slabs of metal beveled with empty, sink-like basins, the upper slab being waist height, the lower, knee height. Yes—a toilet and a sink.

The streamline sink and toilet disappeared into the wall when I was finished but not before I contemplated whether or not to drink the water from the self-filling and hopefully self-sanitizing sink with its burst of steam, and with what I hoped was hand soap.

The water was clear and odorless, something my dry mouth and cracked lips craved, but I didn't risk it. Instead, I paced the remainder of the room, looking for another symbol on the floor that, when triggered, would reveal something, like maybe a water fountain. I found one and touched it.

A dime-sized etching in the shape of a water drop resulted in the extension of another panel, one with a rainbow stream of water that jetted in an arc from a clear tube, landed in a small pool, and drained.

It was clear, odorless, and cool. After letting it puddle in the cup of my hand and giving it a full inspection, I set my lips against the sweep of water and took a long drink. Okay, so at least my captors didn't want me to die of thirst, whoever they were.

Within minutes, the sweet water renewed my spirit and my limbs, each leg slowly recovering from its unexplained weakness and eerie tingle. I stretched, slapped one palm against the wall, and stamped my right foot on the floor as its recoil vibrated through my body.

Had I fallen into some super-secret government site where they did experiments and tests, like before they sent astronauts to the moon? But I didn't think even NASA had the technology to pull something like this off.

And what would they want with me? I was a business

major from San Diego State on scholarship and loans. I had a life, a future I wanted to get back to as soon as possible.

Sniffling and watching the lucid wall trickle, I shouted, "Where am I? Why am I here? How did I get here? Please, someone tell me. Help me, please!"

My mind was sludge. I couldn't remember losing my clothes, when I'd gotten locked in the room, where I'd come from, or how long I'd been here. And then the memory as cold and surreal as this room twisted in my mind, and I remembered.

Maybe I was dreaming? Maybe when we were camping, I'd fallen and hit my head. No, this couldn't be a dream. The stiffness and tingly sensation in my legs were as real as this weird metal floor.

And I knew, with certainty, I'd left Earth far behind.

Today had to be Sunday, I think. Attie, Logan, and Kevin must have returned to our camp at one thirty or two in the morning without me and with a story that would be hard for anyone to believe.

Did people believe them, or did everyone think they went psycho? I was sure they were questioned, dragged one at a time to the police station and into an interrogation room. And what if they blamed the guys for my disappearance, accusing them of raping and killing me and dumping my body in the lake? What if they thought Attie had something to do with my disappearance, too?

My mom? What would she believe when she found out?

My heartbeat rose into my throat, my breathing quickened, and the remaining prickles in my lower legs became a throb of uncomfortable heat.

What if Attie, Logan, and Kevin never returned at all?

Maybe they were here, wherever here was, and somewhere in a room down the hall.

I rose from the corner and took small steps toward the front wall, planting each foot carefully to compensate for its hot numbness. Getting as close as I could without touching the liquid, I screamed, "Attie, are you there? Logan! Kevin! Can you hear me?" My words bounced from the wall, reverberating across my tiny room, as if the wall was made from a misty mat of thick rubber.

Fuck! If I could only touch it, break its seal, and make a run for it. But to where? I didn't know. I just wanted out of there, and as my blood pressure rose and tears threatened to re-spill, I was ready to try and give the wall a test.

My nails reached just past the tips of my fingers. With my teeth, I tore at my thumb, accidentally cutting too close and making my thumb sting, but I had a sliver of nail big enough to throw.

Flying through the air with an over-hand toss, the nail clipping hit the liquid as the wave of its thick paste undulated toward the floor.

It sizzled as a flame plumed from its contact point, obliterating it into a peppering of ash and a spiral of smelly smoke, the first real odor to hit my nostrils since my arrival. Good thing I didn't try touching it with my finger.

A pencil-sized vent opened in the ceiling above the fourth wall, and with a hum, the curl of smoke, along with its smell, disappeared. As the vent closed, leaving the gray ceiling as smooth as before, I hoped that maybe my action would trigger the appearance of my captors.

Watching the dense wall trickle toward the floor, I screamed, "I want out of here! Now! Please! Someone help me!" I stamped my numb feet and sniffled back my tears. "Let me go. You can't keep me here. You can't do this to me. I want to talk to whoever's in charge. Show yourself."

As I balled my hands into fists and tightened my jaw, the hall on the other side of the liquid curtain exploded with light.

Chapter Four

"You need to delete that image. It's hideous," declared Murelle with a clack of her bare feet against the stone floor of my sleeping quarters, and a sneer toward Lestra.

Despite being one and a half years my junior, and of lesser royal stature, my sister continued to override my security settings and enter my room whenever she wanted. She waved one of her powdered arms, stopping to admire the soft, pink film of talcum, sparking red from the glow of the sun coming through the window.

Instead of using our planet's customary muted colors of gold, beige, or peach, she chose to bedeck herself with a trendy collection of pink and purple shell powders and insisted on increasing their color's intensity by adding multiple layers. I've told her over one thousand times that she overdoes it with the shell makeup. "Guys think a little natural shell is sexy," I had tried to explain to her, but she never listened. If my sister wanted to look cheap, that was her problem. Lestra wasn't allowed to wear shell dust or embellished apparel while on duty. But even with her dull exterior, white tunic, and beige leggings, I thought she was pretty.

"And you need my permission to enter my room. We're not children anymore," I rebuked, watching the life-size image of a male human flicker. Instead of telling her about the human our father held in the lab, I relaxed so she wouldn't suspect anything and said, "I got tired of speaking to that generic language simulator, so I transferred its language program to this image I found in our data banks." I tapped the generator, and the backdrop of what our archives referred to as a "typical human sitting room" materialized behind it. "Watch. 'Hello, how are you?'"

"I'm fine. How are you," the image said in a monotone and non-distinct voice.

"And what's that thing?" She pointed to the wooden object next to it.

"It's a chair," I told her.

"A chair? I'd crack my ass on that thing."

"Yeah, you would." I laughed, knowing that every time my sister was pissed, which was quite often, she'd sigh and drop down hard into the closest sitting cube.

In contrast to the soft, thickly padded, and practical furniture of our planet, humans actually sat on highly ornate furniture made from wood, stone, and even metal; materials used for minimal shell contact here, such as walls and floors.

"And it's so cluttered and messy," she added, pointing to a set of floor-length curtains and scowling at the repeated design on the wall.

Like the exterior, the interior of our homes was as smooth and refined as our shells. Panels lowered to cover windows, and the last thing anyone would do is distract from the gentle arches and curves of our high ceilings by covering our walls with decorated paper.

Murelle's face plates dropped. "You could at least put him in a tunic and leggings."

The human image wore the only thing in our data banks that resembled male, human attire—a black, two-piece suit worn by the Scolls, a race of thin-shelled beings two galaxies away. It was a stretch, but it worked for me. I honestly didn't care what the thing wore. Why would I?

"How's this?" I smirked, manipulating the virtual generator's controls. Before Murelle could blink her eyes, the black suit was gone, leaving the male completely naked and oblivious to its indisposed condition. I flipped through the virtual closet flickering before me, searching for a black tunic, thick leggings, and dark shoes.

"Their dicks don't tuck away? They just hang there like that?" The shell around Murelle's mouth turned down at the corners like she had just bitten into an unripe quip.

I hadn't expected her to stand there asking questions, especially questions like those. My goal was to get her to run from my room. The last thing I wanted to do was talk about male genitals with my sister. "Yup, just like that," I said like it was no big deal, which it wasn't—at least not to me.

"It sure is a puny little thing. It looks pretty useless."

"Murelle, I can't believe you just said that. I don't want to hear that shit!" A tap on the controls restored the human's dignity.

"That's much better. Keep it clothed at all times, so it

doesn't offend anybody."

"Why don't you stop barging into my room unannounced and without my permission? Then you won't have to worry about being offended." If only her shell scan couldn't unlock my room.

"Fine," she huffed.

As Murelle left my quarters, she gave the virtual human a kick, slicing through his calf with her foot before going out the door. The man's leg flickered wildly for several seconds before the generator's wavelengths settled back into place, restoring his virtual appendage.

Finally! "Do you have more information on the human?" I asked Lestra, leaning forward.

"Kind of. You'll see," she said, pulling a small tin of shell powder from her pocket.

She pushed her left tunic sleeve up her arm, slid the lid away from the powder box, and gave the puff a generous dip, causing a small glistening cloud to emerge from the container's lip.

"I don't understand how this—"

"Watch and you'll see." Lestra turned her dull inner forearm toward me and gave it a liberal brushing back and forth with the puff, the sweet smell of powder filling my room. Her ashen shell instantly glowed a soft beige. After an additional rub, something else appeared as the powder settled: first a five, a two and then a *U*, nine, three, *Y*, eight, *K*, seven, six, six, four, nine, five, five in that order.

"What in the galaxy is that?" I gasped.

"The code to give you access to the lab and the lab's medical files."

"You damaged your shell? How could you...?" I asked,

still stunned.

"Because my brother, Slaine, is one of the interior guards. He's been assigned to the lab, cellblock three."

"What? That's impossible." The Timuarys were servants and facility and maintenance personnel; they'd never held positions of palace security or planet and inter-planet defense.

Lestra's shoulders dropped.

"I mean, not that your family isn't qualified for those stations," I lied, "it's just that it's not part of our palace tradition."

"He's newly appointed last week—by your father," she said firmly. "You're right. The Timuarys are hard working, but passive. We, too, were surprised but honored by the king's request."

Maybe Slaine was selected because he is taller and broader than the average Timuary male—taller and even more broad shouldered than me—which resulted in two rumors among the royals: he was either the result of a Timuary affair, or he practiced a banned ritual called "forced augmentation," the act of ingesting an illegal substance that keeps the shell from hardening at the end of puberty, thus extending the Enestian growth period.

"Slaine gave me a tour of the cellblocks. But he didn't break any rules," she was quick to add. "He had permission to show them to me."

"Did you see the human?"

"No, but I saw every cell except for the last cell in block three, cell fifteen. Slaine said it was empty and being upgraded. But I know when my brother's lying." Her eye plates widened. "The human has to be in cell fifteen."

"How did you get the code? Did your brother give it to you?"

"Of course not! He'd never go against orders. I used my heritage badge. Secretly etched it while Slaine entered it into the console."

She ran her fingers over her inner arm, and I grabbed her wrist. "You didn't have to do this to yourself."

"Yes, I did. Visitors aren't allowed to bring communication devices into the lab, and I was afraid I wouldn't be able to memorize it," she huffed, poising her hands on her hips. "You couldn't ask your father for access to cell fifteen. Think about it. For some reason, this abduction is different from all the others. Your father assigned a Timuary to guard it, someone he can trust, someone who will keep a secret. Getting the code was the only way."

The bronze finish on the left edge of Lestra's heritage badge was rubbed away, revealing the shinier metal underneath, and some of the metal itself was worn so it was no longer horizontally symmetrical.

"I'm not worried about my badge. It can easily be repaired."

That was true. Heritage badges displayed reputations and wealth with their symbols and intricate designs and were traditionally re-gifted, handed down from one generation to the next. Lestra's badge probably came from a great, great, great, great-grandmother as did mine from a great, great, great, great-grandfather.

But we cannot live without our shells. If Lestra were caught with this intentional self-violation, she would be reprimanded and removed from duty, becoming the first blemish on the Timuary family's reputation.

"I didn't expect you to harm yourself. The integrity of your shell's been compromised. What if someone sees what you've done?"

"I did what I had to do in order to help you. I'm not worried about my shell. If it cracks, it cracks. I'll get it repaired," she said without regret. "As for the code, I'll keep it hidden."

"I appreciate what you did, but still…"

She looked up at me, blinking ashamedly.

"I have a bit of shell paper," I said, hoping my offer would ease my guilt.

"You do?" Lestra's eyes gleamed. "How? It was banned before we were even born."

"I'm a royal."

Each of my family members had a piece, all preserved by a vain and greedy great aunt. I had no need for shell paper. Most males, even those in the royal class, revered our shell's unrefined surface, but I'm sure my mother and Murelle, on the other hand, used theirs profusely, so far without any consequences.

At one time, we used it to buff away the top layer of shell and make our porous shell plates as smooth as glass. It was a short-lived trend. Cases of shell crack quadrupled before its inevitable prohibition.

"Before you leave, I'll memorize the code, then make it disappear."

"Thank you." She gave me a nod and scraped her hand along the inside of her forearm just above the communication cuff at her wrist. Our eyes met, and she smiled. Not her usual friendly smile, but a sexy kind of seductive smile that made me feel uncomfortable. What was up with that?

"Um, let's check the lab's files," I said, taking a step away from her when I stood.

We positioned ourselves at my desk below my virtual monitor, sitting side by side, though I was careful not to let any part of my body touch hers. Lestra displayed her graffitied arm, and I relayed and memorized the precious sequence of numbers and letters that would hopefully give us access to something involving cell fifteen.

"There it is. The file for cell fifteen," said Lestra, pointing to the screen and leaning closer to me.

"Okay, let's open it."

Lestra recoiled. "Is that thing the alien?"

There it was, the human female, its image from the top of its head to the tops of its shoulders engulfing half the screen. The image was probably captured at its arrival when it was lying down, still unconscious, and its vitals and statistics were taken. The lips were turned downward, and its outer covering called "skin," though darker in color than my own off-white shell, appeared paler than that of any human I'd seen in pictures.

"It's so soft and weak," said Lestra.

"To us, but not to them. Human males admire the soft female form. I've read about it in their literature and poetry. According to this, it's fifty-six dimits tall, making her shorter than me. About your height."

"What's that stuff on the head called again?"

"Hair."

Its face was free of it with the exception of two thin, arched strips of the stuff, one above each closed eye, and a row of short, curved hairs along the edge of the skin that is used to cover each eye when the human blinked or slept. Its head was covered with a thick mass of brown hair that hung below its shoulders, reminding me of the mane on a Verilian horse.

"Hair can't be sanitary. I bet it's full of germs," she added.

"Hair is not a carrier of disease. Besides, humans bathe and wash their hair regularly. I think it's pretty, in a strange way. It looks soft to the touch," I said.

Lestra shuddered. "It looks coarse to me. I can't believe you find anything about that alien pretty." Her sitting cube rocked as her body stiffened.

But it was pretty, like I said, even if it was in a strange sort of way, and I wondered if it was now conscious in its cell. Was it scared and confused, its thoughts shifting from one unanswered question to the next, its eyes flickering with pain and agony like the Riften Vole my father keeps in a glass case next to his throne?

Like Lestra said, it did look soft and squishy, but at the same time, it held its shape, meaning that its skin was firm and robust, not as delicate as it appeared. With lips as plump and red as a fresh quip and a nose of flesh that angled symmetrically from its face, I found it not only attractive, but it filled me with wonder, something I now knew I shouldn't directly share with Lestra—especially with the weird way she'd been acting lately.

I skipped back to its file. "Its name is America Novoa, age twenty, meaning it has seen the turn of twenty Earth years, years which are a bit shorter than ours." She was only a year or so younger than me.

I tapped the screen. There were no medical records, only the preliminary information that was gathered during and immediately after the abduction, which took place two days ago from Galaxy One, Sector One, coordinates 32.48

degrees north, 116.26 degrees west.

"An order's been sent to have one of the operating rooms prepped for a pre-mortem analysis," I said with a firm jaw. "That can only mean one thing— My father plans to subject the human to his experiments."

Lestra stood and skimmed her puff up one arm and down the other, then ran it across her neck. "No kidding. He does that to all of his captives."

"I was hoping he'd treat a human differently." My face plates tightened, and I rose to face her. "His tests are cruel and unnecessary."

"So? Why do you care?" Lestra tilted her head, crossed her powdered arms, and walked toward me, breaking my comfort zone.

It wasn't that I was specifically concerned for that partic- ular specimen. But it was a human, a race of beings I'd been studying for years and had grown a slight affection toward.

"You don't actually have feelings for that thing, do you?" she continued, blinking twice and sticking out her chest until her breasts were directly under my nose—and my eyes.

"Of course not," I stated, taking a step backward as a flash of glistening shell powder brought my eyes to the inch of cleavage showing above the collar of Lestra's tunic. "I know nothing of this girl, but like I said, it's an intelligent life form," I stuttered. "I-it shouldn't be treated like the infe- rior beings my father's team abducts for research purposes."

"But it is inferior," snapped Lestra.

She was wrong, but frankly, I was almost powerless, and there was nothing I could do. The female creature would eventually suffer and die under the hands of my father and his team. Still, there was something indefinable about the human, and I had to see it.

Lestra grazed the tips of her fingers across my forearm, continuing to break the spatial barrier between friends. The golden flecks in her eyes danced.

I yanked away. "Lestra! What's wrong with you? You shouldn't be touching me like that, and you shouldn't be standing this close to me. I'm a royal, and you are my servant."

"I'm sorry," she said, shuffling backward. "I never get to wear shell powder. I just wanted you to see it." Lestra rubbed her arms against her leggings, trying to remove the golden dust that so many Enestian girls pathetically obsessed over.

"I already see plenty of shell powder. I don't need to see it on you." Lestra dropped her head. "Besides, you don't need to wear shell powder to look good."

"Really, so you think I look—good?"

"Yes, you're fine the way you are."

Her smile intensified. She took a step closer with her head lowered, smiling up at me, her eyes unblinking, and I quickly moved away to flick off the monitor.

"I'm, I'm ready to see the human," I announced, changing the subject. "Come with me. I'm going to need your help."

Chapter Five

"Is someone there?" I whispered.

The light behind the undulating door dimmed, and a blurred image of a figure appeared through the opaque curtain, a tall figure standing upright on long legs and with arms hanging at its sides. It appeared human-like, but its shoulders were extremely broad, its waist small, and its legs and arms thick like a football player in uniform.

"Human?" asked a muffled voice.

Human? Did it mean me? "Um, yes?" I answered softly, trying to keep my voice level low and pleasant, so maybe it would be sympathetic and help me. My words bounced back in my direction, making me flinch. Please, someone be here to help me and answer my questions. Please.

"Come closer to the wall but do not touch it," the voice warned in a deep, distinctly male tone that was oddly soothing rather than threatening.

Though I was certain whoever it was also saw me in the same fuzzy fashion, I kept my private areas covered with my arms and hands, remained seated, and scooted forward as close as I could without hitting my body against the moving goo.

The strange silhouette lowered to sit on the ground, and while I sat sideways to shield as much of my nakedness as possible, the gray blur faced me and sat with bent knees. Squinting didn't make the image any clearer, and after several seconds of staring at the flowing wave of wall, I blinked hard, releasing a tear.

I needed answers. The confusion and ache of not knowing what was going to happen to me bit at my soul, sending the gnawing pain of hunger residing in my gut throughout my entire body.

"Please, please, tell me. Where am I?" I begged, catching my trembling bottom lip with my teeth and swallowing a rising lump in my throat. *Stay calm,* I warned myself. *Don't make it mad.*

"Enestia."

"What's En…Enestia?"

"A planet three galaxies away from Earth."

The lump returned to my throat, and I shuddered and inched away from the liquid curtain. The woods, the ominous triangle in the sky, the perimeter of tiny lights— Those images were clear. But now others came as I closed my eyes, distorted and indistinct, flashes of lost memories twisting in my mind—a beam of light, a bright room, a metal table, and foreign voices shouting above me.

"So you're an—?" I stopped myself before saying any

more. I didn't want to offend it.

Don't be true. Don't be true, I repeated over and over again in my head as my heartbeat became palpable. But when I opened my eyes, I was still in the dank, gray cell, and the strange being was there. The cold reality of my situation sent my body into an uncontrollable quiver.

"I am an Enestian, a male Enestian," it said.

So it was true. It was an alien, and I was on its planet.

My shoulders bounced in rhythm as I shook and began to sob, muffled cries against my knees that echoed through my cell, pinging from wall to wall. The being leaned closer to the undulating curtain and tilted its head.

So far away from home. No one knew where I was, and there was no technology on Earth that could save me even if someone did. I grew sick, as if every atom in my body swirled with the same fear and uncertainty that wracked my brain.

"America Novoa," he said. "Please do not be afraid of me."

Shouting like a banshee and running around my cell while banging on the walls wouldn't help my situation. If I was going to win my freedom, I needed this person on my side. I swallowed my tears and took a deep breath.

Strangely, I wasn't afraid of him. Somehow I knew he wasn't there to hurt me. Maybe it was the soft, controlled tone of his voice. Maybe it was his twinge of an accent I couldn't identify, an intonation that was soothing instead of jarring. Or maybe it was the way he dropped his head and shoulders when he knew I was crying. I wasn't fearful of him. I was afraid of my predicament.

"How do you know my name?" I asked, tightening my arms around my legs.

"It was in your intake file." My driver's license was in my back pocket, along with my cell phone.

Intake file? That sounded ominous. "Let me go. Please, take me home," I pleaded, wiping the tears from my cheeks and pushing myself so close to the liquid wall I almost touched it with my elbow. The beat of my heart grew stronger, its pulse forcing my throat to tighten.

"I'm sorry, but that decision is not for me to make."

The urge to scream and demand he release me and send me home boiled in my soul, but the being's genuinely sympathetic tone and calm demeanor muted my rage. And if I started screeching, maybe he would leave, and I'd never have an ally.

I swallowed a wail and asked as calmly as I could, "Then whose decision is it?"

"The king of this planet."

"Then I need to see him right now," I pleaded, my voice cracking as I tried to hold back a set of new tears.

"I'm sorry, but that is not possible."

"Then why are you here if it's not to let me go?"

"I wanted to see you, talk to you." He lifted his arm and set it across his knees.

"Why?"

"I understand things about humans that others don't. There are only two Enestians besides me who speak your native tongue. The second is my language professor and the third is my sister. I'm in my fourth year of what's equivalent to attending a university in the United States, and during that time, I've also studied your culture and your literature," he said with sincerity, speaking English so elegantly without a flub.

"Please tell the king to let me go and send me home."

"I'm sorry, but the king does not know that I'm here. I'm not supposed to know about you. If I'm caught, I will be reprimanded." His head shook from side to side, and I yearned to see him, to look deep into his eyes for the hint of sympathy that matched his words.

"Then at least tell me why I'm here. What's going to happen to me?" I begged.

"The king has an…" He paused like he was trying to find the right word. "…an unusual desire to study the unknown, and the unknown includes alien life forms. You are currently under quarantine and observation, and then you will be studied." His voice cracked, and he turned away.

"So I'm being watched?"

"Yes, the guard of this cellblock is required to periodically view all alien captives directly from his station or come to your cell as I have."

I knew they were watching me like I was some sort of caged animal. I could feel it, sense it. My control shattered. "But I'm not the alien. You are, and I can tell you right now that if an alien was on my planet, we wouldn't be treating it like this!" I shouted, pointing my finger toward the shadow of what I guessed was the alien's chest.

"Are you so sure about that?" The being tilted his head in the other direction, and the rumors of Area 51, the mystery and the myth, lurched in my mind as I imagined a flying saucer crashing on Earth and its dead alien occupants being examined and autopsied by the federal government.

With this eerie, eye-opening thought, coupled with the calm manner of the being sitting on the other side of the wall, my voice dropped to a high whisper. "But humans don't go to other planets and steal their citizens against their will," I said, trying to sound as composed and confident as I could.

"That's because Earth is an underdeveloped planet. You lack the technology. If your inferior ships could voyage beyond your tiny galaxy, your people would do the same as us."

The alien's arrogant tone was enough to stoke my anger.

"No, we wouldn't," I said, holding my rage. "I don't believe that. But even if we could and did, we would treat the aliens humanely and with respect, and we would eventually return them to their planets unharmed!"

The being moved closer and spoke coolly with an assertive flare, his shadow slightly elongating. "I don't agree with what the king is doing to you. Like I said, I have a deep respect for humans."

"He's going to send me home, right? When, when he's done"—I licked my dry lips and swallowed hard—"done observing and studying me."

The alien shook his head. "That is information I do not have."

The reality of my abduction and captivity sank deep into my soul. My pulse raced in my ears and the room spun, its walls a slur of gray as ambiguous as the alien blur on the other side of the wall.

My mom— Would I ever see her again? And what about…?

"Are there others here like me? I was with three other people when I was taken."

"No, you are the only human here. You were the only one taken." Attie, Logan, and Kevin were safe on Earth, which was good, but they would be held responsible for my disappearance. No one would believe them… Would they go to prison? How could I stop that from happening?

"But nobody knows where I am—my friends, my family. They might think I'm dead. Can I at least contact someone? Let them know I'm alive?"

The creature shook his head and dropped his chin to rest on his knee. My head spun again, and as I waited for the room to steady itself, I leaned forward against my bent legs to ease my lightheadedness.

"Are you okay?" the alien asked.

"No, I'm not okay. I want to go home," I cried, my face buried against my knees. "Please, let me go. Open my cell before you leave, and I'll sneak away on my own. No one will know you helped me."

But where would I go, naked and alone on another planet? I didn't know. But anywhere was better than here, and if and when I actually came face-to-face with my captors, I'd ask to see the king and demand he send me back to Earth.

"That is something I cannot do. It requires a code and a shell scan."

Shell scan? What the heck was he talking about? He must have meant some kind of card or I.D. What were these aliens, these things that steal people from their planets?

I was so out of place, so far away from my world, my mind teetered as did my body, and I swayed, lost and disorientated.

Everything became hot—my face, my feet, my hands. The room tilted and swirled once again, and as I focused on the wall across from me, my head rocked forward, my body slumped, and I collapsed against the icy floor.

Chapter Six

"America. Can you hear me?"

Her frail body remained limp, a blurry lump of soft, human flesh. One leg finally moved and then the other. With her palms pressed against the cell floor, she pushed herself back into a sitting position, her head lolling to one side.

"Are you okay?" I asked, wishing I had the eyes of a Roccen fowl, so my vision could penetrate the flowing layers of the isolation wall. There was something about her distress that moved me, and I wished there was some way I could ease her pain.

"Yeah, I'm just overwhelmed. All of this is just so hard to believe. I don't know what to think, what to do, I... Do you know how long I've been here?" Her hand went to her forehead, and a shadowy wave of hair fell across her shoulders.

"I believe it's been two days."

The girl brought her arms above her head in a stretch. As a shadowy, smooth figure, she could almost be mistaken for an Enestian female, but I knew it was an illusion. Her elbows and knees were pointy and crooked with protruding bones and joints, and the oval shape and soft curve of her face was produced by skin stretched to conform to the hard skull and mandible underneath.

Despite these flaws, her movements were controlled and graceful, and when she flipped her hair off her shoulder and inhaled, I leaned closer, hoping to catch a glitch in the isolation wall, so I could see her face.

Less than two feet away, a real human sat before me. The two dimensional figures I viewed in their recorded images did not satisfy my curiosity. I had to see it. Maybe even touch it.

What were my father's plans for this human? Pain tolerance tests? Disembowelment? Limb amputation? A live dissection? Those were just a few of the king's favorite pastimes.

As I spoke to this girl and eyed her soft silhouette, my gut started to wrench at the thought of anything bad happening to the innocent human female before I had a chance to study it face-to-face.

She let out a tiny exhale, a sweet sound like the soft sigh of a songflower unfurling its petals, and my sympathy for her predicament doubled.

"I am sorry. You shouldn't be here. You should be on Earth with your family, your husband and children," I said, though I was selfishly enthusiastic about her arrival.

"Husband?" She laughed. "I'm not married, and I don't have any kids, and I don't plan to for a long time. My mom—

She's the only family I have now that my grandparents have passed on. I mean, I have cousins and aunts scattered across the U.S., but I rarely see them."

"What about your father?" I asked, knowing the human family structure is almost identical to that of Enestians, and wanted that fact verified.

"He died two years after my parents divorced." America drew her knees toward her chest in a hug, her soft body conforming to the shape of her thighs. "I was a baby when they separated, so I never really knew him. I've seen pictures of him, though."

"And twenty Earth years have turned since your birth?"

"Yeah, I'm twenty, and I want to see twenty-one and many, many more after that. Please. Help me get back to Earth." Her voice dropped to a soft sob, and I imagined tears running over soft human skin, something I'd seen in many Earth movies.

"The king should not be doing this to you. It is wrong that he's keeping you here." I wrapped my arms around my bent legs and squeezed so hard that I was surprised I didn't crack shell.

"Then help me get home." She spoke so softly I could barely hear her.

In a way, I wanted to help her, and knowing my father, her suffering would eventually end in a slow death. But there was nothing I could do.

"Maybe you can if you find a way to unseal this cell," she added.

Maybe, but then what? Keep her hidden somewhere in the palace so I could periodically interact with her and gain a first-hand experience when it came to studying such an intriguing race? That would be an impossible feat, and I'd eventually have to turn her over to my father or take her back to Earth—another impossibility, considering my lack of resources and the fact that it would be considered an act of rebellion against the throne. My title as prince could only take me so far, and it wasn't something I'd jeopardize for any alien—even a human.

"I don't think I can."

"Please, promise me you'll at least try." She brought her hand to her head and pushed a sweep of hair over her shoulder.

Her desperation surprisingly wracked my heart. "Like I told you before, that's not possible. I'm taking a risk just being in this cellblock. The king cannot know I was here."

"Garran!" Lestra's voice rang through the hall in a loud whisper. "Slaine's returning to his station. We have to go now before he checks the monitors. Hurry! We don't have a lot of time."

"I'm sorry, but I need to leave—now," I said to America, looking from side to side and standing abruptly.

"No, please don't go. I-it's so lonely in here. I'm cold, and I'm scared."

"I'd stay longer if I could, but I can't. If anyone finds out I was here, I'll never be able to come back."

"So you're coming back?" She stood and faced me, the refined, shadowy curves of her body rippling behind the pulsing wall.

One interaction had not been enough to quell my interest. And there was something more about her that intrigued me. I needed to see this female again to find out what it was. "Yes, I'll try to return tomorrow."

"Garran! Hurry," urged Lestra from beyond the hall. "Or we'll get caught."

"Wait," said America. "I don't know your name."

"It's Garran," I told her before I could stop myself. Damn! What if she accidentally said it in front of someone other than Lestra or me?

She repeated my name, but thankfully her human accent and lack of clicks made it undistinguishable.

"Yes, call me Garran," I said, using her pronunciation, and after a last glance at America from over my shoulder, I jogged down the hall to meet Lestra, my footsteps echoing, hoping I had one more chance to speak with America before my father started his experiments.

Chapter Seven

AMERICA

An explosion of white light obliterated my sight. "I can't see. Where am I?" And how in the world did I get here, out of my room, if I was, in fact, no longer in my cell? My hands grasped the cold edges of the table as I lay flat on my back unable to move. My heart pounded strong enough to drum a hole in my chest.

Was someone there? "Who are you? What are you doing to me?" I asked desperately, using all the oxygen in my lungs, gasping and coughing to refill them again. My throat tightened with an onset of tears. My blood pumped harder, and I gasped at the reality that I was immobilized.

Trying to lift my head from the table resulted in the pulling of my hair at the base of my skull, as if a vacuum hose took hold of it, sucking and drawing my head to rest once again on the hard surface beneath me. Lifting my arms and legs was just as futile. Any bit of movement resulted in the same force, the suction of air against my skin, keeping me pinned to the table, naked, vulnerable, and freezing cold.

Ready to explode with fear and anger, I ordered my legs to kick and my fists to beat, striking and hitting anything or anyone I saw, but nothing moved at my mental command. "Let me go!" I screamed.

I blinked through my blindness, straining to see someone or something, concentrating, sharpening my senses, trying to gauge where I was and what was happening to me. Turning my head from side to side, a wave of claustrophobia sent my pulse spiking so fast that I could barely catch my breath.

Was I awake or in the middle of some horrible dream?

No, this definitely wasn't a dream. Strange noises erupted to my left, rhythmic but distinctive, punctuated by pauses and responses—a language—it had to be, but not like anything I had ever heard before. An odor, something chemical and unpleasant, came next, something that burned my nostrils, making me cough, gag, and swallow hard, trying to remove the bad taste it brought to the back of my throat.

"Stop! I can't breathe," I gasped, filling my lungs with the fouled, stagnant air, my head spinning, my eyes blinking wildly.

But who or what was I speaking to—the passengers aboard the triangular ship that took me away from the woods? The alien who visited me? His words replayed in my mind: *the king has an unusual desire to study the unknown, and the unknown includes alien life forms.* No, not him. He said he didn't agree with what the king was doing to me.

A deep sting erupted at my ankle. Was it the touch of an alien syringe in an alien hand? My jaw clamped shut, and my mouth closed and sealed, as if the soft inner skin of my lips was rimmed with dots of superglue. Who was doing this to me and why?

Calm down, America. Calm down before you lose your mind. There was no sense in fighting.

Don't kill me. Please don't kill me. Every muscle in my body trembled, pulsing with panic. Closing my eyes increased the nausea pulling at my gut and the horror bubbling in my brain, coiling it into a spiral of thoughts I couldn't contain. Maybe I was dying or already dead.

I'd never see any of them again—my mom, my family, my friends. This was it. I'd never be a wife and mother, live the American dream.

I don't want to die. I don't want to die.

And what would they do with my body when I'm dead? I imagined my naked corpse in a tube of formaldehyde, the side of my face sunk against the glass as gravity took its toll.

No! No! Stay alive. Stay alive. Breathe. Breathe.

Breathing through my nose was difficult, but I managed to suck in deep, burning lungfuls of air and talk myself through the pain as it radiated up my leg and into my hip while I tried to regain control of my thoughts.

From my hip, the pain exploded into my chest, making my back arch uncontrollably and bringing down the crown of my head to meet the table. A series of three labored breaths through my nose eased the pain as it slowly retreated back into my lower legs. Is this what death felt like, or was this worse than death itself?

The remaining pain doubled with a jab of something cold against my thigh, something that pushed and twisted, something sharp that stopped when it hit bone. The sides of my face and my ears were warm and wet, but from what? Blood was my first thought. My stomach tightened. My chest heaved. And then I realized it was from my tears, thick, warm tears I couldn't control.

Take a breath. Feel your chest expand. Another deep breath. Yes, that was it. I was still alive. *Breathe. Breathe. Inhale. Exhale. Inhale. Exhale.*

Ouch! No! Another pain, a deep poke, cut into my wrist. A bath of warmth came next, something wet, maybe this time blood. *Stop. Please stop.* A slow prickle worked its way up my spine, colder and colder, settling into my chest and limbs.

Now was I dead? My eyes were opened. Was I blind? The smell was gone. The voices were gone. Everything was black and quiet and still. My nostrils flexed. No, this wasn't death, but it was almost just as bad.

My emotions continued to twist and turn like my stomach as I blinked against the darkness, trying to move my limbs and fighting the fatigue and a sudden flood of exhaustion that was strong enough to make me believe I'd die in my sleep.

Stay awake. Stay awake. Stay awake.

More cryptic voices.

My muscles became limp, my thighs, my calves, my arms, and the suction at the base of my head released. I wiggled my fingers, my toes. A pair of hands caught me at the ribs, a grip hard enough to break bone. Cold fingers encircled my ankles, and I was lifted from one table to another, the back of my head banging against its surface with an odd twang.

Blinking and straining to see my surroundings, my hair caught a small breeze as I was whisked to who-knows-where, the table being pushed or pulled in one constant direction.

I turned my head to the side and closed my eyes.

Please, please! Let me see!

My eyes burned and watered, but I was still partially blind when I opened them. White walls appeared, fuzzy and nondescript, curving as they met a high ceiling dotted with lights that stole my restored vision the longer I looked at them.

Someone was at my right, walking briskly beside my table. Another was to my left, and as I strained to hear, I caught the quick breathing of a third behind me. With my compromised vision, all three were as blurry as if they stood on the other side of the wavy wall of my containment cell.

Where were they taking me? A place to continue my torture, something that would lead to my death, or was I going back to my cell?

No! No!

Adrenaline shot through my veins, and with a deep breath, I pushed up from the table and rolled to the side, straining to see, struggling for strength. My feet hit the floor, and staggering, I burst forward in a clumsy sprint.

Where was I going? I didn't care. I just wanted away from them, away from there.

Voices behind me. Male voices. Strange shouts. Rapid clicks and odd vocalizations.

My shoulder hit the wall to my right and then to my left as I rebounded to the other side of what I guessed was a long hall. A dark, rectangular shadow ahead—a door, maybe. I slammed against it, searching for some kind of knob or lever.

But hands met my back, pinning me to the door, and I turned my head, longing to see more than the blurry, human-like silhouette that pulled me into the hall and threw me to the ground. My knees hit first, and I dropped forward, catching myself with my palms.

Another pressed his knee into the center of my lower back and I collapsed, my cheek meeting the icy floor. With its next move, my arms were behind me, and its hands, thick as if gloved, burned bruises into my tender skin as I fought against an iron grasp.

I caught an arm with my hand, and as it jerked its body away from me, my fingers scraped against the oddly hard yet smooth bicep beneath its shirt sleeve, and I could only assume it was wearing some type of body armor.

Something thin, cold, and wiry bound my wrists. I jerked from side to side, kicking to rise to my knees, but fighting was futile beneath their weight.

Through my misty vision, I saw the glint of a long needle, and with a sting, it penetrated my upper arm.

Keeping my arms crossed over my breasts, I withdrew toward the corner of my cell. The skin on my arms chilled. How long I had been unconscious, I had no clue, but I was so tired and so weak that it took every bit of strength I had to make it to the gray wall. Thankfully my sight had been restored.

Two feet away lay a metal tray on the floor, holding three colored, brick-sized blocks: one green, one brown, one yellow. I leaned forward with an outstretched hand, hooked the edge of the tray with my fingers, pulled it toward me, and was met with some familiar odors—some kind of meat, vegetables, and I wasn't sure about the third. They were sol-id, manufactured bricks of food, but my stomach was too upset to eat. My mouth and throat were too dry anyway. I needed to drink some water, but my body was too stiff and exhausted to stand.

Flexing my back and stretching out my legs, I saw the possible cause of my new weakness. The skin covering a large vein on my wrist was bruised, purpley-blue with a tiny red dot in its center. Someone had taken my blood. But when? While I was asleep? And how? What happened to me? Was I removed from this cell unconscious and taken somewhere else? And then I remembered the bright light and the pain that screamed through my immobile body while I was being examined by alien captors I couldn't see.

"What the hell did you do to me?" I yelled with raw lips, finding the strength to stand and using the wall for support before making my way to the water fountain.

The water seemed colder than it was before, making my teeth hurt. I trembled, rubbing my arms, bringing my thoughts back to the mountains where I stood with Atlanta, Logan, and Kevin, looking up at the strange object in the sky.

I was cold, so cold! I needed clothes. "You could have at least given me a blanket," I shouted at the undulating wall.

My left thigh was swollen on one side and bruised at the hip, a hard knot of a bruise the size of a golf ball. When pushing upon it lightly with my finger, a familiar pain returned, one that burned and blurred into a faint memory.

A table, a bright light, strange voices, and deep pain—Yes, I remembered the blinding light and lying upon a hard, cold table with edges so sharp that they cut into my fingers when the sting came, and I tightened my muscles, forcing my hands to lock beneath it. And I remembered stumbling through a dark hall, half blind, and then being caught, restrained, and drugged. A deep bruise encircled my wrists, and my ankles were dotted with plumb-colored fingerprints.

I dropped to the ground and gave the tray of cold bricks a quick kick with my foot, sending it toward the curtain of cloudy crystal. All three bricks rolled from the tray, hit the liquid wall, sparked, sizzled, and turned into a puddle of ash.

Rounding my back, I leaned forward and closed my eyes, letting my long, brown hair fan about my shoulders. What was my mom doing right now? How was she handling my disappearance? Was she scouring the woods for evidence that I was still alive, hoping she wouldn't find my dead body? Was she holding news conferences so she could beg my kidnappers to let me go? Was she at home, lying in bed, depressed and crying, asking why this had to happen to me? Or maybe she had done all three.

The unanswered questions roiled in my mind again and again, again and again, sending me into a spontaneous fit of panic. But after their tenth rotation, like counting sheep, the repetition made me drowsy. My heartbeat slowed, and the pulse in my neck became undetectable.

Stay positive. Stay positive, I told myself. *Be strong. Crying won't help.*

Slumping against the wall and closing my eyes, I decided I'd rather sleep than think about my uncertain fate. But just as I was about to drift into a self-forced slumber, the vent in the ceiling opened, filling my cell with its annoying hum as it sucked away the smoke and smell of the burning food cubes.

Chapter Eight

GARRAN

"Garran, is that you?" America was a mere lump of a shadow, with two small projections, her feet extending from one end.

"Yes, it is me," I told her and settled next to the containment wall, drawing my knees toward my chest.

"I was hoping it was just a dream." Her figure lengthened, and in the next minute she was in a sitting position across from me, the curves of her soft body oddly Enestian.

"I'm not sure what you mean." I had anxiously checked her file several times, but it hadn't updated since the day before.

The silhouette of her arm showed, and her shadowy hand ran the length of her body. "Ouch," she said when her palm crossed to her hip. "But it wasn't. It was real." The cadence of her voice faltered, and with her next words, I knew she was crying.

"Oh my God! What did they do to me?" She wept.

"You are in pain." That bothered me. More than maybe it should have. She was just another alien, right? But at the same time, I wished I was in her cell, not just to see her foreign form face-to-face, but to give her some comfort, a hand to hold or maybe an arm around her shoulder.

"Yes, I, I was on a table. I couldn't move. I couldn't see. I thought I was dying. I tried to get away, but they, they…" She broke into a sob. Her head dropped, and a sweep of hair fanned against her body like a snow sparrow unfolding its wings.

Damn. Heat erupted under my brow plate, and my jaw casing locked in place. Time was running out, and I realized I cared not only because I wanted more time with this creature for curiosity sake, but also because she didn't have much more time. I had to get inside that cell and do what I could to soften her sadness.

My father had already completed his first stage of alien examinations. There were three stages. What each entailed? I didn't know, since I avoided the lab and any part of my father's experiments that used live specimens. But I did know each round of tests progressively became more invasive until he finished with the creature's live dissection and death.

The soft blur behind the rippling curtain rose, stumbling as America came to her feet. Her hand came to her head, which I assumed was to wipe the tears from her cheeks, and as she turned, she pushed her hair from her face.

"I am sorry this has happened to you," I said as I stood. And this time, I genuinely was, her suffering slowly overriding my ethnocentrism.

So Enestian she appeared from behind the oozy containment sheet. The soft curve of her chin, the rounding of her shoulders, and just like my planet's females, her upper body sloped inward to a tiny waist and turned outward again to defined hips and thighs. I wondered what it would be like to touch her skin. Draw my hand along her body. Would her flesh depress or was it firm? Would it feel smooth or would my palm catch upon the contour of a crooked bone or rough hair, something reminiscent of a prickly dew plant?

"Then make it stop. Please!" she whimpered. "Make them not hurt me again. Make them let me go."

"If I could, I would, but like I've explained before, I have little influence over the king."

She sank her thin arms down, reaching to hug her drawn-up legs once she hit the floor. "I want to go home," she said softly. "Three days but it feels like three weeks." Her head lowered to the top of her knees. "I missed my shift." Her words were muffled, and I imagined her pale lips from her intake picture resting against her knees while she spoke.

"Your shift? I do not understand." I lowered back to the floor and scooted as closely as I could to the rippling containment wall.

"It's Monday on Earth. If I were home, I would have worked today. I had the afternoon shift—one to ten. I love my job. Most of my friends hate theirs."

"And what is your job?"

"I work at a coffee shop called Rock n' Robusta."

"Robusta? I am not familiar with that word."

"It's a type of coffee bean. We use only the highest quality beans at Rock n' Robusta. We use Arabica beans, too." She lifted her head. "Do you know what coffee is?"

"Yes, I researched it after I watched the movie *Pulp Fiction*. The character, Jimmie, says, 'I don't need you to tell me how fuckin' good my coffee is, okay? I'm the one who buys it. I know how good it is. When Bonnie—'"

"'—goes shopping, she buys shit. I buy the gourmet expensive stuff because when I drink it, I want to taste it.'" America gasped. "Oh my God. I can't believe you've seen *Pulp Fiction*."

"I've seen it many times. Like I said, I've studied your culture, and in doing so, I've viewed many films produced in the United States."

"It's my favorite movie," the two of us said in unison. "At least my favorite in English," I added.

"Wow, that's crazy," said America as she laughed. Lacking the hard clicks of my language, her laugh was rich yet delicate, and I was thankful our change in conversation had brought her some temporary happiness. Something warm rushed through me. It felt good to hear her laugh. "I wish I was there now—at Rock n' Robusta. I'd order a large coffee." She straightened her back.

"We have something similar to coffee—tarla beans. When placed in a cup of water, the beans immediately sprout, and the infusion process begins as the leaves develop and open. The beans are removed when the first bud appears, or the blooms will sour the brew."

"It sounds more like a tea than coffee. Rock n' Robusta sells tea, too."

"So your job is to prepare and serve coffee and tea?"

"Yeah, and scones and cookies, and sometimes I sell records, too. There's a small record store inside the shop. It's pretty much the only place around that still sells vinyl. Because of that, a lot of bands come in—not just the locals—but pretty much any band that's on tour and playing in San Diego. We get them to sign photos and album covers, and sometimes they donate memorabilia, and then we hang them on the walls. We play rock music, too, all kinds—hard, alternative, classic." She dropped her hands in her lap. "Oh, I'm sorry. You probably have no idea what I'm talking about. I'm just rambling on and on..."

"Motley Crue, Led Zeppelin, Nirvana, The Beatles..."

"You've listened to them?"

"Yes. Earth music in English, like movies, has become part of my independent studies. I'm familiar with most genres, but rock is my favorite. Enestian music is..." I paused to find the right words, and America tilted her head to one side and leaned closer to the containment wall. "It's melodic but one-dimensional. It holds no inspiration or influence." I inched forward. "American rock music has a culture all its own. It impacts fashion, attitudes—even your language," I said. "It's..."

"Raw emotion, energy, it moves—"

"The soul," I said, and opened my eyes as wide as I could as I gazed at the blur that was America's face. If only I could see her clearly while we spoke—her tender human lips, plump and meaty, the apples of her velvety cheeks as they lift with each word. "And with its weave of rifts and drum beats, it suppresses all fears, all uncertainties, leaving one's spirit whole and comforted, if only for a moment."

"Yes, that's exactly it," she said enthusiastically, her human voice and accent pleasant against my ears, but a moment later, she set her chin against her knees and let her hands drop from her lap.

"America?"

"Yeah," she said weakly. She sniffled, and I knew she was crying again, softly. Again, I wished I could touch her.

My hand upon her could offer some sympathy.

"I should go. I want to stay. I want to learn more about you, but I've already stayed too long. If I get caught, then I can't return."

I sighed and imagined her at Rock n' Robusta, making coffee and other alien brews like I'd seen so many times on American television programs. In my mind's eye, she measured, mixed, and tapped on a strange machine until a dark liquid flowed into a cup she held, her hand soft and bumpy with underlying bone and cartilage. To hold her hand, even comfort her, I should like to do that very much.

"I know. Go," she said, as I stood and straightened my tunic.

Lestra was at the end of the hall. "What's wrong with you?" she asked when I reached her. "Fifteen minutes— That was more than fifteen minutes. I can't keep my brother distracted for much longer than that." She walked ahead of me, and once we were out of the lab, her steps turned into a stomp.

"Nothing's wrong with me," I finally said when we reached my quarters. "Something is wrong with my father. It's obvious at first glance that humans have more similarities to us than differences. Like I said before, their thought processes are—"

"How can you even think that?" Lestra's lips came together with a hard click. "That alien is nothing like us."

"It speaks a language. It can reason. Its cognitive abilities surpass any of the inhabitants of Reelio Seven."

"That's not saying much. Reelians are weak witted."

I sat onto the edge of the bed, my body slumped like the gray blurry figure of America when she had sat in a ball in her cell. "She was examined this morning by my father."

"As to be expected," said Lestra as she sat next to me.

"He hurt her. How could he do that?"

"Simple. The way he always does." She scooted closer, and the bed sunk with her weight, rocking her body against me.

I stood and crossed the room. A tapestry depicting an ancient raid upon our kingdom hung against the wall. It was intricate, delicately hand woven, each detail a small bud of colored thread. "But it's different this time. She's different. She's not like the others." I gave the tapestry a punch, hitting the stone wall behind it. Dust emanated from its primordial fibers, and the smell of rot became heavy in my room.

"What are you doing?" asked Lestra as she ran to me. "You're going to crack your shell." She grabbed my hand and held it, then ran her fingers along my knuckles.

"I'm fine," I said and ripped my hand away.

"You're not fine. You're obsessing over something that's out of your control, something that shouldn't even be your concern."

"Lestra, just go, please. I want to be alone right now."

"Why, so you can lie on your bed and listen to that awful alien music you like so much?"

"Go, please."

She stormed from my room, and as she caught the light next to the door, I could have sworn she was wearing shell powder again.

Obstinate palace maid. And how could she be so insensitive? My father's cruelty had to end, not only toward beings that possess higher order thinking skills, but all living creatures. I turned on my monitor and blasted Motley Crue, envisioning America sitting beside me as we sang the lyrics.

Chapter Nine

AMERICA

"No. Not again. Please!"

Blinded by the bright light and immobilized, I screamed until my lips were sealed shut by a force not my own. Voices, more voices. Words I didn't understand. And clacking sounds—not metal upon metal or plastic upon plastic—the sound was dull, and at times there was a scraping, not like sandpaper, but like smooth surfaces gliding across one another. The sound an ice skate makes against the ice.

What were these things? These things with human-shaped bodies and a language made up of sounds and clicks. If only I could see them.

What are you doing? No! Don't!

Something slid against my body, something hard and cold. It stopped at my hip, found my previous puncture, and with a thrust re-entered the wound. A spark of hot pain radiated through my abdomen, shot down my thigh, and ended at my foot. The left side of my body burned as the probe dug deeper, twisting and grinding.

Hands clasped my legs, hard yet rubbery against my skin. *No! No!* My knees were separated, and my legs, now numb and heavy, were pulled apart. My heart pulsed, heavy thumps that rattled in my ears. Each intake of air took strength and thought. *Breathe, Breathe. Breathe*, I told myself. But the heaviness in my chest remained, and though the room smelled of chemicals and raw meat, my lungs burned and yearned for a deep breath.

Just do it! Kill me now! I don't want to live if I'll never see my mom and my friends again! I can't live in that cell another day!

Garran. His blurry body erupted in my mind as I strained to see my captors. He made me laugh the day before, brought back good memories, but his sympathy, his company, it wasn't enough to give me any prolonged hope — not now, not when I was here, like this.

No! I want to die. Let me die now. Death, please save me from this humiliation! My eyes closed.

The re-punctured wound at my hip throbbed. Around its swollen edge, a bit of blood was crusted, but it hadn't turned into a scab. I rose to the right wall, and when the sink retracted, I caught water in my hand and gave my body a splash. The cool water eased the sting of my wound, but when I sat down again, the pulsing, fiery ache returned, along with the memory of the second time I'd been brutally violated by my alien enemies.

The tray that had held the colored cubes of food the day before was still in my room and icy cold to the touch. I gently propped it against my hip, hoping it would alleviate the swelling.

I was still alive after what they did to me, but for how long?

A whip of fear lashed up my spine, and the walls of my cell appeared to close in upon me, crushing my freedom and sucking the air from my lungs. My muscles and my mind pulsed with a need for freedom, for an escape if only for a minute's time.

I had to get out of here. I could do this.

The urge was too strong to resist. The food tray was cookie-sheet sized and harder than any metal I'd seen on Earth, its strange sheen reflecting my face in a blur of gray and gold as I held it, angling it in the dim light. Yes! I had to try. Why not? Sitting in my cell and waiting for another round of torture or even death left me little hope. What if Garran never returned? Then what? Any chance of survival would be gone, too.

I sat, my legs drawn but facing the lethal wall. After placing my palms in the center of the tray, I raised it above my head. Would the integrity of the tray shield me from the fatal wave of jell?

In one quick motion, I pushed the metal through the liquid curtain. Sparks flew and pinpoints of tiny lights spurted in all directions. The fall of goo split, spilling over the edge of the tray while I remained shielded, hunched, and digging my heels into the stone floor in a crawl that inched my body forward.

But the tray's thinner rim began to melt under the wall's caustic wave. Like drops of hot wax, a shower of molten metal rained at my sides, a splash that hit my arms in several places. If the tray buckled or a hole burned through its center, the wall would undulate downward like the blade of a guillotine, severing my head from my body.

Just one more foot!

The smell of burned hair filled the narrow hall as my head slipped through the divided wall, and I sat up on the other side, catching my breath. The tray was warped, its sides solidifying in the hall's dank air, and as I set what was left of the metal to my right, I noticed a hunk of singed hair, dry and wiry, lying across my shoulder. It gave with a yank, crackling into ash that peppered the floor.

Coin-sized drops of metal, aluminum foil thin, trailed my arms, leaving stinging, red, and hairless patches of skin when I brushed them away, but I ignored the pain. I was free. And even if it didn't last for more than a few minutes, it was enough to hold my sanity.

Now what? Right or left? Did it really matter? How far could I get without being caught?

Right, I decided, and crept down the hall, the small lights in the ceiling sensing my presence and becoming brighter as I walked beneath them. This was not the same hall I'd been in before. This hall was lined with cells on the left, cells identical to mine.

"Empty, empty, empty," I mouthed as I passed each barren room, its containment wall deactivated, but as I came across the next, its fourth wall intact and rippling, a deep howl cut through the thick, misty liquid.

A small body, a four-foot high, broad-shouldered blur,

hobbled forward, and I stumbled, my back knocking against the far wall.

A series of grunts came next, dark and haunting, making my skin prickle and my shoulders jerk into a hard shudder.

"Shhh, please," I said, looking left and right.

But the creature continued its mad rant even after I sprang forward into the shadows of the next dormant cell.

Voices. Clicks. "Damn!"

Something hit my calves, a dot of pain erupting from the source. Instinctively, I raked my hand across my lower leg and found a small, liquid-filled dart that spun under its own power, feverishly drilling into my soft flesh as if it was designed for the tough, armored hide of a rhinoceros.

My vision blurred, and my body thudded against the cold stone floor.

Two failed escape attempts within a twenty-four hour period, both resulting in a medically induced state of unconsciousness, left me too weak to cry, though the last attempt had been liberating. Knowing what lay beyond my cell gave me the needed dose of determination I needed in order to keep my sanity.

Like before, I had been returned to my cell. And I was still alive—for now.

That was something I needed to ask Garran about again. I needed to know my fate. He had to tell me.

But who was Garran, this strange alien who liked *Pulp Fiction* and rock music? Three galaxies from Earth, and he knew about the Fab Four? He understood what music meant and what it did for me, and apparently rock music did the same for him, too.

Not many people understood that. Attie hated my taste in music. Country music was her thing, and though rock was our coffee shop's theme, even some of my co-workers complained and were tempted to switch it up to a pop music channel as soon as the owner left.

But not me. Like Garran said, rock moved my soul, and in a strange way, so did my conversation with Garran. Now that I was back in my cell, the bit of hope his last words left me with returned, like maybe the king would eventually send me home. It wasn't anything specific that he said. I wasn't sure what it was, but something about him gave me a sliver of faith. And something more. I liked the way his voice sounded. Odd, different, yet it wrapped around me when he tried to console me.

I wanted to see him again. I needed to see him again, and in the process, I had to convince him to help free me. But what were these aliens? Garran said something about shell, but his shape was human in so many ways.

"America." Garran's fuzzy figure appeared on the other side of the slithery wall. Thank God, my botched escapes didn't jeopardize his ability to sneak in here and see me. He didn't need to know about either one of them.

"How are you feeling? Have you eaten? I checked your file before I came. It indicated that a meal had been delivered," he said.

"There was one meal, but I didn't eat it, and now it's gone." I remembered the sick, charcoal-like smell of the burning food cubes and the melted tray. "And I haven't been given any more food since." And maybe never again, considering what I had done.

"That's unacceptable. If I can, I will try to find out why and have meals delivered to your cell regularly."

"Thank you," I said, touched by the fact that he seemed to really care about me.

He eased to the floor, and I studied his silhouette when each of his legs bent and his palm met the ground to hold his weight while he settled into position. As I lowered across from him, pain rushed to my hip, my arms gave, and I collapsed.

"Are you okay?" asked Garran. He moved forward, rising on his palms and stopping just shy of catching the top of his head in the goo of the containment wall.

"I was taken again," I said as I delicately held my hand against my hip and rose to a sitting position. "They—"

"It was your second examination. I know what they did," he said shamefully.

"I don't think I can survive another." The memory of the crippling highest point of pain returned. My throat tightened as my pulse spiked, and I gasped before swallowing hard.

"No, you can't. I mean, you need to try, to stay strong, to…"

"What's going to happen to me?"

"I'm not sure."

But there was something about his tone and hesitancy to answer that made me think he knew more than he was leading me to believe, and I shivered as the cold in my shoulders rode the back of my neck. I wanted Garran on this side of the barrier, his arms around me, making me feel safe. Somehow, I knew I would like that.

He shifted his weight, and one hand dropped from his

knee to the floor.

"They're going to kill me the next time, aren't they?" I rose until my body was square with his and without covering myself with my hands. Why care about my nakedness when I was going to probably die anyway?

He lowered his chin.

"Aren't they? Please, tell me! I want the truth."

He lifted his head until we were eye-to-eye, and through the rippling curtain, his face appeared skull-like with dark sockets and a defined chin. But that didn't frighten me. If he were next to me, comforting me, I was sure his eyes would hold a special softness, and I could bear his answer, even the one I didn't want to hear.

"Yes," he said. "I am sorry."

The minute I was cruelly examined by my captors, I knew this was my fate. I just didn't want to believe it until now.

Every nerve in my body pulsed, and the hair on my arms rose. My stomach wrenched with a sudden, explosive pain, and I sucked in a quick breath until it subsided, and I was left feeling sick all over.

"How? Tell me!"

"I'm not sure. I've never participated in the king's experimentation with aliens, nor do I ever wish to. I am only familiar with the initial examinations."

I slowly dropped onto my right hip and lay with my hands pillowing my head. I drew in each knee until they were parallel with my belly button. The cold stone floor brought a bone-deep shiver through my body, and I blinked several times to stop my tears.

"So much I wanted to do," I said softly. "And now I'll

never... What does it matter anyway?"

"It matters to me," said Garran. He mimicked my position, shifting gracefully until he was horizontal and across from me. "Please tell me."

Why tell him and torture my already heavy heart? But there was sympathy in his words, and as I peered through the fuzzy screen at someone more foreign to me than anyone on Earth, the urge to tell him bubbled through my body.

"To buy Rock n' Robusta. Judith, she's the owner, plans to sell it in five years. By then I'd have my degree and enough money saved up to buy it. Then a few years after that, I'd open up two more locations."

"An entrepe... I, I don't remember the word."

"Entrepreneur. But not quite. I'd be just a business owner."

"Just? Managing a business requires an intense work ethic, the ability to solve problems, and manage a staff. It is a position of authority, one to be respected."

"I wish my mother could have seen it that way." I laughed. "She wanted me to become a doctor. Her brother, my uncle, is a doctor. I had the grades for it. I was accepted to John Hopkins—that's a university with an excellent pre-med program—but in the end, I opted for San Diego State and majored in Business Administration."

"And your mother did not approve."

"Yeah. When I enrolled at State, she pretty much flipped out, and I tried to calm her down by pointing out that the tuition at state was more doable for her and for me, and I'd also be able to afford my own apartment."

"She should understand that you are capable of making your own success and in the career of your own choosing."

I closed my eyes and imagined Garran squeezing my hand with those words.

"I know, but she did have a point. Fifty percent of all businesses fail in the first year. She was just watching out for me. Up until my sophomore year in high school, all I talked about was being a doctor one day, so she was shocked when I changed my mind."

"What happened during your sophomore year?"

"Fetal pig dissection." The sick smell of formaldehyde filled my nostrils as I recounted how each preemie pig's rubbery tongue extended several millimeters from the pig's mouths, and how Jimmy Bradley, my lab partner, cut off the tip and tossed it at me. "I almost puked and had to sit in the hall of the science building for the rest of the period. In fact, I had to sit in the hall for the rest of the week until the last day of dissection. After that, I knew I could never make it through med school."

"I understand," said Garran, and he chuckled. It was an odd chuckle, human-like but infused with a click when his lips met, but it was sort of cool. "I avoided intergalactic biology for the same reason. One of the course requirements includes the live dissection of a…" He rolled onto his back. "There is no English translation for the name, but it is a small, thick-shelled, four-legged creature. When in pain, its labored, high-pitch screech forces one to wear protective ear caps." He turned back to face me. "I could not perform such a task, much to my father's disappointment."

He moved his arm, letting it slip from his side to the floor in front of him, and as he did so, I caught the crisp outline of his body, his wide shoulders and narrow waist.

"Does he also want you to become a doctor?"

"No, a scientist, a researcher, and eventually…" He sighed. "Like your mother, he believes his chosen path for me will lead to optimal happiness and achievement. I've avoided following his course, but my destiny is set. My choices are limited, and I cannot go against my father's wishes. If I could change the manner in which he conducts his practices, it would be different. That's something I want to do, but…"

"Is this true for everyone? Are careers pre-selected by parents?"

"No, but things are different for me. My family is…" He lifted up onto his forearm. "My family holds important positions, positions that are filled by the next generation."

"Like a family business?"

"Yes." He lowered his upper body back to the floor.

"So, if not a scientist or researcher, what do you want to do?"

"I want to be a pilot."

"And fly a ship like the one that brought me here?" The bit of hope Garran gave me doubled.

"Yes, and others, the entire royal fleet of flyers."

"Royal fleet? You mean flyers for the king?" I rose up onto my elbow. Maybe he had more influence upon the monarchy than he'd led me to believe? "Can you fly one now? Take me home?" Tears rose on my lashes and dripped to my cheeks. "Please."

"I cannot. I do not have the code that will override a shell scan." He sat up. "I wish I could." He abruptly stood and brushed off his body with his hands. "But I have no means to do so." He shook his head. "My time with you has expired. I need to go."

I jumped to my feet and faced him through the sludge of

wall. "So this is it? The end? The next time I'm taken from my cell, I'll be…"

But I couldn't say the last word and only uttered, "I'm a prisoner on death row."

And I was being punished. For what? For being a human, and that was all? Maybe I'd die before then. I could continue starving myself, and then like a fetal pig, my body would be opened and explored by curious and cruel beings.

Garran remained silent. I dropped back to the floor and rolled onto my stomach. With my face against my hands, I cried, not caring how each sob became louder than the next and that each time I caught my breath, my body heaved and buckled against the cold stone.

After several minutes, I took in a long, controlled draw of air. My crying subsided, and my body relaxed limply against the floor. My hair wet and sticky with warm tears, I turned my head toward the cloudy wall.

Garran was gone.

Chapter Ten

GARRAN

"If only the code into the lab would also open her cell. I need to find a way to get inside," I said the next morning as Lestra and I studied the lab's updated files on the monitor in my quarters.

"Why? You talked to the thing. Isn't that enough?"

"No, I want to see her before… I'm not sure how many days she has left." I ached to see her, to comfort her, to touch her, which brought pleasant but strange feelings I felt not only in my heart but in my body, something that made my lower plate tingle. But I wasn't ready to share that with Lestra. I wasn't in the mood to deal with her reaction.

"Well, that's not going to happen. You know that would take a shell scan. I helped you get into the lab, and I distracted my brother for you each time, but I can't be a part of helping you enter its cell. If I get caught, I'll be reassigned to a palace substation."

"I'll order you to help me. Then if we get caught, you won't get in trouble."

Lestra's lower jaw plate dropped, but she didn't say anything. Like mine, Lestra's shell was ecru, but in the light of my room, my exposed shell slightly yellowed and shimmered naturally, a royal trait, while Lestra's appeared dull and ashen.

Like I said before, she was a pretty girl, though. Her eye sockets were large, and the plates around her mouth naturally curved upward at its corners, giving her a sexy smile even if she didn't mean to. Her face was slightly contoured, her nose a minimal projection with small nostrils, and the shell surrounding the well of her ears expanded delicately and deeply into her ear canals, another desirable characteristic. She'd certainly make an attractive wife for another high-ranking servant.

"*If* we get caught? Don't you mean *when* we get caught? We're lucky we didn't get caught last night. I can only keep my brother away from the monitors for so long. I was afraid he was beginning to suspect something."

"Yeah, too bad Remlin wasn't assigned to her cellblock instead. He's as dumb as shell."

Lestra's lip plates buckled. Being related by blood or marriage to our primary staff, Remlin was either one of Lestra's cousins or another one of her brothers.

"I don't want any of my family members involved in this, especially Slaine."

"We won't get your brother in trouble. Don't forget the authority I have," I said, giving her upper arm plate a squeeze with my cupped hand. Not that I had a lot of authority at this point in my life.

She yanked her arm away and pointed to the screen. "That's odd. Three pithes of human blood were added to the laboratory's blood-housing unit two days ago, and another three were added this morning."

"Not odd, she was taken and examined twice."

"But now there are twenty-seven pithes of human blood in storage."

I opened my eyes and mouth so wide I thought I would be the next dumb-ass Enestian to crack my shell and get rushed to one of the two in-lab emergency rooms at the palace.

My insides knotted as I imagined America's frail body, a clump of shadow through the wall. Six pithes within only a few days' time was a lot of blood, but twenty-seven? "I don't think a human could survive that amount of blood loss." I was shaking so hard my shell plates clacked. I didn't want her to suffer. I needed to be with her, see her, hold her.

"Humans are feeble and vulnerable. They probably bleed all the time, and it doesn't affect them."

"I don't think so. Unintentional bleeding isn't mentioned in their writings," I announced, gripping my stomach. "That means America isn't the first human abducted by my father. Why did he take her? Why did he need another one? I want to help her. I don't want her to die like the others."

"*Help* her?" asked Lestra, closing the file. "That would require breaking every security protocol and defying your father. Talking to it has to be enough. You can't do anything more for it."

She was right. I crossed my arms, clacking my shell hard.

"And you shouldn't care if that thing dies anyway. It's an inferior being. It's disgusting," she continued.

"But I do care, now that I've communicated with her."

"I shouldn't have told you about the human," she scoffed.

"Then why did you?"

"I don't know."

She didn't need to give me an answer. I knew exactly why she told me. She was hoping to become my personal adjutant when I saw the turn of my twenty-third year. Though part of the servant class, royal adjutants were among the most highly regarded and respected citizens in the entire galaxy.

A royal's personal adjutant shared the same meals as his or her royal, were given comparable living quarters, and ruled his or her own set of loyal subjects—a team of lesser servants.

For Lestra, stretching her role of palace maid into a semi-friendship with me brought her closer to this appointment. She'd never say "no" to me even if she wasn't under my direct orders, and on top of that, I could trust her. She was a Timuary, after all. It wasn't just tradition; it was in her blood to be my confidant. And because of that, I also didn't have to worry about her telling my father or anyone else that I'd compromised lab security and visited the human.

"I want to actually see *her*, not her gray figure. I'm going to find a way to get into her cell no matter what."

Maybe once I saw her I would understand why I felt more attraction to her than Lestra, who powdered her shell for me. Why my plates tightened when I imagined holding her. Why her impending death affected me more than it should. We shared an interest in music and films, something I didn't have with anyone else on this planet.

Or maybe it was merely because she was so different. None of the girls in my class interested me. They were more concerned about their shell makeup and fashion than they were about getting an advanced degree. America wanted to graduate, save her credits, and own a business. I respected that. She wanted to make something of her life just like I wanted to be king to change how we established our dominance over the Millennius.

I tossed my virtual generator to the floor, commanded it to display a replica of the palace, and enlarged it until the research lab engulfed the center of my room. "I need to avoid the shell scan. There has to be an override code."

Lestra tapped her jaw shell and tilted her head. "If there is, I don't know how to get it. I'm not supposed to know about her, either. My brother would never open her cell in front of me, so it's not like I could copy another code onto my shell, and—"

"And I would never ask you to do that. I would have never allowed you to do that the first time."

"Well, I can't just ask my brother for it, so you're just going to have to be satisfied with talking to it before it dies and not actually seeing it."

Why all the secrecy when it came to this girl human? Why were humans different from his other intergalactic specimens? But I couldn't ask my father for unbridled access into the lab and its cellblocks without a good reason. The last time I demanded entrance into the lab he had told me, "Young princes are not privy to all palace matters, especially those involving our facility's private research endeavors."

He still resented the fact that my chosen course of study did not involve domestic and intergalactic research—his passion, or should I say, obsession. My father, a quizzical man with a sardonic mind and a hard heart, could sever the limbs from a conscious Sallentarian without as much as producing a watery eye or grimace.

As the future king, I thought my father would be pleased when my choice of advanced curriculum involved galactic politics, combat strategies, and alien languages, but "a king," my father once told me, "only needs a thorough understanding of his enemy's minds and bodies, inside and out, to remain the most powerful ruler in the Millennius, my young prince."

Young prince? Damn him! Why did he always insist on calling me that? My shell plates were hard and fused, indicating I was well beyond puberty and ready to take my fated position as a royal ambassador to Enestia. It was time for all palace matters to become what mattered to me, especially this one.

I couldn't turn to the queen for her support and influence on my father. As with tradition, their marriage had also been arranged. It was obvious they'd never fallen in love, but like a dutiful queen, she gave him two heirs despite the fact that my father's outward affection for her only went as far as a pat on the shoulder—and even that was rare.

She purposely distanced herself from all palace affairs, including my father, to the extent of taking one long galactic vacation after another. Currently she was on Verla Three, enjoying their low-thermic atmosphere, and I wouldn't have been surprised if her enjoyment also included another man's company.

Murelle wished she was vacationing on Verla, too, but I didn't. Verlians were friendly, passive beings—too passive for me. I was always in the mood for a little conflict, and I certainly didn't want to lie around all day on the lake shore under the harsh Verla sun. That was paradise to my mom and Murelle, but to me it was a solid bout of boredom.

The only thing I was missing out on was checking out all the Verlian girls. It's a well-known fact that Verla is home to some of the hottest females in the galaxy with their naturally-glistening shell plates and eyes like purple flux.

But I couldn't think about Verlian girls right now, not when there was an Earth girl suffering in cell fifteen, weak from blood loss and a lack of food.

"Hey," said Lestra, turning her attention back to the human's files. "Her file was just updated. Another meal was delivered to its cell."

Finally they brought her more food.

"It is now scheduled to get three meals a day," she said after a few taps to the simulated screen.

"Breakfast, lunch, and dinner," I said in English and under my breath. Meals were scheduled? That meant they planned to keep her around longer than I suspected.

"And there is something else." Lestra sucked in a deep breath. "Her final examination has been arranged. It's in fifteen days."

Fifteen days? That was a long time. My father never kept specimens in the lab for that length of time.

Fifteen days... King Seiljan from Terinow— He was going to be visiting our planet in just over two week's time. Now it made sense.

My father was saving America for Seiljan's arrival, so Seiljan could watch—a private demonstration of my father's power and what he was capable of if anyone in the Millennius ever challenged him. My father was a sick man.

Chapter Eleven

AMERICA

"America," came a voice from the other side of the watery curtain.

"Yes?" I said.

"Are you okay?" My heart smiled at the sound of his voice. I wanted to rush into his arms, have him hold me. And more. I wanted more.

Garran's blurry figure lowered to the floor in the same spot where he had sat the day before.

I eased down across from him, and the bruise on my hip exploded with pain as I met the cold floor, reminding me that his people were responsible for my fate. "No! I'm not okay," I snapped, angry that he'd let this happen. "My hip still hurts from whatever they did to me."

"Bone marrow extraction," he said.

My bottom lip trembled, and I drew it into my mouth

while sucking in a deep breath to stop my tears. How could I allow myself to feel anything for him when he let them hurt me? Because I believed he was as powerless to intervene as I was to get out of here.

"Standard procedure for all specimens. I would have stopped them if I had the authority."

"That's what I am," I said weakly. "A specimen."

"Yes, to all Enestians except for me." He tilted his head, and I yearned to see him. To see if the sincerity in his voice was mirrored in his face.

"Standard procedure. What else did that include?" I wanted to know everything. The nip of the cold floor rose up and into my lower back, and I shuddered when its chill reached my shoulder blades.

Garran drew his knees closer to his chest, and I heard him exhale. "I'm-I'm not sure. After preliminary tests are performed, additional examinations are dependent upon the type and origin of the species."

"I don't want to die." I choked. My throat tightened, but my eyes remained dry. I was out of tears, dehydrated. I hadn't had the motivation to take a sip of water.

"I will do what I can," he said softly and lowered his chin to rest upon his knees.

We were both silent for several minutes, and if I closed my eyes and concentrated, I could hear his steady breathing before and after the undulating wall hit the ceiling or the floor and made its next ascent or descent.

"I want to stop him. It needs to end." Garran's voice had a new timbre to it—stronger, steelier. But maybe his intonation meant something else. "Not just with you, but with all of them. I will change things when I am…"

"When you are what?"

"Fifteen days," he said softly.

"What? What do you mean, fifteen days?"

"Your next examination takes place in fifteen days."

That meant I had just over two weeks to live.

I gasped in a series of spasms, trying to catch my breath as my body shook and became ill with an explosive wave of dread that settled like a heavy, foreign mass in the pit of my stomach. Dead at twenty. To die here on a strange planet I'd never seen and without any friends or family. Except for an alien named Garran.

"America."

"Yes, Garran," I managed to answer, my voice raspy from tense muscles in my throat. I calmed my body just enough to part my lips. I liked his name. It matched his build—tall and strong—from what I could make out through the milky wall. He was big—much bigger than I was—I wondered how small my hand would look in his palm, and something tightened low in my stomach.

"How old are you?" I asked. I knew he was completing his second year of higher education, but I still didn't know his age. I wanted to know. Needed to know everything about him.

"Twenty-one, according to Earth standards. Since my birth, Earth has orbited its sun one and twenty times, while in my galaxy Enestia has circled its suns two and twenty."

"Suns?"

"Yes, there are two, one providing more thermal energy than the other."

"So, is the temperature of your planet higher than mine?" Maybe this room was climate controlled to match that of Earth's.

"No, they are similar, but two suns create a climate that is consistent on all four hemispheres. Earth comprises five, um, what's the English word? I apologize for my mispronunciations when it comes to your language. I think the word is biomes. Enestia only has two of them."

"Mispronunciations? Your English is awesome for an alien," I said. In fact, there was so much more about this guy that made me want to be near him. Like his bravery in coming to see me, despite knowing he'd be punished. He wasn't like the one who hurt me. He was different. I wanted to see how different.

Garran described Enestia's forests, rich with flora and fauna, and explained the makeup of the planet's atmosphere, its troposphere being composed of oxygen and nitrogen in percentages equivalent to that of Earth. The images were so vivid in my mind. I closed my eyes and saw patches of moss he called jessom stretching over boulders, and cherry bees buzzing past my ear, their bodies glowing red in the sun.

"I want to see it. Take me outside," I said, lost in Garran's words, momentarily forgetting that I was naked, confined to a gray cell, and slated to die in a couple of weeks. "Something beautiful. I want to see something beautiful before I…"

"I'd like to," he announced. "I'd take you to the palace gardens now if I could, and then I'd take you home."

His posture stiffened, he raised his hand, and for a minute, I thought he'd push it through the thick goo of the containment wall. But he stopped short, his palm an eighth of an inch from suffering the same fate as my fingernail and food cubes.

I lifted my hand to meet his on the other side, bringing

my palm close enough to feel a ripple of soft airwaves, a byproduct of the wall's undulation. Garran spread his fingers, and I did the same, matching his movement.

His hand was bigger than mine, the fingers thick but well-proportioned to their length, the blur identical to that of a human's. And as I held my palm in place, but coming as close as I could without touching the crystalline wave, heat grew against my skin, and I wished it generated from the warmth of Garran's hand instead of the pasty goop.

What did this alien look like? With a hand so comparable to that of a human's, how could the rest of him not be similar?

"I want to see you," I blurted.

"And I you," said Garran.

His admission sent my insides into a pleasant spin. Maybe I was mistaken, but his tone promised he was interested in more than just studying me. Like he wanted to see me because we had a connection we both wanted to deepen.

He pushed up from the ground and stood. I followed, our movements in unison until we were face-to-face, two non-descript smudges of color to each other like gingerbread cookie cutouts, a boy and a girl.

"You look like a human," I said, and as I looked him up and down, noting his broad shoulders and the V cut of his upper body, the chill at the base of my neck became a warm tingle. Once again, that my life would end in fifteen days was pushed to the back of my mind.

"And you an Enestian." He laughed.

"Is there a difference?" I asked, wanting to know so badly. I produced an image of him in my mind, something I hoped he looked like—tall, built, and handsome with the blue surfer eyes I adored.

"Yes, very much so. A difference you cannot see from behind that wall."

"And what difference is that?"

"Our bodies are covered in shell."

"Shell?" He'd said something about that before, something about a scan. The picture I constructed in my mind withered and redeveloped as a human covered in something like that of a chicken egg.

"Yes, that would be the translation in English," said Garran.

"How, I mean, wouldn't it break…?"

But a voice shot from the other side of the wall, high pitched and foreign, a string of words and awkward blend of clicks and delicate intonations.

"I need to go and quickly," said Garran. "The guard assigned to this cellblock is returning to his station." Another blur joined his, a petite form that threw its hip to one side as it stood across from me. "I can't let him find me here."

"Fifteen days. Please, stop it from happening, Garran. Please, don't let me die."

"I'll do everything I can to stop it. I—"

The blur grabbed Garran's upper arm, and just as I was about to ask him when he could return, both of them were gone, and I was left with a shell-covered human form in my mind's eye. It didn't seem gross and disgusting like it should. It was something I desperately wanted to see.

Fifteen days. I had to see Garran before I died. "Fuck this place," I screamed.

Chapter Twelve

GARRAN

I had two weeks to gain access to the human's cell and the lab. But now, actually seeing her might not be enough. Maybe I could stop my father and his team. To do so would be an act of treason, and I knew the consequences. But could I sit back, do nothing, and let America die a slow, cruel death? I wasn't sure, considering the cost—my title, my fortune, and maybe even my life. America's soft silhouette erupted in my mind, and her last words to me eclipsed any price as I sat down at the dining room table.

"Father, may I have a moment?"

"Just a moment, or more?" my father said gruffly, tugging at his embellished tunic and brushing a crumb of kismick bread from his lap. It fell onto the sleek, glass tabletop to join several more and glow amber within the table's under lights.

"Maybe more. It depends," I answered, setting down my goblet of fermented quip nectar. "I have a question. Actually, it's more like a proposition." Now was the perfect opportunity, since Murelle decided to skip dinner with us and dine with a cousin.

"A proposition from a prince to the king? Ask, my naive prince."

Naive? Hardly! My skills in weaponry and aviation exceeded my father's. He was a scientist, a man of inquiry and investigation. He stayed out of wars by advertising our wealth and the fact that our Enestian defense systems could destroy a small planet. My father could never lead an army, but due to his experiments and clever propaganda, he probably wouldn't have to anyway.

"I've been thinking, Father, that I've been doing myself a disservice by not following in your footsteps." My father straightened his back and leaned forward on his sitting cube. "Lately, I've been finding my studies rather daunting, and in many ways, unnecessary. With your permission, I'd like to accompany you to the lab on a daily basis and assist you with your research. And I'd like to withdraw from advanced piloting class and replace it with intergalactic biology if that's okay with you."

He didn't speak right away. His eyes narrowed as he reached across the table for another glasshouse grape. He popped it into his mouth and snapped his fingers in the air. A Timuary holding a narrow-necked decanter rushed to the dinner table to refill the king's glass with quip wine.

"Fine. The next time I have a relevant specimen in my lab, you're free to join my team."

"Relevant? What about the Erublian you told Murelle

and me about over dinner last week?" And what about the earthling, you liar?

"The Erublian lasted no more than a few days. They are uncivilized, nomadic, soft-shelled creatures. No match when it comes to the Enestian deterrents."

"And the Erublian was the last of your relevant captives?"

"I'm afraid so." My father glanced away and snatched his glass from the table as he continued to lie, but why? What made having a human within the walls of cell fifteen so different from any other creature my father felt was worthy of examination?

"That's too bad. I was really looking forward to trying something different," I groaned. It couldn't wait. I had to get involved in my father's work as soon as possible.

"No one's stopping you from enrolling in intergalactic biology. If you want to follow my lead, that's a good start," he said with his nose in the air.

"Do you think I can at least come to the lab every day after I leave the conservatory, you know, to start learning about the research equipment, the containment cells, and the quarantine and examination procedures?" That might grant me access to America's cell with a shell scan.

If I was caught, I could handle the formal reprimand and blame my actions on my curiosity and spontaneity, two traits my father, on more than one occasion in the recent past, had proudly admitted that I'd inherited from him.

But to save America from death? Did I dare to defy the king?

My father's brow ridge lifted. "And this is all about following in my footsteps?" he asked, tapping his finger against his thick chin. "This is coming from you, the boy who at the start of the term challenged my authority and the way I rule this planet. You suggested that peace could be gained through negotiations and mutual trust rather than enacting terror in the minds of our contemporaries, claiming it would be a more effective way of maintaining our, let us say, caustic yet noble reputation?"

"Yes, Father. But now I know I was wrong. I freely admit that I've come to my senses. When I'm ambassador, my skill in the art of rhetoric will be most advantageous, but secondary when it comes to instilling fear throughout the galaxies," I said, leaning forward and purposely holding my goblet exactly the way my father did, with my index finger extended. "Honestly, Father, was it that foolhardy for me to believe in dialogue, debates, and compromises? And what does that matter, now that I understand the veracity of your ways and the errors of mine?"

My father reclined in his chair, the cube's high back bending to accommodate his weight, took a long sip from his golden cup, and plopped another glasshouse grape into his mouth.

"It's just amusing you should ask about joining my team." He chuckled, his eyes glazed from drinking too much quip liquor.

"Why? I see nothing funny in wanting to expand my knowledge of my father's duties."

"Because Murelle asked me the same question less than an hour ago."

"What? I had no idea."

What in the galaxy was that sister of mine up to? There was no way she could have known of my desire to obtain access to the research lab and its adjoining cells, but if she had, asking for admittance into the lab is exactly the first thing she'd do. She would do anything to one-up me and jeopardize my cause.

"Did you—"

"No," my father interrupted after taking another slug from his goblet. "Your sister has no business in the lab. You, on the other hand, should learn the basic principles of abduction and dissection if you're going to, as you suggested, follow in my footsteps. With your eventual rule of Enestia, those skills are a must."

"Then, Father, I'd like to begin right away. I don't want to wait until the next relevant abduction."

"Fine." He snapped his fingers in the air, then spoke jovially into his communication cuff while a Timuary topped off his goblet with the flux-colored wine. "Huskus, prepare the Trispian for dissection. The prince thinks he's ready to join us in the lab."

Huskus, the lead scientist, joined my father briefly in a laugh before he stopped himself and spoke. "Yes, your royal."

"Come, my young prince." As the king stood, the violet wine sloshed from the top of his cup and dripped from his fingers. "I'm ready for some post-dinner entertainment."

Entertainment? Was I ready for this? No, but it was necessary if I decided to eventually sneak into the lab, see America, and try to save her from death.

The security of the lab and its adjoining cellblocks were true to the map Lestra and I generated days before in my room. When we reached the Trispian's cell, my father stood, his shoulders locked, and a narrow beam of light broadened in fan-like fashion to ride the contours of his ridged frame.

To override my own scan, Slaine Timuary typed a code into the monitor, but my attempt to get a peek at the code was futile, with his body partially blocking the monitor. It would have been too long to memorize anyway.

"Come, my boy," said the king as a double door unsealed and opened. "Let's see if you're ready to become a real man."

I met his comment with a false smile and followed him through the door. The poor Trispian was huddled in the corner and cowered when my father, holding a shock rod, approached it and nudged it from its cell. Two shocks from the rod were enough to force the creature into the hall and down to the lab. With each shock, the Trispian's back had arched, its jaw clamped shut, and it let out a wail between tight teeth. I grew sick with the knowledge of the creature's fate.

I'd never seen a Trispian in person, but I'd heard of their planet—Trispia. This specimen was larger than the one I'd seen at the virtual zoo when I was a kid and more Enestian in appearance than I'd remembered. Wearing a white coat, Huskus met us in the hall and ushered the soft-shelled creature into the lab, and my father and I followed. It was my first time in the there.

To my left and right, long counters held the products of my father's research—clear, cylindrical jars stuffed with the remains of many aliens. Heads, arms, torsos, some shelled and others de-shelled, their unsupported internal structure a globular mass of unrecognizable tissue, were suspended in liquid, along with internal organs and fetuses from beyond our galaxy.

At half the height of the average adult Enestian male, the Trispian met Huskus at the hip as it stood waiting and shaking. When my father stepped toward the alien again, it wailed, a hollow screech that hurt my ears but pulled at my heart, making my face plates drop. The king immediately poked it with a shock rod. The creature's body jerked, and it became silent.

And you consider this creature irrelevant, I wanted to ask when the Trispian's watery eyes met mine, but I held my tongue, knowing my tone would be one of indignation.

"To the table," my father ordered. "The prince will assist you." He winked, and Huskus motioned for me to take the Trispian by the legs as he took its arms.

Once our hands were firmly about the alien, my father gave it a long shock with the rod, holding it at the Trispian's neck for many seconds while it winced and groaned. The alien's limbs became limp, and in one motion, Huskus and I lifted it to the table.

Its mobility slowly returned, and just as it tried to wiggle itself from the metal slab, it was sucked back into place by the table's vacuum. For a creature that normally stood with a rounded back, the act of being pulled flat was more than painful. It screamed, trying to turn its head from side to side, causing the table's suction to double, and within minutes, the gruesome crack of shell was heard as the pull and weight of its body shattered its rope-like tail.

Hiding my disgust and horror was difficult, especially when my father and Huskus smiled at me, expecting me to do the same, and my father broke into a cruel laugh at the breaking of the Trispian's shell.

"Are you ready, my dear prince?" asked my father. All I could do was nod and shift my eyes away from the ailing creature. "Then we shall proceed." He held out his arms, and Huskus quickly fitted my father in a lab coat and gloves identical to his, although my father's lab attire was in the royal color of green.

"And the prince?" asked Huskus.

"He is here to observe, not to participate," my father answered sharply. That was a relief. The light hanging above the table illuminated. The Trispian gasped and let out another cry as its sight was obliterated by the bright light, and Huskus tapped a button that sent a small, invisible force from above to seal the alien's lips closed and pin its limbs to the table. A compartment opened in the wall, revealing an array of shiny dissection knives, and my heart began to pound as wildly as the creature's upon the table.

The shell plates covering the Trispian's chest heaved, and its eyes blinked erratically, the pin-dot pupils lost within its yellow irises. This alien was irrelevant to my father, but it was relevant to me. Behind its eyes lay a brain, something more than just a bundle of nerves. As the alien cried with eyes pleading for compassion and the end of its pain, I knew it was a creature who could think, learn, problem solve, and communicate with others of its species.

To me, irrelevant was a bog slug. Relevant was anything above that lowly plated terrestrial mollusk on the Enestian taxonomy. I couldn't watch a tri-horned hog dissected and killed any easier than I could this Trispian.

My whole body became ill, beginning at my stomach and working its way up my throat. With the ting of metal upon metal as my father selected a bladed tool from his collection, the plates at my spine locked, and for a moment, I thought my knees would buckle, sending me to the ground.

"But it's still alive," I blurted as my father approached

the alien. He glared at me from over his shoulder. Did I dare question the king? "I, um, I mean, I always thought a dissection took place on something that was dead," I lied.

"I always begin with a live subject," he said with a wink. "It will be dead shortly, and in the meantime, I can observe its tolerance to pain."

I swallowed so hard that I felt the lump in my throat knock against my shell as it went down. America would be given this same fate, tortured until her death, cut into pieces, and displayed like an award. I couldn't let that happen.

My father's shell-spitting tool flashed under the light. As the Trispian's eyes bugged, I felt mine do the same. As its chest plates overlapped, scraping with each breath, my own breathing became labored, and my eyes watered uncontrollably. This was what my father considered being a man? Yes, a man could do these things—a cruel, selfish, unforgiving man whose need for power overrode his sense of dignity and appreciation of life.

At that moment, I knew I could never be my father. I could never take his place as king if I was expected to continue his gruesome legacy. During my ambassadorship, I'd be expected to partake in every dissection, supporting my father's quest to rule the galaxy by exposing the weaknesses of fellow races.

I'd have to change things, find a way to eliminate that requirement of my post, and then as king, I'd find the support to stop this barbaric practice altogether.

The shell at the Trispian's waist split under the spike of the blade and the king's strength. The Trispian's eyes closed under a pain I couldn't imagine. I drew away from the table as my communication cuff fluttered with light. It was Lestra.

I answered, turning on my heels.

"Yes, I will be there in a few minutes," I said loudly and before she could speak. "Father," I continued, spinning to face the table. "I'm sorry, but I've been called back to the palace." Staying composed was almost impossible, especially after I spied the Trispian's bright orange blood pooling underneath it on the table. "Maybe I can witness a more relevant dissection. I've actually become bored with this one," I lied again.

The plates above his eyes came together. "Very well. We can continue your integration into our practices tomorrow. We'll begin with a complete tour of the lab in the morning. That should give you some satisfaction until my team seizes a more appropriate alien specimen for study. I'll inform Slaine Timuary of your impending visit, as he is lead guard. In addition, I'll expect your presence at our next team meeting," he said, his breath thick with the smell of fermented quips.

"Thank you, Father, my king," I said, excusing myself with a bow and diverting my eyes away from the bloody knife in my father's gloved hand.

Slaine met me at the door to escort me from the cellblock, and as the door resealed behind me, I heard the chilling crack of shell echoing from the back of the room. I could only hope the Trispian was already dead, and its suffering had ended.

In the hall leading to my quarters, I let my feet stamp the floor hard to settle the contents in my stomach, and I thought of America, her soft, delicate shape, her light voice, and crisp, ear-pleasing laugh. So helpless. So vulnerable.

And then I imagined her in the lab, writhing and

screaming under my father's knife, her soft skin erupting like the squeezed casing of a ripe quip. The pain would be unbearable. She'd flail and fight against the restraints, her back buckling like that of the Trispian's, while the contents of her veins pooled into the wells of the table.

My father— I'd never let him get his hands on her. Now I knew I had to stop him, but how?

My chest tingled within my shell as I longed to touch the human, hold her shell-less hand, and tell her everything would be okay—a promise I wish I could make.

"Hello, dear prince," Murelle snickered, entering the hall.

Damn Murelle. That dissection almost made me forget about her meddling into my business. Whether she meant to or not, she was always ruining or almost ruining something for me. Why her sudden interest in lab work? She must have known I was going to ask, but who told her? Lestra? She's the only person who knew my plan. But she wouldn't betray my trust.

"And why are you so smug? I'm the one who won this battle." Although at that moment, I almost wished I hadn't.

"What are you talking about?" She stroked her golden arm.

"Father gave me access to the lab, not you. I get to work with his team and at his side."

"You? You asked to work with Father?"

"Oh, don't play dumb with me, Murelle. Someone told you I wanted to work in the lab. Who was it?" Lestra entered the other end of the hall, her drab tunic stiff and cone-shaped. "It was you, wasn't it, Lestra?"

"Me? What, your royal? What are you talking about?" She blinked hard.

"You told Murelle that I wanted admittance into the lab."

"No, I didn't. I s-swear," she stuttered, looking almost as sad and displaced as the human girl we saw on the monitor in my quarters.

"Oh, leave her alone, Brother. She didn't tell me anything."

"And how do I know you're not lying for her?"

"Because that girl would never betray you." Murelle stroked the jewels on the top of her hand.

"How do you know?"

"Because she's in love with you."

I didn't answer but shot a glance at Lestra, who turned away from me and clasped her hands behind her back.

"Oh, come on now, princey. Can't you tell? Think about the way she looks at you, how her hands shake when she's next to you, how her wardrobe has changed over the last few months, showing just enough cleavage to give you a peek at her tits." She faced Lestra. "As if a servant had a chance." My sister laughed.

"Leave her alone."

Was she really in love with me? She *was* acting funny lately, telling me things she wasn't supposed to and getting too close so I'd notice she was sporting shell powder. If it was true, she was going out of her way to help me, not because she wanted to be my royal adjutant, but because she wanted to be more than just my personal servant, something that would never happen.

"And what about my shell powder, Lestra?" Murelle continued. "One of my tins is missing, and you were the last one in my room. I know you took it." She glared and her shell lips turned up awkwardly.

Lestra gave Murelle a cold stare and maintained eye contact until Murelle blinked and crossed her arms. Without acknowledging me, Lestra turned and marched down the hall. My sister was right. Everything she said about Lestra was true. I just never wanted to believe it. I didn't need the complication. Even if I were interested in her, Lestra could never mean more to me than a friend.

"That was fucked up, Murelle."

"So?"

"So, she's a Timuary. She warrants some respect. She doesn't deserve to be humiliated. You're as spiteful as you were before the turn of your nineteenth year. Grow up." I moved forward, backing Murelle up against the wall.

"What do you care, unless you love her, too? So, do you, big brother, have your heart set on a mere maid?" Murelle sneered as the fan of shell on her chest rose with a deep breath, and her black and purple-rimmed eyes showed a tad of fear.

"I have a better question for you, little sis," I said, putting my hands on Murelle's shoulders, pinning her against the wall and concentrating all of my anger toward my father on to her.

"Stop. You're going to crack my shell," she said, blinking and turning her head from side to side. With quick breaths, Murelle's shells clacked, and I released her.

"Then answer this: why your sudden interest in the research lab?"

"I don't know," she shouted.

"Yeah, you do, and you better tell me."

"Move aside, or I'm going to tell Father."

"You'll tell him anyway, so what do I care? I'm not going to let you leave you until you tell me the truth."

"Okay, okay. It's…" She gave me a kick and dodged to my left, but I caught her by the shoulder.

"It's what?"

"It's Slaine Timuary, okay? He's, you know, hot, and he's no longer just a servant. He's head guard now. He's moved into the guards' quarters, so I don't see him anymore. And yeah, I know he's still off-limits, but Dad's going to marry me off in a few years." She turned her cheek to the wall. "Who knows what my husband will look like, and if I'll really love him. So, I figure I might as well lose my virginity to someone decent looking while I have the chance."

That was the last thing I wanted to think about—my sister having sex.

My stomach soured, and I made a face. "You're fucking Slaine?"

"No, not yet. I mean, he doesn't even know I want to. I'm still working on it."

"And you criticized Lestra?" I sighed, releasing my trampy sister. "Slaine would never break his oath to our family and take you into his bed, and just because you want to fuck Lestra's brother doesn't give you the right to embarrass her like that."

"Oh, so you *are* in love with her." She took a lungful of air.

"I'm not in love with her, but I do care for her. Enough said."

"Okay, maybe so, but why *your* sudden interest in the lab? I know you hate father's research, or you would have taken intergalactic biology the minute you had the chance."

"I don't need to explain myself to you, little sis. Remember, I am going to rule this planet someday, not you."

"Fine. Don't tell me. I'll figure out why on my own," she said, sneering at me from over her shoulder as she turned down the hall.

I walked to the end of the hall, hoping Lestra was waiting for me outside my quarters, but she was gone. Why had she called me from the lab?

As much as I wanted to know, now was definitely not the time to find her and ask.

Chapter Thirteen

An alien stood on the other side of the glass curtain, as still as a Buckingham Palace guard, but it wasn't Garran. This Enestian was taller and broader, and his head sat upon a shorter, thicker neck. I could only assume it was a male, and he was the guard assigned to my cellblock.

Why was it here?

Fifteen days hadn't passed, only five, maybe six at the most. It was hard to tell without the light of the sun or glow of the moon to give me a hint at the time. It had been a day or more since Garran's last visit, and I could only hope he hadn't given up on helping me.

My body tightened, and I cringed, choking out a soft cry against my cupped hands. I was so cold and so hungry. This morning when I awoke, there was another tray of food bricks on the floor of my cell. I took a nibble from the brown one, but it had been so dry and tasteless I didn't take another bite.

I had to get out of here! I had to get home!

With cheeks hot and eyes ready to spill tears, I approached the thick, waterfall-like wall and leaned forward to study the alien's profile.

"My name is America," I said slowly and with an exaggerated motion pointed to my chest. "America." The alien remained silent. "America," I repeated. "From Earth."

What was the use? This alien was definitely not Garran's sister or Garran's language professor or it would have spoken to me in English.

But just as I was about to plop to the floor, the alien stepped closer. "Slaine," he said, motioning to his chest the same way I had. "Enestian," it added.

"Slaine," I repeated. "I'm cold," I said and mimed being so by shivering and rubbing my arms.

And then he turned and walked away. I stepped closer to the wall, but the blur was gone, and I sank to the floor, sick with being lonely again and afraid, but relieved I wasn't being taken somewhere to be examined and killed.

Garran. I wanted Garran for comfort, the sweet, gentle Enestian whose tone alone let me know that he understood my pain. My insides warmed as I closed my eyes and envisioned his strong, humanly profile and the line of his sharp jaw behind the flowing wall. What did he look like, this sweet, sympathetic being covered in shell?

But why? How could the blurred outline of something non-human elevate my heart rate pleasantly when I thought of him? Why did I wonder what it would feel like if he touched me? Maybe even kissed me? Or more? Fuck. I was going to die in two weeks and would never know what *more* really was.

"America."

It was Garran. I straightened my back and moved closer to the cloudy wall as my pulse increased. He dropped to the floor across from me.

"Thank you for coming back." *For caring about me. For wanting to see me.*

"You don't need to thank me. I wanted to come."

I folded my chilly arms across my breasts, and when I took a deep breath, my cheeks warmed. "There was someone here a few minutes ago."

"Yes, that was Slaine. The guard assigned to your cell."

"Where is he now?"

"Distracted. If he knew I was here, he'd report it." He rubbed the top of his head. "I'm not sure how much longer I can visit you without it being detected. Yesterday, I was granted access to the lab. I hope to gain entry to your cell within the next few days, and then…"

"And then you'll take me home?"

"If I can, but first I need to get you out of here and away from the lab, then—"

"Home?" I asked, and rose to my knees.

"Yes, I'm not going to let you die, I promise," he said confidently and unblinking. "I will do anything to stop that from happening, but getting you to the Laguna Mountains will be more difficult than freeing you from this cellblock."

The Laguna Mountains. He pronounced it like La-gun-a, making me smile. I closed my eyes and imagined Mount Laguna, majestic and unyielding. Where I live. How I missed it so much, even the stupid little things like how one of the cabinets in my kitchen would never quite close all the way, how the guy in the next apartment would play his music way too loud on weekend nights, and how Attie always left crumbs on the counter after making a sandwich. I'd like to show Garran where I lived. Maybe take him for coffee at Robusta and play him a Motley Crue album.

"I've seen pictures of your Laguna Mountains. They were full of snow. I've never seen snow before. The rain on Enestia doesn't freeze."

"Then you're missing out. Snow can be fun."

"What can you do with snow?"

"You can ski on it, sled on it, and pack it into balls and throw it at people." I laughed, remembering my last snowball fight with Attie.

Garran tilted his head. "You hit people with snow?"

"Yeah. It's a game. It's called a snowball fight."

"So, if we were on Earth together, and it was snowing, would you throw a snowball at me?" He laughed.

My insides sparked. "I sure would," I teased. And then we could warm up later with hot chocolate, snuggling together under a blanket. I'd put my head on his shoulder…

"Is that what you were doing with your friends before you were taken and brought here, having a snowball fight?"

"No, it wasn't snowing at the time. It only snows in the winter. Right now where I live, it's spring." Spring—my favorite season. The daffodils and tulips I planted in the big terracotta pot on my apartment balcony were about to bloom, something I'd now miss, just like I'd never see another spring. My stomach burned, the sensation rising in my throat.

"And you were there with your friends."

"Yeah, Atlanta, Logan, and Kevin."

"A female and two males?" Garran asked, tilting his head.

I nodded. "Logan is Atlanta's boyfriend."

"And Kevin, he is yours?" Garran asked slowly.

"No, I don't have a boyfriend. Kevin and I hardly knew each other."

I swallowed hard. Kevin, even with his hot athletic build, would have never become my boyfriend. The two of us just never clicked.

But here I was instead, talking to an alien I'd never seen and who made my heart jump when I studied his smooth profile.

"Your snowball fight reminds me of… Um, I don't know how to translate the words. There are amphibians on our planet called knulls. During a heavy rain, they form a thick, clear bubble of mucus around their bodies. Once the rain stops, the knulls hop away, leaving their bubbles behind. Enestian children find them and throw them at each other. The bubbles pop when they hit, leaving a smear of mucus," he said.

"Yuck." I laughed, as something about this alien continued to put me at ease and paused my homesickness and fear of death. He promised he wouldn't let me die. I had to believe that.

"Yeah, I never played when I was a kid, but I've always wanted to."

"Why didn't you?"

"I wasn't allowed. It's not considered a dignified form of recreation for a—" Garran lowered his head, and his shoulders rose with a long breath.

"For a what?"

"America, there is something I haven't told you." He paused and swallowed. "I'm a prince," he said softly and diverted his eyes away from me.

Shock zoomed through me. "You're a prince? The prince of this planet," I said, pissed because he'd kept that from me.

"Yes, I didn't tell you before because I thought you'd expect more from me. I am a prince, but I am a prince with little authority until I am king. That's why you are here and not back on Earth. I don't have the permission or the means to—"

"Then don't ask his permission. Just do it. Sneak me out of here. Please, don't leave me alone again. I don't think I can handle another day of this, knowing I'll be killed in ten days if you can't free me and not knowing what's happening on Earth. I miss my family and friends, and I know they miss me. Please, send me home," I pleaded, as a set of tears freed themselves from the inner corners of my eyes with a blink.

"I wish it were that simple. I told you I will do everything under my power and abilities to help you, but this building is highly secured and under surveillance at all times. It would be impossible for me to take you out of here undetected, so I need to come up with a plan."

"But as a prince, you've got to have some kind of pull and—"

"And it doesn't matter. At least not to my father. His authority is golden. In his mind, I'm just a naive and overindulged prince. Until I'm ambassador, he won't recognize my intellect, abilities, or accomplishments, and even then, my authority will be limited."

"You're going to be the Ambassador of Enestia?"

"Yes, in two years, upon my twenty-third year of life. It's my destiny. What I've been groomed for—taking one course after another at the royal conservatory, studying our planet's history and the legacy of my family name." He sighed and his shoulders slumped. "But I just don't know if I really…" He stopped and sighed again.

"If you really want to be the ambassador," I said. "Because you want to be a pilot."

"Yes, but I could be both." He squared his shoulders. "And I would be both if I could eliminate some of the duties ambassadorship entailed. I'd be king, too, if I could govern differently. Right now, I don't want to be king—not if I have to rule the way my father would want me to. He prefers the threat of war over the peaceful words of negotiation." He crossed his ankles and straightened his back. "There are many things, kingly traditions, that come with being a prince and ambassador that I'd prefer not to follow."

"Like what?"

"My eventual marriage. It will be arranged at my father's choosing when he thinks I am ready to take a bride."

"An arranged marriage? That's awful! Are all Enestian marriages arranged?" The thought of Garran being with someone else made me a bit jealous.

"No, like humans, we prefer to begin a family based on emotions, not convenience, with a formal courtship, love, and then commitment and marriage. Family units are encouraged, a husband, wife, and their eventual children if they wish, but for a royal, the rules are different. The goal of my marriage will be to gain a political advantage over another planet in our galaxy."

"What about having a girlfriend before you're slated to

get married?"

"No, for me it is forbidden," he said softly, though his tone was tinged with what I could only interpret as being resentment. "I've known my fate and my duty to Enestia since I was a child, so at first I accepted it," he said, his shoulders lifting and settling as he inhaled deeply enough for me to hear it. "But now I want to make my own decisions."

"I wouldn't want an arranged marriage, either. I'm going to marry for love—only love. That is, if I get back to Earth. Sometimes I still can't believe this—any of this—until I relive that night in my mind. The ship, dark and expansive, triangular with tiny lights, how it was above me, and I fell and became numb."

"That ship was a dual propulsion galaxy cruiser with long-range travel capabilities, the flagship of Enestia's fleet."

"And you can fly a ship like that?"

"Yes. As a prince, there is one thing I don't regret—the education I was required to receive. All royals are trained in intergalactic flight."

"Then *you* can take me home."

"If I can gain access to a ship. Activating a flyer's controls takes a proper shell scan, and I have not been given clearance. My first priority is to get you out of this cell. Then I'll try to find a way to get you back to Earth."

"Thank you," I said, smiling as hope kindled in the center of my chest.

"And if I hadn't been forced to take an intergalactic language, I wouldn't be able to communicate with you."

I couldn't see him smile, but I heard it in his words. His voice cradled my soul, and I longed to keep its sweet cadence in my ears, to let it rock me gently and give me some comfort even after he was long gone from my cell, and I was left alone, once again, to huddle in the corner and pray I'd last another day.

"When you talk, I forget that you're not human."

"And I forget you're not Enestian. I used to think the English language was harsh and lacked depth, but when I hear you speak and imagine your soft lips forming each word, your language is one of the most beautiful things I've ever heard in my life."

A euphoric sensation rose from deep below, flooding into my warmed chest. "Come closer," I whispered. "As close as you can."

Garran pushed up from his palms, leaning forward as I did the same, and our faces came within inches of each other. The wall's warmth pulsed against my lips in small puffs, and I yearned to kiss this unique alien creature.

"You're beautiful," said Garran.

"And how would you know?" I laughed as my body tingled.

"I've seen you."

"You've seen me?"

"Your intake image when I looked at your file, but even if I hadn't, I'd still think you were an amazing being."

"I don't remember a picture being taken."

"You were unconscious," he said in a tone that sounded like an apology. "Your eyes were closed," he continued softly. "Your eyes, what color are they?"

"Brown, but sometimes, depending on the light, they look green," I said. "What about yours?"

"They're a bit hard to describe. You'll just have to wait and see them for yourself," he teased.

My chest expanded without taking a breath, and I imagined his body with a layer of shell, smooth but masculine, defined yet indistinct, the thought stimulating instead of repulsing me. I pictured someone like Batman with his strong, amazing body covered in a muscular superhero outfit. "What about your lips— Are they covered with shell?"

"Yes, but it's different from the shell that covers the majority of our bodies. Shell lips are porous instead of solid, forgiving instead of stiff."

He turned his head slightly to the side. His jaw lowered as his lips parted, and even with the wall rippling between us, I could just make out the tip of his tongue as he licked his lips. I thought he was beautiful, too, this statuesque blur of a creature whose nose was straight but faint, and whose sharp chin cut to the clean lines of a throat and neck.

"I want to touch you," he said.

"And I want to touch you." But even more, I wanted his touch upon me, his shell against my skin.

"I will do everything I can to see you, even if it breaks protocol. I'm touring the lab tomorrow. I will try to see what I can do."

My heart beat hard, and I closed my eyes, imagining the prince, a human form with shell-like skin. I heard a high-pitched voice, and when I opened my eyes, a second form appeared behind Garran, but it wasn't Slaine. I recognized its shape from the day before. It was the female, and she was there to tell Garran it was time to leave.

Chapter Fourteen

I found Lestra in the servant wing of the palace, dumping a load of dirty tunics into the steamer.

"Thanks for keeping Slaine occupied for me again while I talked to America," I told her.

"You're welcome," she said without looking at me.

"And you still haven't told me."

"Told you what?"

"What you wanted when you called me at the lab yesterday. We never got a chance to talk about it."

"I honestly don't remember," she said as she continued to keep her eyes from mine.

"Here, let me do that," I said, reaching for the clothes bin.

"No, I can do it," she snapped, pulling the bin away to shake out the last of the tunics. "This is the work of a

Timuary, not a royal. A prince doesn't even belong in this room. You should leave at once."

She was right, but normally she wouldn't care. Why did she have to be so damned difficult? "Come with me to my quarters, so we can talk."

"Is that an order?" She fidgeted with her tunic, pulling at the hem.

"Yes, now come on. I know what's bothering you. Just forget about it. You know I could give a shit less about what my sister has to say."

"How can I forget it?"

"Easy, just get over it, okay? I don't believe her anyway."

"Why not?" She sighed. "It's true." She left the room, walked into the hall, and I followed.

What? I gave her an out, and she didn't take it? I didn't expect that response. Well, maybe I did. I don't know. Most of the girls I was around were either cousins or servants, and because of my fate, in terms of marriage, my interaction with eligible Enestian females had been limited because it was simply unnecessary.

"I don't know what to say, Lestra." My shoulder plates tightened.

"You don't have to say anything. I know I shouldn't have these feeling for you, but I can't help it. I really care about you."

"I'm sorry, Lestra. Did I…"

She finally lifted her head and bit her bottom lip of shell.

"Did I do anything to make you think…?"

"You mean did you lead me on?"

"Yeah, I guess that's what I mean."

Like me, Lestra's life was pretty sheltered when it came

to romance. Serving our family since birth, she led a very isolated existence. The only boys she had any real contact with were either part of my royal family or the sons of high-ranking military officers—both groups were off-limits to all servants, even servants with the last name Timuary.

"Well, yeah, kind of." She stared back down at the hall's black stone floor worn glassy smooth over time by the padding of many royal boots.

"Like?"

"We spend a lot of time together, Garran. You request my services more than you do any other palace maid. You ask for me personally."

"That's because you're smart and dependable. And those are traits I admire, traits I hope my wife someday will have. But you know the rules. Even if my feelings for you extended well beyond our professional relationship, we could never be together. It's not allowed. No exceptions. A royal could never—"

"But you're not like that, Garran. I know you too well, better than your own sister. You'd break tradition and defy your father for someone you loved."

She was right. She did know me as well as she claimed. If I found myself falling in love with a palace maid, I would break the royal rules and disappoint my father by asking for her hand in marriage. But I didn't love Lestra.

"You must not know me that well because I'd never do anything to disrespect my father in terms of my marriage obligations," I lied.

"Yeah, go ahead and say that. Play the role of the prince, but you don't have me fooled. You're defying him right now, lying about your interest in intergalactic biology in order to see that thing in cell fifteen. You'd break your oath to marry at his choosing in a heartbeat."

"Shhh," I whispered, scanning the hall for untrustworthy ears like Murelle's. "It's different when it comes to the human. A life is at stake."

"A human life. So what?" She marched down the hall, her arms folded and her steps harder than usual.

"It has feelings. It's…" I said as I walked behind her.

"And I don't?" She stopped when we reached the dining hall, and I almost ran into her back.

"Of course you do, and I care about your feelings, and I care about you—just not the way that…you know." For all the years I'd known Lestra, I wasn't quite sure why this conversation felt so awkward.

"Yeah, I know—now." She turned and gave me a hard stare.

"Lestra, to me you're not just a palace maid. You're a friend." I took a deep breath and exhaled so forcefully air whistled through my shell. "A good friend. I trust you. Not just because you're a Timuary, but because you are who you are."

"So what does that mean?" Lestra stroked the top of her hand as if it were donned with precious jewels.

"It means that I *want* you in my life, not just now, but for a long time. I'm considering you for the position as my royal adjutant."

Did I just say that? Not that it wasn't true—it was. But the fate of an adjutant's marriage lies in the hands of the adjutant's royal, meaning me. Just as my father had my married future in his grip, it would be my duty to choose Lestra's husband for her at the turn of her twenty-first year.

"What's up with you two?" interrupted Murelle as she sashayed into the dining hall. Bellow Timuary followed, carrying a tray of ripe fruit. Following the rules for servants, Lestra and Bellow didn't make eye contact, although I'm pretty sure they were first cousins.

"None of your business, sis."

"So, did you two kiss and make up?" she teased as she selected a cape apple from the tray and took a bite.

"Come on, Lestra. Let's go. It suddenly got too cold in here for me."

As I crossed the threshold into the next room, there was a crash behind me. Turning, I saw the tray of fruit scattered on the floor and Lestra standing with her hand against her mouth. A handful of grapes rolled to meet my boots.

"You did that on purpose!" Murelle screamed.

"I am so sorry, my royal. How clumsy of me." Lestra's sorry tone was almost believable.

Bellow chased after a grape and retrieved it, then came down on one knee to collect and toss the soiled fruit back onto the tray. "Sorry, Bell. I couldn't stop myself," I heard Lestra whisper when she knelt beside her relative to help.

"I'm going to report this." Murelle scowled.

"It was an accident. Get over it," I said, coming to Lestra's defense. "Besides, any report you file against Lestra would be negated with a report I'd submit about her exemplary performance over the last few months, so don't waste your time. Come on, Lestra. Let's go," I continued, taking her by the hand.

"Now you're both on my shit list," I heard Murelle mutter as Lestra and I left the room. My sister sure had a lot of class for a princess.

"I'm sorry about that, Garran. She just made me so mad. I'm a Timuary. I'm not supposed to feel anything but love and respect for the royal family we serve, but right now all I want to do is break your sister's shell."

"I don't blame you." I laughed. "You have no idea how many times I've thought about doing the same thing to her."

Lestra tightened her grip on my hand. "Um, Garran," she asked, "would you really do what you said, you know, save me from a reassignment by filing a report on my behalf?"

"Of course." When we reached the foyer and stopped walking, I gently pulled my hand away from hers. Her hand was a hand used to hard work, a hand smooth at the palm but rough at the fingertips.

She took a deep breath and sighed. Her eyes told me there was something stirring inside of her, something that erupted from my touch and kind words, something that made her hand shiver in mine, despite the fact that her hand was so hot. If I didn't know better, I'd think she had a fever.

She was waiting, waiting to sense the same emotions from me, emotions she would never find. Lestra, as pretty and graceful as she was, couldn't send my heart beating a zillion times a minute like hers was beating for me right now. She desecrated her shell for me, not out of duty or because she thought it might bring her closer to a royal post, but because her feelings for me went well beyond what they were supposed to be.

"Like I said before, I respect and admire you, Lestra. You're loyal and trustworthy, and I enjoy our time together. You're a good friend." Her smile faded with my last word, and I felt like a total jerk. The truth needed to be told, but at the same time, the last thing I wanted to do was break her heart. It was time to change the subject. "So, when you called me last night, what were you going to tell me?"

"I don't know. I told you. I forgot." She didn't forget. She was getting moody all over again.

"Well, anyway, I need to thank you for calling me when you did," I said, heading toward my quarters. "It gave me an excuse to leave the lab. I was about to witness something unbearable."

"What? You went to the lab?" she asked, jogging up behind me. I knew that would break her bad mood.

Once we were settled in my quarters, I told her about the Trispian, my graphic tale leaving me almost as sick and angry as I was while witnessing the horrific act of what I'd call murder.

"I can't believe it!" Lestra jumped from her sitting cube. "I can't believe your father would do such a thing in the first place, besides making you watch the live dissection of an innocent alien."

"Why wouldn't he? That's what I'm going to be expected to do." My shell plates clacked as I shuddered.

"I'm going to talk to your father about this right now," she declared while pacing my room. "I'm going to tell him there's absolutely no reason to subject you to the mistreatment of galactic life-forms. Someone else can do it. It doesn't need to be you."

All I could do was laugh. "So you're really going to find my father and say these things to him?" The king didn't even know her name. He'd immediately dismiss her to a lesser planet for her impudence. "Besides, I asked for access to the lab, remember? Now do you understand why I need to see that human before my father gets his hands on it?"

My mind was flooded with the image of America, but this time, she was on the examination table in my father's lab, her eyes holding the same terror I saw in the eyes of the Trispian. I couldn't let that happen to her or to any of the other creatures my father's team stole from their home planets.

I had to see her as soon as possible, force my way into her cell if I had to, as long as my father wouldn't find out.

"I want you to come with me on my tour of the lab. Your support in this would really mean a lot."

"I'll come with you, Garran." She dropped her head and looked up at me. "But I still think your dad needs a good talking to by me. I'm not afraid of him."

I wasn't directly afraid of him, either. I was afraid of what he could do to me with his power, and she should have been, too.

As expected, Remlin Timuary kept his post just inside the main entrance to the lab. He nodded when he saw Lestra and me approach and went as far as engaging the door before we were close enough to trigger it open ourselves. Obviously my father had told him to expect us.

"Good day, my royal." Remlin smiled and led us into the reception area. One of the scientists on my father's research team passed us in the corridor. He stopped to give me a bow but didn't say anything. I wondered whether or not he just left cellblock fifteen, whether or not he was the one responsible for drawing America's blood and extracting bone marrow from her hip. The thought burned under my shell.

Slaine stood at the first cellblock, his feet set apart on the stone floor, his hands behind his back. "My royal, it is an honor."

"Thank you, Slaine. Oh, and congratulations on your new assignment. You are the first Timuary to become lead guard. My father chose wisely."

"Thank you, my royal."

"So, tell me. Where will our tour begin and end?"

"It will begin here, at cellblock one and end at cellblock three, cell fourteen."

"Fourteen is next to the research lab?"

"Yes, it is."

"And what about fifteen? I do believe there is another cellblock after fourteen?"

"Yes, my royal, but cell fifteen is currently under renovation. The king specifically—"

"I'd like to see those renovations."

"I am sorry, my royal, but—"

"Slaine, do not challenge my authority. If I want to see cell fifteen, I will see cell fifteen. It does not take my father's approval. You are a Timuary. I am a royal. It is your job to do as I say."

My stomach churned. I heard a click and knew Lestra's shells were tightening with anticipation as were mine. I hated using my royal influence against this humble Enestian, but it had to be done. I had to see the human.

"I'll need to contact the king."

"You will do no such thing, Slaine. Listen to me." I grabbed his arm. He didn't flinch. We were almost of the same height and build, but his head was slightly larger than mine, and the shell plates above his eyes were thick and protruded slightly. "I cannot tell you how or why, but I know about the human in cell fifteen, and I want to see her. I want to enter her cell."

He shot his gaze to the floor.

"Have you seen her?" His eyes shifted back to mine. "Answer me," I demanded.

"Yes. I have seen it one time. It was cold. I gave it a blanket from the guard's quarters."

He'd *seen* her, something I'd longed to do for days. Had he touched her, too? Slaine had been in her cell, given her something I couldn't—comfort—and maybe even put his palm on her shoulder. Or held her hand. Something I should be doing. He had definitely seen her naked. The plates across my chest overlapped hard with my next breath, and my jaw locked uncomfortably.

Sure, I was glad for what he did to keep America warm, but I was jealous...yes, jealous...that he had helped her, while I, a prince, was powerless.

America had been on my mind continually since I'd last been with her. But I had been absent from my activities far too often and didn't want anyone to become suspicious, especially Murelle. So I stayed away, even though it killed me. I was taking a risk each time I saw her, but as I came to know her better, I found myself willing to take a chance just to hear her voice. Make her laugh. America Novoa's well-being was becoming more important to me with each passing day.

I thought of the hours she spent alone, huddled, afraid, lonely, and I wanted to burst through that wall to see her. Touch her.

Kiss her.

Show her I was more than a helpless prince with no

authority.

"Slaine!" snapped Lestra, dragging me from my thoughts. "What were you thinking? You could lose your position."

"I know, but this specimen is different from the others. It is Enestian in many ways."

I seized on Slaine's compassion. "Yes, she is. That's why I need to see her. I speak her language. You are to take Lestra and me immediately to her cell, and you are to tell no one."

The plates between Slaine's eyes overlapped. "Opening the specimen's cell requires a shell scan. Each scan is logged into the specimen's files. The king will find out, and I will be reprimanded and demoted. Prince Garran, please!" he said and took a step toward me. "I cannot disgrace my family."

"You opened it when you gave her a blanket. How is this any different?"

Lestra gave her brother a cold glare, her shell lids becoming mere slits, and Slaine's shoulders stiffened as if he was heeding some kind of warning. But what kind of warning? Was it something that went beyond Slaine entering her cell in the first place?

"I, I overrode the shell scan. I have the code."

"Then use it again."

"Your royal, I took an oath."

"And as a royal, I am ordering you to — "

"Garran, please, don't put this kind of pressure on my brother. I have the code. It's actually the same one we used to enter the lab before you were given permission to do so. You can override the scan yourself," said Lestra.

The code we had did more than open medical records? She lied to me. Kept me from America.

"Slaine." Lestra stepped toward her brother and spoke,

breaking the rule for Timuarys not to speak to one another while a royal is present.

"Lestra, hold your tongue!" Slaine's chest puffed with the scrape of shell.

"Do not rebuke her, Slaine Timuary. She has my permission to speak to you. Your sister is on the path to becoming my royal adjutant. Anything she says or does is under my guidance and with my consent."

Slaine snapped his shoulders back.

"I'm sorry, Brother," continued Lestra, "but we are both under Garran's direct orders, and though the king's wishes certainly outrank those of the prince, I am asking you to abide by Garran's commands without question and without alerting the king."

"Do you understand what you're asking me to do, my royal?" Slaine addressed me directly instead of answering his sister.

"Yes, I do understand," I said and rested my hand on top of his shoulder. "And I also understand there's a human female destined to suffer under my father's unnecessary experiments and die in a week's time. The king is a sadist. He cares for no life except his own. Please, Slaine, take us to cell fifteen."

Slaine blinked, his eyes, blue and amber, like his sister's and mine, flashed with doubt and fear. "And if the king finds out that I've—"

"If my father finds out, I'll tell him that I deceived and threatened you, and that I stole the code. But if you do as I say, it won't matter, because he'll never find out about this. Now, take us to cell fifteen."

"As you wish, my royal."

"Thank you, Slaine. And thank you for helping the human."

My heart rattled against shell. I was so anxious to see her. The one-dimensional photo in her file came to mind, and I remembered the dark circles under her closed eyes and the thin, pale lids that covered them. Everything in that photo expressed weakness and fragility, something that didn't define the girl I grew to know. But there was beauty in that photo as well, the turn of her soft chin, the plumpness of her lips, and the shine of the stuff they call "hair."

I couldn't wait to meet this female human called America.

Chapter Fifteen

America

Something rough rubbed me under the chin. I opened my eyes, stretched into a yawn, and found a blanket draped over my body. It was thick but light in weight, the weave of the fabric rough but slick as I ran my fingers along its edge.

Slaine! He must have understood that I was freezing my ass off in here. He was gone, or I would have immediately thanked him. He had kept his watch over me, off and on during the day, and had the decency to leave when I activated the toilet and sink to eject from the wall. Even though he couldn't really see me, it still would have been uncomfortable and awkward to see his shadowy form while I peed.

Although we couldn't communicate, seeing his fuzzy figure on the other side of the liquid wall gave me some comfort, especially when I was thinking about Earth and missing Garran's presence.

Garran. I was amazed at how much he and I had in common, even though we'd grown up galaxies apart. For all the guys I'd known on Earth, I never felt as connected with any of them the way I did when Garran and I talked about music, about what we wanted from life. Sure, I was initially irritated when he told me who he really was, but I got that he felt powerless and didn't want to get my hopes up until he figured out a way to rebel against his father in order to help me.

I stood and wrapped the blanket around myself. It was a bit itchy, but it was warm, and although I had started to get used to my nakedness, it felt good to cover up. My whole body ached from lying on the cold floor when I slept each day, but my skin was smooth and soft from the semi-bath I gave myself earlier, using the soapy liquid I discovered in a compartment built into the sink.

The soap also made my hair manageable and shiny, and though my teeth had chattered when I dunked my head into the basin of cold water, it was worth being clean and smelling good. I'd give anything for hot showers, real food, and my mom.

What was happening on Earth? I'd fallen asleep with that question on my mind, and it still lingered. My family and friends were probably worrying and crying about me, just like I was on another planet three galaxies away worrying and crying about them. I hoped they weren't still being interrogated by the police, or suffering because of my disappearance.

I missed everyone, even Lois, the bitchy neighbor in the apartment below, who'd yell up at me from the stairwell when I played my music too loud, at least too loud according to her standards. I would have given anything at that moment to be in my apartment getting hollered at, even with Lois holding her cell phone and threatening to call the police.

If I ever got home, I'd never again take anything for granted.

Yes, Garran would do it. He'd save me, protect me from the possibility of death even if he couldn't take me back to Earth, and I simply remained "missing" for years.

His promise gave me hope. The chance that he could help me, as impossible as it sometimes seemed, was the only thing that kept me from losing my mind—that and recounting Garran's sweet words...and his hot body.

A body covered with shell? How could he move and bend so freely while encased in something so hard— It had to be hard or it would break with his weight.

I closed my eyes and pressed my back against the far wall of my cell, savoring his masculine form in my mind. Holding my blanket, I slid downward until I met the floor.

Three shadowy figures appeared on the other side of the wall. I recognized Garran's form right away, and my body relaxed with his close proximity. Another was Slaine, and the third, shorter and thinner shape, was probably that of the female Enestian I saw with Garran the day before.

I stood and approached the wall. The wave fluttered and then froze, something I hadn't seen it do before.

What? Was it going to open? My heart thumped hard. A sizzling sound came next, along with a sweet, zingy odor I couldn't recognize, and I caught myself holding my breath as the cloudy wall rose slowly. I was finally going to see these beings of shell, and maybe go home if they were here to free me. And how thankful I was to not be naked as I stood in anticipation, clutching the folds of the wrapped blanket at my chest.

The first thing I saw were two pairs of boots, one pair deep green and velvety, another gray, lacking definition, reaching mid-calf, and then a third set of smaller black shoes with pointed toes and tiny, one-inch heels.

Black pants were tucked into the tops of the boots, billowing slightly over the boots' neck before tightening and clinging to the legs underneath. The green boots were Garran's. The athletic thickness of his legs was undeniable. The gray boots were Slaine's, and the black, pointy shoes were worn by someone with thin but well-defined legs that were covered in black leggings.

The hands appeared next, and I held my breath, staring as my mind discerned the fact that instead of skin, ridged shell-like plates encased each finger and wrapped up and around the top of each hand. The arms and torsos became visible next, and I released the air in my lungs, eager to see their faces.

Garran wore a green shirt that matched his green boots, a shirt embroidered with gold thread in strange angular designs that cut, curled, and zigzagged. In great contrast, Slaine's shirt was white and non-descript, with the exception of a large pocket over one breast, and the female was dressed in beige, an A-line tunic with long sleeves.

I took a step forward as the last bit of the clear curtain of confinement retracted into the ceiling.

I think I gasped. I wasn't sure. My heart pulsed so strongly I could hear it in my ears and feel it heavy in my chest, wrenching my whole body.

"America," said Garran.

What had I expected they'd look like? I wasn't sure. I could never construct it my mind, and now after seeing them, I knew I could have never come up with their images on my own.

Instead of frightening me, Garran's appearance was amazing. There was nothing to disappoint as he reflected the same silhouette I had come to adore. His face was smooth, curving delicately at his cheeks and chin, but he was masculine and athletic with his broad shoulders and thick upper arms, making him distinctly humanoid with his muscular build. But what did he think of me? Now I was real, no longer just a photograph and a voice.

Garran's eyes rode my body. When we made eye contact he smiled, and my heart bounced. Slaine said something to Garran in their native tongue, plates of shell overlapping at his cheeks when he spoke, in sounds that twisted and purred and clicked, and with words that were sometimes fuzzy and sometimes so distinct they seemed almost human.

When I imagined aliens, I'd always pictured short, thin creatures with big heads and huge eyes—ugly things—but these aliens were true to the sleek forms I'd viewed through the wall. And despite being hairless, they were attractive and humanoid with hard exteriors, making them appear as if they were carved from stone.

In contrast to their matte shells, their clothing glimmered unnaturally under the light as if each molecule of thread was alive and twinkling in unison with each other, and a badge of sort was attached to the upper left of each of their shirts. Garran's badge was much more elaborate than the others, with its array of large, multi-colored jewels, while Slaine's and the female's were plain, lacking jewels or stones and made with the simple turns of filigree upon gold.

The female's long tunic dropped to just above the knee, and as she stood and teetered to the left to rest most of her weight on one foot, I could see that her body thinned at the waist and rounded at the hips just like a human female's. She was at least a foot shorter than Garran and Slaine. Her nose was smaller, too, and her cheeks curved down to a pointed chin, and though I had a blanket to keep myself covered, I felt naked again as the female's eyes scanned my body. Bright blue and dotted with amber, her eyes, judgmental and empty, were intriguingly beautiful.

"America," Garran said again.

"Garran," I said, tightening the blanket wrapped around my body and tucking it to hold it in place. "Are you here to take me home?" I asked, rising up on my toes in anticipation of leaving my cell.

"No, I'm sorry. I just, I just wanted to see you."

"Oh." I sighed and dropped to my heels so hard a dull echo followed. Home—not today—but Garran was a welcomed distraction to my predicament.

He said something to Slaine and the female, motioning with his hand for them to leave. Slaine turned, but the female held her ground, the place above her eyes coming together as she rattled off something in Enestian. After another exchange, she walked away, her body stiff, the plain filigreed badge she wore flickering when it caught the light. She peered at me through the constricted slits of her eye plates, and the liquid wall spilled back into place behind her and Slaine.

Garran came closer. His beauty alone was enough to make me swoon as our eyes locked. As he approached, my insides lit with a pleasant heat radiating from my lower abdomen.

"Can I touch you?" he asked gently.

"Y-yes."

I trusted Garran, although we barely knew each other. Whether it was the warmth in his eyes, the most unique eyes I'd ever seen, or the calm in his voice, I didn't know, but something told me he wouldn't hurt me or do something to make me feel awkward or uncomfortable. I wanted to touch him, too.

Garran took another step forward, and my heart rocked in my chest. He lifted his index finger to my face and gently set his fingertip on my cheek. His hand met my mouth, pushing my bottom lip delicately, then tracing its shape with two additional fingers.

I closed my eyes, and for a moment I thought I felt his warm breath against my skin.

But Garran had only rested his fingers on my chin. I opened my eyes and trembled with his touch as he stood in front of me, his chin lifted, his head tilted slightly to one side with his bright blue and yellow-dotted eyes focused on mine. Eyes full of confidence and pride, eyes that were loyal and sympathetic, yet full of energy and the need to accomplish a chivalrous quest—the eyes of a knight.

His body, clad in protective plates of shell like a suit of armor, matched the passion I saw within, but could this being, this Enestian Prince, rescue me like a knight in shining armor? What was it about this strange being with sheets of shell for skin that made me suddenly feel safe on a planet I had never seen before and knew nothing about?

Something about this alien made me smile despite the

fact that my body ached and my stomach wrenched with pains of hunger. His movements were sharp and purposeful like that of an athlete's, but there was a hint of elegance and an air of sophistication in the way he tipped his head and how his shoulders settled gracefully when he took a deep breath.

Why did the feel of his soft fingers make my blood pump noticeably in my throat and send a warm shiver through my body, this thing with hard hands but with a warm shell? His touch was innocent, yet sensuous, an extension of his passion, and I marveled at how the grazing of his fingertips upon me could ignite desire.

Was he experiencing this, too? Were the parting of his lips and the deep, eye-closing breaths a sign that he hoped our innocent exploration of shell and skin was a precursor of what might happen between us if we were truly alone?

"Am I what you expected?" he asked. He smiled and the shell plates on his cheeks and below his eyes lifted.

A loud sigh, followed by a trail of abrupt Enestian words barred my answer. The female's fuzzy figure appeared on the other side of the wall. Garran glanced over his shoulder. His forehead crumpled, the plates coming together as his eyes tightened. He shouted something at the female, his tone harsh, and his words abrupt. She spoke in return, saying something with clicks and sharp, foreign words, and Garran responded by shaking his head. She stepped away and disappeared.

"Who is that?" I asked when she was gone.

"Lestra Timuary."

"Lestra," I said, but without shelled lips, there was no way I could pronounce it correctly by giving it a sort of clicking tone.

"She is a palace maid, my servant, and she is also Slaine's sister." He slid his finger from my chin to my throat and then my collarbone.

"What did she say? It's obvious she's upset about something."

"She's just concerned for my safety, but I've assured her that you've undergone the proper period of quarantine, so there's no need for her to be worried."

Lestra was afraid of catching a disease from *me*? I was the one who should have been afraid, yet those strange but oddly familiar aliens, with their impeccably unblemished shells, led me to believe they couldn't possibly harbor any type of illness or disease, especially the prince.

He set his jaw and inhaled. "And she told me that what I'm doing is not appropriate. Touching a female," he said, his words so breathy and seductive, the fire inside me danced. "Having your body so close to mine when we aren't betrothed or married is considered scandalous for a prince, a blemish to my reputation if anyone was to find out."

"Only for a prince or for others, too?"

"Intimacy before marriage is not against the law. It's based upon each Enestian's personal beliefs, just as it is for humans. But it's different for the royals, since I won't meet my bride until my wedding day."

I sighed and watched the shell sections under Garran's shirt overlap and slide with each breath while I tried to shed the thought of my so-far-happy and productive life ending before I graduated from college. He gazed up at the ceiling like he was thinking of the right words, and I looked up at him from under his chin, studying the gentle curves of his nose and the two small holes—nostrils—at its base. My nose was big compared to all the Enestian noses I had seen so far—not that I'd seen a lot.

Our eyes met once again as he lowered his chin, eyes so alien with their unique coloring. My hand, still poised on his forearm, shook along with my lower lip when I took a deep breath.

He inhaled and leveled his shoulders against the wall, his body beneath his green tunic and black pants smooth with the occasional rise and fall from the place where muscle would protrude on a human. I imagined myself slipping my hand under his shirt and feeling skin instead of shell.

"This is beautiful," I said and grazed my hand over his shirt, tracing one of its designs in gold thread, my finger making a spiral before settling my palm against his shoulder. His shell plates stiffened under my hand, making a muffled rubbing sound.

Garran took one of my hands into both of his, giving it a sweet squeeze, and my swirling insides exploded in a bath of pleasant heat. Instead of being jointed and fitted with plates of various sizes, the inside of his hand was one continuous sheet of soft shell that flexed when he moved. His lips and much of his face consisted of the same malleable shell, and when he wasn't talking or smiling, his face was smooth and human-like.

He ran his index finger along the top of my hand, following the length of bone rising up from my skin. "Those are bones," I said.

"We have bones, too. We just can't feel them through our shell. In fact, our internal structures are supported by a skeletal system almost identical to yours."

"Then you are more human than you think." I smiled.

"Or you are more Enestian than you think," he teased back.

"Are all of your body parts covered in shell?" I asked innocently before I realized it could be taken the wrong way. Though now that I thought about it, I was curious about that, too. "Sorry. I didn't mean to get too personal. I'm just so lost here. I don't know what I'm saying half the time."

Garran's chest plates rose, and the side of his body met mine when he took a big breath. "You don't feel lost now, do you?"

"No, not when you're here."

He lifted my hand to his face, and I touched his lips, pressing lightly. He made a soft clicking sound as I pulled away. His lips were softer than they looked. Like the tips of his fingers and the insides of his hands, the shell of his lips was well defined and leathery tight like a piece of canvas stretched upon a frame.

His eyes burned into mine, and as alien as he was, I still felt connected to him.

"You smell good."

"It's jessom moss oil. Jessom moss grows all over our planet. It's treasured for its dark green color and unusual but pleasant fragrance. The royal wardrobe is indicative of jessom's color," he said softly and close enough for his lips to nearly brush my cheek.

A pleasant shiver radiated through my chest until the enormity of my situation hit me. Seeing Garran, an alien from three galaxies away from Earth, standing inches away, exuding a strange, although beautiful, scent cemented the reality of my abduction and captivity, and my head whirled and knees buckled.

He caught me under the arms, his biceps hard against my ribs, and lowered me into a sitting position before joining me on the cold stone.

"Are you okay?" The shell sections above the bridge of Garran's nose came together.

"Yeah, I'm okay."

"I didn't hurt you, did I?" he asked, flexing his hands.

"No, not at all." His body heavy against mine felt pleasant. "I'm fine now. I just got a little lightheaded for a minute. I haven't eaten much since I've been here. Just a bite of one of those."

"Those are nutritional food replacements," said Garran, noting the tray with the food blocks on the floor next to me.

"They don't taste very good."

"No, they don't." He laughed. "But you need to eat." He picked up the brown cube. "If I had to pick a favorite, this would be it."

"What is it? Some kind of meat?"

"Yes, kertrish. It's been processed, blended with dietary supplements."

"Kertrish," I tried to repeat and completely missed the clicking sound after the first syllable.

"A small, thick-shelled animal, raised for Enestian consumption. Kertrish do not make good pets. Their plates are rough and pocked, and their bite can crack shell." I imagined a wolverine with the thick, leathery hide of an armadillo. "Try it," he said.

He brought the brown block to my lips and held it under my nose. I took a whiff. Its smell made my mouth water, but, remembering how the yellow block had tasted, I was still leery.

Garran laughed. "Its taste will please you. I promise." He brought the cube to his mouth and took a small bite. He chewed and swallowed and as the plates along this throat rippled, the smell of cooked kertrish, something meat-like but gamey, became thick in my cell.

"Okay, I'll at least try it." I took the cube, held it delicately to my lips, opened my mouth, and let my teeth sink through the buttery-like substance. There was no crunch, no need to chew twenty times before swallowing. It melted against my tongue and at the back of my throat, its taste true to its smell. My empty stomach appreciated it more than my taste buds did.

"Not bad, I guess," I said after swallowing. "It's better than that one." I pointed to the yellow cube.

"Yes, that one's made from tartemlow and bestripe root. Its flavor is questionable even among Enestians, but it contains nutrients vital to shell health.

"Well, that counts me out," I said and ate what was left of the brown cube slowly, not desperately and frantically like my gnawing stomach wanted me to. The green cube came next. It tasted like vegetables, but its slightly sweet flavor was a bit off-putting.

"Bleglosh," said Garran. And he described how its thick stocks are harvested and boiled.

"Do you feel better?" he asked when I finished the green cube.

"Yeah, I do." The burning in my stomach ceased, and for the first time since my abduction, all my strength had returned to my limbs. "So, did you figure out a way to free me and take me home?" I set my hand on the prince's forearm, expecting it to be cold, but instead it was warm, and I dared to give it a gentle squeeze.

"No, but I will do everything in my power to help return you to your planet if possible," said Garran without hesitating.

I believed him.

Chapter Sixteen

GARRAN

The shell plates around my mouth locked into a smile as I ran my fingers once again down the side of the human girl's face. America shuddered under her blanket.

"Are you cold?"

"No," she said, and leaned close enough for me to feel her warm breath against my shell.

"Are you afraid?"

"Afraid yes. Not of you, but of what's going to happen if you can't get me back to Earth." The skin above America's eyes wrinkled like a dried filbian plumb.

"I don't want you to be afraid." My fingers slid below her chin, and I felt the bone beneath her skin. My body boiled pleasantly beneath my shell, starting below and coiling upward through my chest.

"Why me? Why did your father pick me?"

"You were—what's the saying—in the wrong place at the right time. Once a planet is selected, the precise location is determined by many factors, such as how easily one of our ships can slip into that planet's atmosphere undetected. Once our research vessel has breached a country's air-defense systems, a healthy native being is taken quickly. We want to spend the least amount of time as possible in a foreign orbit, especially one that contains underdeveloped planets. Not because we fear the planet's combined armed forces but because we don't want them to know we exist. Enestians are the most powerful beings in the Millennius, and to stay that way, we need to keep other aliens ignorant of our technology."

Why had I said that? I sounded as arrogant and ethnocentric as my father.

"And when they're done with them, they always kill them, like your father plans to do to me?"

"Yes." Somewhere on Trispia, a family was missing one of its members. "But I'm not going to let anyone hurt you," I told her. But deep in my shell, I knew she would die, too, if I couldn't find a way to stop it.

America lifted my hand away from her face and held my fingers. When our eyes met, I shivered on the inside like a piece of ice had been wedged beneath my shell.

"I thought you would be harder." She smiled.

"Our shell is hard, but in certain places, like the inside of our hands and the bottom of our feet, the shell remains thick but flexible."

"It feels leathery," she said as she pressed my palm. I knew the word. Leather was earthling animal skin, but I couldn't imagine what it felt like until now.

"You aren't as mushy as I thought you'd be. Your skin is soft but firm."

"Thanks, I guess." She laughed, shook her head, and the stuff called hair shifted across her forehead. I slowly reached forward and touched it.

Her hair was soft and billowy between my fingers, and as I leaned closer, I caught the scent of husstle blossoms and jintz bark. She obviously found the personal hygiene station and was keeping herself clean, and now her sweet scent combined with her humanly beauty made me wonder what it would be like to kiss her lips.

"Sir Lancelot," she whispered, still holding my fingers. With her other hand, she bent each of my fingers forward, curling them into my palm and then straightening them, watching the shell plates slide and buckle, and each time her fingers slid up and then down mine, I imagined how it would feel if she were doing the same to my lower plate.

"Sir Lancelot?" I struggled to focus on what she'd said.

"One of King Arthur's knights. Your shell is like a suit of armor, the way it's divided up into plates that overlap at the joints when you bend."

"Ah, yes, I have read your Arthurian legends."

"You have?" America straightened her back. "So have I—all of them. Including *A Connecticut Yankee in King Author's Court*."

"Yes, I've also read the works of Mark Twain," I said.

Her blanket slipped a little, and as she tucked it under her arms, I noticed her breasts under the blanket were large—at least by Enestian standards—and wondered if they were soft but firm like her cheeks. My blood pulsed hard beneath my shell as she continued to explore the workings of my hand.

"Like I said, I've read much of your literature. A Knight of the Round Table, a table, round with no head, suggesting that everyone who sat there shared equal status with the king."

She stroked my palm and lightly squeezed my shell at the wrist. "But unfortunately in this kingdom, my father sits at the head of the table, enjoying his power over the Millennius," I said, lifting her hand in mine to inspect the soft lines engrained on her skin at the joints and brush my fingertip across the flat, hard pieces of red shell at the tips of her fingers.

"Fingernails," she said. "They protect the top of our fingers, and I've painted mine for decoration."

"Our shells are also for our protection, and female Enestians dust their shell with powder to make them sparkle. It's also for decoration."

"But your shell is a lot thicker and stronger than a human fingernail. Our fingernails are made from keratin, the same thing our hair is made from." America stroked her hair with her free hand. "What is your shell made from, bone?"

"Yes, that would be a good translation."

"Human bones can break."

"Yes, and I've read humans can survive these breaks." The sound of the Trispian's shell cracking infused with my thoughts, making it momentarily difficult for me to concentrate on America's words, and I shuddered under my shell.

"Yeah, we can, but there are certain breaks humans sometimes don't survive, like if we break our spine, or neck, or fracture our skull. But most bones can be reset and healed," she said, meeting my hand palm to palm and pressing lightly. "What about your shell? Have you ever cracked it?"

"Our bones do not heal, so it's best that we never crack our shells or do anything to weaken them. We can't live without our shells." A shrill howl pierced my mind with the continued memory of the suffering Trispian. "From a very young age, we're taught to respect one's shell, treat it with dignity, and never do anything that would jeopardize the integrity of it. A scratch can lead to an undetectable hairline crack. A hairline crack can lead to a larger, noticeable breach."

"You'll die without a shell?" The skin around her eyes creased at the corners.

"Yes."

"Then what happens if it does crack?"

"A team of doctors fuse the shell back together, using an enamel patch, a temporary and dangerous fix. It is done here at this lab. Last year, one of the researchers fractured a face plate when his shuttle malfunctioned and crashed into a building. If you look closely, you can see a horizontal line across his cheek that's slightly lighter than the rest of his face, right here," I said, running my finger lightly across the thickest part of America's cheek and watching her skin gently sink with the pressure. "But one's shell is never the same, even after a good repair. It is more likely to break again, and if a section of shell shatters into pieces too small to put together, a plate of artificial shell has to be used instead."

"So what's underneath your shell?" she asked warily.

Under my shell? What kind of question was that? I never thought about what was under my shell before. Why would I? There was nothing under our shells; our organs were inside our shells.

"Not under our shells—inside our shells," I responded. "Like humans, Enestian interiors contain a distinct set of systems: circulatory, respiratory, digestive, skeletal, muscular, nervous, and many more, although I don't know all the English translations."

"But what is under the shell if a piece comes off?" she persisted.

"The systems I just listed. They would be exposed. Our shell defines our shape. It keeps our systems of organs intact. If I lost a shell plate right now, my exposed interior would spill out onto the floor of this cell. That's why a minor crack is so dangerous. Careless Enestians kill themselves every year by taking chances and doing something dangerous that cracks their shells."

I flinched at the thought of losing a piece of my shell or having it purposely split under the will of my father. America's hand shifted against mine, and I turned my wrist to hold her hand.

"And careless humans die every year when they take chances and rip their skin."

A soft sigh came from her lips, and she interlocked her fingers with mine. Heat exploded under my shell once again, and I longed to keep touching her, to pull her soft body against my chest and hold her and tell her everything would be okay, that she'd be released and sent home.

This being was having an effect on me that Lestra never could, but how? Was it America's soft form and delicate movements, her clear voice, sharp and penetrating, grating at my soul, her dark eyes, reflective and warm, her mouth outlined with soft, red flesh in the shape of a Hestian flower? I didn't know. Or maybe it was just pity, simple compassion pulling on my heart, telling me to break any rule I had to in order to set this miraculous being free.

Whatever it was made me ache with the desire to explore not only her body, but also her mind. Everything about this creature filled me with raw, determined emotions, emotions I hadn't experienced before, but would need in order to save her.

"Do you think you will be able to help me?" asked America. Her delicate lips puckered.

"I will do everything I can," I said.

She blinked, and I reached out to touch the tiny hairs that fluttered above her eyes. Several droplets of water fell to my finger. America was crying silent tears accompanied by a sniffle here and there, not like Enestians with our loud exasperation of clacking shell when we shivered and cried into our hands.

It had been a long time since I last cried. In fact, I didn't even remember the incident. Crying, especially uncontrollably, wasn't fitting for a prince. But with princesses, it was okay. Murelle was moody and cried all the time.

"I'm so sorry this has happened to you." My own eyes became watery like they did when I watched the Trispian wince under the glare of white light, and it took everything I could to stop it.

"I know. I'm glad you're here. It helps a little, knowing someone will be trying to find a way to get me out of here. I, I just want to go home." She brought her arms around me, and I held her while she sobbed against my shoulder, her body hot and trembling against mine.

"And I will take you there if I can. If not, I am going to at least make sure you live." But how I'd do that? I still didn't know.

The sound of the wave of wall retracting made me turn my head. "It's time for me to go."

"No, please, don't leave. Not yet," said America, tightening the blanket around her body as I stood and pulled her up with me.

"I have to. It's too risky to stay any longer. I'll come back tomorrow, and maybe by then, I'll have more answers."

"Wait," she said, and just before the last bit of wall disappeared into the ceiling, she rose on her toes and kissed my lips. I burned to pull her against me, lengthen the kiss, and let my hands travel the soft curves of her body, but the wall was gone now, leaving us exposed to the hall.

"Thank you," I said in a tone I hoped let her know that her kiss was more than welcomed and that I was leaving her wanting more.

Lestra approached. She stood, her eyes set first on me and then on America, her jaw fixed and the small plates around her nostrils flaring like a mad vinyip bull.

"Tomorrow," I said, slipping my hand from hers. "And I'll be alone this time. I promise."

Chapter Seventeen

AMERICA

Alone time with Garran. That's what I wanted. If I couldn't go home, being with him at least helped stave my fear and loneliness.

The wall descended with a sizzle, and I watched Garran become all shadow as he turned and walked away.

"Strange but so beautiful," I whispered as I touched my lips with the soft pad of my index finger. It was an unusual sensation kissing him, missing the cushioned give of flesh against flesh, but his firm lips were smooth, warm, and well-defined, and their unique tactile pressure was more than pleasant against my tender skin.

"I hate this," I said, my words ricocheting around my tiny room as I stood wrapped in my odd blanket. "I'm bored. I'm hungry. I'm scared," I said to Slaine's blurry figure.

And I wanted Garran. His gentle embrace had consoled

me while I wept. And I liked his kiss so much I wanted more. Thinking about Garran settled me somewhat as I rekindled his words and gentle touch in my head while awaiting his return. His lack of skin didn't matter. His shell was immaculate and smooth, warm and comforting against me, and the more I remembered the curves of his face and the unique sparkle in his eyes, the more handsome and regal he became.

"I must be going crazy," I moaned as I sank to the ground. But I wasn't. The yearning for Garran and the rustling in my soul was unexpected, but it was real.

I closed my eyes, and when I opened them, Slaine was there, wavering a bit as he shifted his weight between his feet. A moment later, the curtain of my containment solidified and withdrew, leaving a trace of the unidentifiable odor as it slowly revealed Slaine's sizeable frame.

Why was he entering my cell? With my heart pounding, I scooted to the corner and adjusted my blanket, giving it a pull and re-tucking a corner against my chest. I didn't fear him; I feared what he may have been ordered to do, such as escorting me to an examination table.

The urge to jump to my feet and dodge left to freedom was there, but even at full strength, there was no way I could bring that being down if he caught me. His shell casing alone was probably twice my weight, and these creatures were unbelievably agile, their movements unrestricted and graceful despite their hard exteriors. Besides, again, where would I go?

He said a few words strung together, his voice deep, but in an eerie way, oddly soothing as he stood above me confidently; it didn't take a human to see that I was miserable, and those unusual eyes of his held sympathy as he tilted his head and the plates around his eyes shifted.

Slaine watched me as he crouched down, his thick legs bent at the knee, the thin fabric of his pants revealing the outline of several plates of shell overlapping at the joint. These aliens were so human, yet not so human at the same time.

I searched the deep blue of his eyes, blue eyes that sparked with flecks the golden color of a lion's hide, like Garran's but different. They were strong, but naive and dutiful — Tarzan eyes.

In the dim light, his shell was shadowed blue in places, accentuating the contours and hallows. He wore a short-sleeved shirt today, giving me the first chance to see a set of bare, Enestian arms. Though covered in a shell as hard as stone, they were as defined as a body builder's, as if the shell itself had been molded from a human male arm. I could only assume the muscles and tendons underneath mirrored those of a human being.

Slaine said something. The words were foreign, of course, but the look on his face and his body language were as readable as a human's with his overlapping facial plates coming together between his eyes. He pulled something from a lower pocket on his tunic and opened his hand. In his palm was a cluster of round, grape-like fruit, their yellow skins so shiny I could almost see my reflection as I peered down at them.

"Thank you," I said and took the string of fruit, noting its green, spindly vine.

He reached out to touch my hair with his index finger. A stray strand hung over my shoulder, its ends cascading over his hand before he stood and backed away, his blue Tarzan eyes searching my soul like he wanted to understand what it meant to be human.

A moment later, he rose from the ground and made his way from my cell. The milky wall lowered, and while Slaine stood once again outside my room like a Buckingham Palace guard, I plucked the largest fruit from its stem and popped it in my mouth. My tongue bathed in unimaginable sweetness, I took a small breath through my nose and savored the fruit's rich juices.

I was so appreciative of Slaine's small kindness and hoped that meant Garran might find enough others to sympathize with my plight and help him take me home.

Chapter Eighteen

"I still can't believe you touched it," said Lestra when we arrived at my quarters. She threw her hands in the air, and I realized how lucky I was that she didn't witness America kissing me. I didn't need any more of Lestra's shit.

"And I still can't believe you knew that the code to enter the lab would also override a shell scan. You should have told me."

"I was trying to protect you."

"Protect me from what?"

"From any kind of alien diseases it might be carrying. But now I know that wasn't the only thing that needed to be protected."

"Yeah, like what?"

"Like your feelings for it. The way you touched it— It wasn't like a scientist examining a foreign life form. You did it in— "

"And you wouldn't have known I had if you'd followed my orders and stayed down the hall with your brother until it was time for us to leave," I said, taking a seat on the edge of my bed.

"But you did it in a lovingly sort of way, like you cared about that thing," she continued.

"It's not a thing. She's an intelligent being, a human being, with thoughts and feelings just like you and me."

"It is a weak, ugly creature."

"Being shell-less does not make her ugly or weak, but she does need our help, or she'll end up like the Trispian."

"So?"

"So, you were pissed when I told you about the live dissection. I know you don't agree with my father's experiments, so your continued apathy when it comes to America doesn't make any sense."

"Yes, it does. She's shell-less," she huffed. "She's an inferior being."

"She deserves to live, and I'm going to make sure that happens."

"You did what you initially wanted to do. You saw it, and you talked to it. Isn't that enough?" she pleaded.

"No. Not anymore." Now that I'd felt her touch, I couldn't stop wanting to learn more about her and touch her again.

"Well, it has to be enough. There's nothing you can do for her. There is no point in visiting that thing again. You'll never be able to stop your father."

Lestra threw her hip out to one side and folded her arms, and I noticed for the first time today that she was wearing a fitted dress rather than her usual leggings and tunic. It was a plain dress, coarse and beige — servant's colors, so she wasn't breaking any rules — but I could swear her arms shimmered in the light when she moved, as if they were covered in a fine dusting of shell powder.

"Garran, I am not trying to be mean. I'm just thinking about your feelings. Remember the Verlian snup you received at the turn of your tenth year?"

"Yes," I said with a sigh. Why did she have to bring this sad subject up? That was over ten years ago.

"That day when it split its shell, your father wanted to take it to his lab and have it euthanized, but no, you threw a fit and insisted on trying to nurse it back to health. And what happened, Garran?" I dropped my head to my chin with a clack. "It died a week later," she continued.

"So, what's your point?"

"You grew attached to it during that week, making its death more difficult for you. If you had let your father — "

"The snup was an animal. The being in cell fifteen is a human girl." I was already attached to America, and in a way that made me hot under my shell. I just hoped Lestra couldn't see how attached.

"Well, I don't see the difference."

As she continued to stand there so smug and judgmental, I was tempted to tell her to wash off her shell powder, but I didn't.

"I'm going to see her again today. Alone. I trust you not to tell my father about it. Don't forget that your brother is involved in this now. If I get reprimanded, so will Slaine," I warned her.

"He's only involved because you practically forced him to be."

Oh, the impudence of this palace maid. If she spoke this way to Father, she'd be demoted to a lesser planet, though I was too angry to remind her of that fact. "Yeah, but I can always leave that part out of my story if I get caught," I threatened, even though I would never selfishly betray Slaine like that.

"Get caught doing what?" Murelle stood in my doorway, sparkling with bright pink shell powder.

"Why do you insist on barging into my room all the time? Get out," I snarled, shooting up from the bed, "before I crack!"

"Calm down. What's wrong with you? You two sure have been spending a lot of time together. I know why she wants to be around you, Garran, but why do *you* want to spend so much time with her? What are the two of you up to anyway?"

"We're not up to anything. Now leave!"

"Really? I'm not so sure about that." Murelle strolled across my room until she was face-to-face with Lestra. "Why are you in my brother's quarters?"

Lestra lowered her head and bowed. "What do you mean, your royal?"

"Leave her alone, Murelle. She's here because I asked her to…help me with my studies. That's all. Now go away."

Murelle laughed, a horrible, high-pitched laugh accompanied by the clacking of her jaw shells. "Your studies? As if she'd know anything about dual propulsion systems. Why are you really here?"

"Don't answer her, Lestra. I outrank my sister by almost two years. You know the rules. You need to answer to me first, not her."

"Are you wearing shell powder? How dare you!" she scowled, grabbing Lestra's arm to give it an inspection. "That's *my* shell powder. The one that disappeared from my room days ago. I knew it had to be you. You're the only Timuary I ever see near my quarters."

Lestra jerked her arm from Murelle's tight hold and stood facing my sister, her shoulders square and her height elevated by rising on her toes. She already beat Murelle by a half dimit, and as Murelle cowered, it was obvious Lestra could beat her in a brawl.

"How dare you," snapped my sister. "I'm going to report you to—"

"You're not going to report anybody. I'm the one who gave Lestra the shell powder. I'm the one who took it from your room. You have so much of it. I honestly didn't think you'd miss one little tin. I gave it to Lestra and told her she had my permission to wear it, a light dusting, but only in the evening, after most of her chores were done."

"Timuary's can't wear shell powder. It is against the rules. You can't give her permission to wear it. Why would you? Think about it, Garran. If she wants to wear shell powder, it's because she wants to wear it for you. What happened to your standards?"

"I have standards—high standards, but they don't exclude me from being kind to others," I announced as I wedged my body between Lestra's and Murelle's.

"Oh, so being kind includes spending time conversing with palace maids unnecessarily?" she scoffed. "I've been watching you, big brother. You've been acting strangely the last few days, distant and distracted. Does Dad know you failed your last intergalactic biology test?"

"Jump in a black hole," I said, instead of using the profane word I had ready.

"Don't think I won't find out what's going on with the two of you, because I will. Your position as ambassador isn't a certainty like you think. One mistake and that commission will go to me," she threatened, stepping backward toward the door without losing eye contact. "And you"—Murelle pointed at Lestra—"you better watch yourself. One more incident like that, and you'll be off this planet."

When the door separated from its frame, Murelle walked through it slowly, continuing to stare at me through narrowed eye plates. I didn't breathe until she disappeared and the door resealed, pulling back into its frame.

"Do you really think she's been watching us? Do you think she knows we've been going to the lab?" asked Lestra, rubbing her forearm.

"No, she's just doing something she's good at—being a bitch. She doesn't scare me, and her threats are certainly not going to stop me from seeing America. Just forget about her."

Lestra set her hand on my shoulder. "Garran, thank you, um, for you know, taking the blame for the missing shell powder." Her shell lips puckered. "I won't wear it anymore. It just makes me feel pretty, that's all."

"Like I told you before, Lestra, you don't need shell powder to look pretty." Maybe I shouldn't have said that. Was that "leading her on" again?

"And I'm sorry for what I said earlier about letting the human die. What you want to do—save it—that's a noble thing, I guess. I'd hope you'd want to be there for me if someone was going to hurt me."

"Of course I would, Lestra. I told you, you're my best friend."

She smiled and stepped closer. "And you're mine," she said, her lips parting slightly. "Do you know what I want?" With another step, she brought her face inches away. "A first kiss from someone I care about. I don't want it to come from the man appointed to be my husband."

Like me, since the day she was born, Lestra spent her days and nights surrounded by relatives. The chance of her, or even me for that matter, kissing someone other than a future spouse was more than limited.

"What about you?" With her index finger, she traced a curvy line of embroidery on my tunic at my chest.

"Like you, I am waiting for my first kiss," I told her, though I just had my first kiss, and in my mind, had already relived the feel of my Enestian lips upon America's more than a dozen times. "How long that will be? I'm not sure. But that first kiss cannot come from a Timuary." I gently pulled her finger from my tunic, and her hand slipped from mine.

"Fine," she huffed and popped up from the bed. "Wait until you're married. That could be ten years from now, depending on your father."

"Fine," I said and shook my head.

She pulled at her crumpled skirt and left my quarters with her nose in the air. Was she angry enough to sacrifice our relationship and tell my father that I'd been visiting the human? I didn't think so, but at the same time, her behavior raised my anxiety level.

Chapter Nineteen

Garran's familiar shadow appeared on what I calculated to be the next day. This time he was alone as promised. I closed my eyes and took a deep breath through my nose as I stood at the back of my cell. As I exhaled, my whole body shook with anticipation. A sizzling sound came next, crisp and wispy, and my nostrils were filled with the same smell as before, but this time I recognized it—ozone—and I knew the crystalline wall separating me from Garran had rippled away and disappeared.

The pungent smell only added to my fervor, heightening my five senses.

"Hello," he said softly.

I loved his voice, deep and silvery, marked with a royal flare and Enestian accent that sent euphoria through my chest, spiking my pulse, a voice that, as we grew closer each day, made me burn with the desire to see him face-to-face.

"America," he repeated.

My eyes remained closed as I savored each word like a soft, breathy kiss against my ears.

I had lain awake last night wishing for morning, yearning to touch the being whose words alone left me wanting more.

One more deep breath, and I lowered my head and opened my eyes.

His deep green boots emerged from under the rising wall, the boots' shaft folding at the top to hit mid calve. When his legs, clad in clingy, black pants appeared, I swallowed hard and stole a quick breath.

I slowly worked my eyes to the top of this amazing creature, my white knight, his shirt as green as his boots and patterned in interlocking circles with thick, gold thread, as it billowed gracefully where it tucked into the top of his pants. Long, willowy sleeves became tighter at the cuff and ended with his hands of thick, leathery shell.

With another breath, my whole body shaking, I lifted my head and studied his flawless Enestian coating, shadowed with the deep arc of his cheekbones and cut jawline — a face so uniquely beautiful I let out a sigh.

His creamy beige shell bordered on taupe in the dim light. I held my breath, and a fluttery feeling entered my chest and expanded, causing me to break my gaze and inhale deeply.

Damn, he was hot. Even hotter than I remembered from the day before.

"So, am I what you expected?" Garran took another step forward, and my eyes shifted to ride the length of his body. "You didn't get a chance to answer yesterday." He smiled, the corners of his mouth curving upward ever so slightly in such a provocative, alluring manner. I had to part my lips in order to catch my breath.

"Yes, and more," I managed to say.

"You're not disappointed?" The place where eyebrows would be lifted, and his eyes widened, their golden sparkle bewitching.

"No, not at all. What about you? Am I what you expected?"

"Disappointed? No. Enamored? Yes." He licked his lips, and when he swallowed, the plates along his throat rose. "You're beautiful, America." Heat washed across my chest and into my cheeks. "Can I touch you again?"

At that moment, any fear I could have had in terms of our differences melted, and my sudden curiosity and desire for him to touch me were keen. My knees became weak, and I took a step backward to brace my back against the wall.

"Yes," I said, closing my eyes as my throbbing heart became palpable in my chest. I wanted nothing more than for this alien to kiss me.

I opened my eyes, and he slowly raised his hand and rested his index finger against my chin. His gaze riveted me to the spot.

Then his hand met my mouth, pushing my bottom lip delicately before tracing the length of my neck with his fingers. I tried to control each breath, inhaling through my nose, wishing his fingers drifted to explore other places.

"I'm not hurting you, am I?" he asked gently. His forehead casing wrinkled with concern, and I was amazed at how his smooth, visually inflexible countenance could be so expressive.

"No," I said through a breath.

"I want to feel you so badly, but I need to remember that skin is more tender than shell."

He brought his hands to my shoulders and dropped his fingers to my naked collarbone, his touch so magical against my skin, that when my blanket started to slip I hesitated before pulling it back into place. As his hands inched down to my waist, following the curve of my torso, I sighed softly.

"Touch me," Garran said, his palms slipping up my arms.

I brought my trembling hands to his shoulders.

"I can barely feel that," he teased and in a tone so sexy I arched my back against the wall and increased my grip, my fingers biting into his hard shell.

"Can you feel that?" I chuckled, clasping his shoulder even harder.

"Yes," he said, and his chest expanded with a deep inhale.

Keeping the same pressure, I moved my hands down his arms, stopping at each joint to feel the places where shell plates overlapped. When I reached his wrists, I edged my hands up each sleeve, my fingers drumming across the hard shell of his forearms.

At his elbows, the tips of my fingers traced the edge of shell as it disappeared beneath another plate, and I guessed the soft tissue of my fingertips could be pinched between them if he suddenly moved.

"I want to see it," I said, "your shell." Closing my eyes as I drew my hands back to his wrists, I plunged them upward again, this time pushing both sleeves forward until they were gathered at his shoulders.

He sucked in a breath and lowered his head as my fingers wrapped against his hard forearms. As if fashioned from marble, each plate curved to match the bulk of tight muscle beneath its protective casing, his biceps and triceps humanly distinct and packed with power.

"A tattoo?" My eyes followed a set of black lines at the top of his left arm, streaks that swirled and turned in the same pattern as the gold thread on his shirt.

"The mark of a royal."

"I want to see more," I said quickly, unable to control my hands as I increased the pressure against his shell.

His lips parted, and for the first time, I saw that his tongue rested behind a set of human-like teeth that were perfectly straight and bright white. He swallowed hard, and with shaky hands, fumbled with the top clasp of his shirt. His breathing was as deep and unsteady as mine as he fought each golden fastener, twisting it away from the swell of fabric.

"Ah," I said as he undid the last hook, and his shirt fell open.

The tattoo continued up his arm, spilling with intricate detail to his shoulder and ending at a plate of shell above his right pec. "It's beautiful," I said, noting that one line was affixed with small jewels of green and yellow.

His chest plates were smooth and budded in each center with a knob of shell indicative of a human male nipple. The plates covering his abdomen buckled with each breath he took, each part of his six-pack overlapping a half inch with an inhale and then coming back into position. Centered above his waistband, an indentation the size of a dime was in the place where a belly button would be. How amazing that his shell seemed so close to the definition of male human anatomy.

When my palms smoothed along Garran's chest, a soft

breath left his lips, and I rested my forehead against the top of his shoulder while I explored his body. My fingers tense, each tip pressing deeply against his shell, my urge to discover every bit of him felt primal. Like I was driven to learn more, press harder, get closer.

My hands traveled to his back. Thick plates covered his shoulder blades, each sliding beneath another piece of shell as he brought his hands first to my waist and then around my body. An intoxicating chill raced up my spine, and he groaned when the tips of my fingers hit his waistband and stopped.

Holding me close, his breath against my neck, I took in his scent, something sweet and woodsy, and my whole body trembled. Garran lifted his head, and our gazes locked.

"Can I kiss you this time?" He smiled, and I brushed my index finger against his bottom lip. With vertical creases like a human's, it was taut and leathery, and though it lacked the soft puffiness I was used to, I wanted nothing more than to feel them damp and hot against mine.

"Yes," I whispered.

"I won't hurt you," he whispered back. "At least I'll try not to," he warned with a laugh.

I smiled and closed my eyes as he drew closer, and his lips met their mark. My fingers dug into his back, my nails rapping against shell, and he launched his soft, human-like tongue into my mouth. My lips hungrily working upon him, my tongue twining with his, a swell of something hot and euphoric shot through my chest, and my knees buckled.

"Too hard?" he asked through a kiss, his body rocking against mine to hold me steady.

"No," I said, dropping my hands to his buttocks and

feeling a similar burst of heat below my waist.

Garran gave my bottom lip a gentle bite. I held his handsome face in my hands, and as his breath hit my neck, I wondered how this amazing being with shell for skin and eyes so tense they burned my soul, could make me feel so safe on a planet three galaxies away from home.

Would I have time to explore more of a relationship with him before my days ended? What would it be like to really be with him? It should have seemed weird, but it felt so natural. I relaxed into his embrace, his kiss, and prayed I had the chance to find out.

Chapter Twenty

America closed her eyes and lifted her head as my tongue cut across her jaw and down her neck. Her body arched and her pelvis pressed against mine, causing the pressure behind my lower shell to double. I marveled that her responses were so like what I'd expect from a female Enestian, yet even more sensual, more passionate.

"Are you sure I'm not hurting you?" I asked, my breath hot against her tender neck.

"No," she said. Her fingers clasped my buttocks once again, and my lips and tongue came down upon her neck, followed by a restrained bite as I worked my lips to the top of her shoulder.

"Oh," she said in a breathy exhale that sent my heart pounding so hard each beat reverberated against my shell and thumped in my ears.

She gasped and her hair fell forward, brushing the side of my face. Soft and glossy, I raked my fingers through a thick strand, each fiber igniting the sensitive pads of my fingertips. Her nipples were erect, tight buds poking through her thin blanket, and I brushed my hand across them, restraining my urge to tug the blanket away.

After cupping the back of her thigh as lightly as I could, I ran my hand down the length of her leg. She was so beautiful, so soft, so delicate, every curve of her body kindling a sensation deep within my shell that I'd never felt before. I wanted her.

The pressure in my lower plate mounted, and I groaned, my voice trembling as she brought her leg up and around the backs of mine. My hand slipped higher, meeting a sweet roundness that fit perfectly within my palm.

Her fingertips rippled downward against my chest, followed by her tongue, its tender wetness slipping between each plate of my abdomen. Heat rocketed under my shell with her next lick while my hands feverishly slipped under her blanket to stroke her naked back.

I pushed against her, tightening my lips and holding my breath to prevent my lower plate from opening.

"You feel so good," she moaned.

"So do you," I said, bringing my body away from hers in another attempt to control my plate, the rush of cool air helping me keep my shell in place.

"We should stop," she continued between breaths.

"I'm sorry. I should have never let it get that far." I shook my head. "But I couldn't help myself. You're just so amazingly beautiful, America, and I respect and care for you." I gave her hand another kiss. "I lost control—something a prince should never do."

"It's my fault, too. I really like you, Garran, and the fact that you're so, um, hot, makes it even harder to—"

"Hot? Temperature influences human sexual behavior?"

"No, that's not what I meant." She laughed, and this time gave *my* hand a kiss. "It means…" she began, looking up at me with a gaze so sensual that previously dispersed heat returned to my lower plate. "That I'm physically attracted to you. That I think you're incredibly good looking."

"Oh," I said, as the warmth below moved into my cheeks.

She nuzzled my hand against her face and sighed, the warm air escaping from her mouth and brushing against my palm.

"Slaine," she said a moment later, looking over my shoulder and loosening her hold around my neck. I turned my head and a blur developed behind the wall, clearly becoming Slaine's.

"It must be time for me to go."

"No," she said and smacked the cold floor with the palm of her hand.

"I'll come back tomorrow, and I will make sure I'm alone again."

She kissed me, something light and soft this time, though it did little to settle the adrenaline pumping through my veins.

Her hands slipped away when I stood, and I bent down and gave her a long but equally tender kiss before I left, my lower plate surprisingly staying in place. I backed away from her slowly as she sat up, our fingers stretching to maintain our touch before her hand slid from mine.

The security wall hit the ceiling, and as I walked into the

hall and the wall bubbled back into place, America's body became a shadow. She whispered, "Good night, Garran."

And although I loved how she spoke my name with un-clear Enestian clicks, it was a warning I couldn't ignore. If my father got to America before I could help her escape, would she cry out for me in terror? Would the king recog-nize what she was screaming? Had my repeated visits to her put not only myself, but Lestra and Slaine in danger?

Chapter Twenty-One

AMERICA

I rolled to my left side. My right side ached at my hip and shoulder from the cold, hard floor. I was ready for a shift. That's what I did when I slept—switched back and forth from one side to the other when it became too uncomfortable to bear, and I awoke, stiff and sore, to rotate onto my other side. My hands were my pillows, and they too hurt from the hard cartilage of my ears pressing into them, making them numb from the lack of circulation.

Was it day or night? I didn't know, but Garran's last visit left me pleasantly drowsy, and I pulled my blanket to my chin and imagined he was still kissing me.

And in my mind's eye, that kissing led to more, his body pressing against me, his hands working to take off his clothes and mine, our bodies connecting in a magical rhythm of passion and pleasure. But could *it* even be possible? Maybe *it* was bigger than a human's, and what if *it* was covered in shell? *It* needed to be hard, but what if *it* was too hard, and I couldn't respond to him the way I'd just imagined I could?

Sex was supposed to be amazingly sensual and intense, at least that's what Attie had told me so many times that I'd lost count. "Sex is something too hard to describe," she'd said. "You just need to do it and find out." I did want to do it, especially now before I died, but with Garran and on Enestia, I was not only the alien— He was a prince, and I was Cinderella before the ball.

"Human female."

I sat up so quickly I banged the back of my head against the wall behind me. I caught the edge of my blanket and pulled it back up, then tucked it under my arms and spread the other end across my legs to cover my cold feet.

On the other side of the clear, undulating wall stood three figures, tall and slim, with the third person much taller and broader at the shoulders than the others. Slaine was one, but who were the other two?

"Human female." The voice was deep, a man's voice, monotone, and tinged with the Enestian accent.

I stood, wrapping the odd blanket around my torso like a sarong, tucking its tip into the fabric against my chest. The wall froze and drew into the ceiling slowly, and as their faces came into view, I shifted my eyes away from Slaine and studied the other two—both men.

The thinner male wore a simple gray shirt, black leggings, and black boots. The other man was taller, broader at the shoulders, and wore a velvety green shirt embroidered with the same gold pattern as Garran's.

His shell echoed Garran's color and stature, but its matte

finish appeared rough from age, with the creases between his face plates deep. But he was still handsome and regal, his confidence palpable as he lifted his chin and his eyes rode the length of my body. There was no denying that I had been given a visit by the king, and he entered my cell as the last few feet of the creamy wall disappeared above them.

Unlike Garran and Slaine, I immediately feared this man. His assertive grace and royal air alone were enough to raise goose bumps on my arms. Knowing he had a "perverse desire to study alien life forms" only added to my apprehension.

"Human female," said the thin man.

My palms hit the cold wall behind me first, then my back, my shoulders, and my head as I tried to dissolve into the wall and disappear.

"What do you want with me?"

He turned and spoke to the king while Slaine remained rigid, staring at the wall.

"You are a guest of the king."

"Where am I?" I asked, playing dumb.

"Enestia. A planet. A planet three galaxies away from your Earth," his shell lips clacked. Garran's English was much better than his.

"Why did you bring me here?" My voice shook.

"You are a guest of the king."

"Let me go. Take me home," I demanded, my voice cracking as I looked directly at Garran's father.

The king's eye plates narrowed, and without breaking his eye contact with me, he said something to the other man in Enestian.

"You are a guest of the king," said the other man.

This guy was a fucking broken record. "Am I allowed to leave this cell?" I took a step forward.

"No," he clicked.

"Then I am not a guest. I am a prisoner." I took another step, bringing the distance between us to five feet.

Plates of shell rippled on his forehead, and he blinked hard, lash-less eyelids while he tilted his cue-ball head. "Prisoner? I do not understand that word."

"It means to be a captive, a detainee. It means you will not let me leave. That I am not free."

"Yes, you are not free."

My throat tightened. "Then I am a prisoner," I blurted.

The being tilted its head in the other direction. "You are a guest of the king."

"Are you going to ever let me go?" I asked, pulling the blanket tightly against my body.

"Let you go? No."

"What are you going to do with me?" I asked slowly, making sure my pronunciation was perfect. For a moment, the pain in my thigh returned, an icy prick that came with the memories of what they had done to me.

"You are a guest of the king."

"If I was a guest, you would let me go."

"You are a guest of the king."

Balling my shaking hands into fists, I dropped my shoulders, lifted my chin, and dared to take another step toward him, and then another. The alien hesitated and then took a step backward to create more distance between us. The king, on the other hand, had not budged, but his eyes remained on me in a concentrated glare.

"Who are you?"

"Sessman Glitch," his shell lips clacked.

"And him?" I asked, throwing a nod at the king.

"King Meallian, the King of Enestia."

"Tell the king," I said in a gutsy tone, "that he can't keep me here. I am a citizen of Earth, and I need to be returned there immediately."

Glitch translated, and the king smirked with a breath of air exiting his nose.

"People will be looking for me," I threatened, raising my voice. "They will find me," I lied as I looked straight into the king's eyes, "and when they do—"

There was a flash of white shell, and my jaw wrenched as the king's palm hit hard. Warm liquid hit my lips, and I knew that my nose was bleeding. "Fuck you," I screamed and lunged toward the king, my fists ready. One good punch landed against his chest, and just when I was about to launch a left jab, the king grabbed me by the wrists and squeezed. Slaine rushed forward. The king shouted, and Slaine retreated.

I thrust my knee against the king's groin, but the king didn't budge. Two more knee jabs where I figured his balls were, and the king still didn't flinch. He pushed me against the far wall, holding my wrists vise-like, and spoke, the tone of his words ripe with cruelty and hate, and the glare in his gaze seething with evil thoughts.

His face only inches from mine, saliva sprayed from his mouth with his words, and I turned my head and closed my eyes. With a last push, he let go of my wrists, turned his back to me, and left my cell to stand next to Glitch, who had already entered the hall. My blanket had fallen and was at my feet.

Slaine, Marine-like with his shoulders square, arms crossed, and feet apart, took his post next to the king. His shell covering was slightly darker than the king's, but despite his calming coloring, I knew he could crack my head like a nut under his arm if the king ordered him to do so.

"You are a guest of the king," said Glitch.

"Damn it," I said as I caught my breath and rewrapped my blanket around my body. I attacked the king. What the hell was I thinking? What would Garran think? Would he care?

My eyes welled with tears as I lowered my chin to examine my sore wrists. They were bruised in perfectly shaped rings of purple. When I opened and closed my mouth, my jaw ached, but my nose had stopped bleeding. The skin on three knuckles bled from meeting the king's badge with a punch.

My knee hurt, and when I lifted my blanket, I found a knot on my kneecap that was beginning to turn blue. What the hell did they have or didn't have down there? Whatever it was, it was extremely hard.

The watery acrylic wave dropped from the ceiling. Slaine blinked, and his lips moved, twisting upward at one corner. It was a smile. Was there a hint of sympathy there, maybe just a touch? Was it a smile of compassion? If it was, then did it also contain pity, because he knew my fate was dire—especially now?

Chapter Twenty-Two

Garran

"Damn, when did this happen?"

"Slaine said about an hour ago." Lestra plopped down on my bed and leaned against a head cube.

"That bastard. He better not a lay a hand on her again. Now he might want to kill her even sooner than planned. I'm surprised he didn't do it right there, but then again, that wouldn't have been as fun as doing it in the lab," I said sarcastically, remembering the tray of torture devices my father had ready for the Trispian. "My father deserved a punch in the chest and more."

"She dishonored him and in front of two people. Four days remain before her execution and dissection, but I wouldn't be surprised if he changes that."

"Then I need to get her out of there as soon as possible."

"Yeah, and then what? Your shell scan can't activate any

of the ships in your father's fleet."

"I know. I'd have to hide her until it does."

"You can't keep it here. Your sister already suspects…"

"I know." I stared up at my stone ceiling, following its gentle curve at the top of each wall. So many thoughts shot through my mind I could barely speak. And then I thought of the perfect place. "The Ring of Reverence."

"What? You can't take her there! It's not allowed." Lestra jumped from my bed to face me.

"No one would know."

"But it would be a desecration, a snub at the Enestian legacy. Where's your Enestian pride, Garran?"

"Pride? There's no pride in watching a fellow being die. She'd be safe there."

"And where would she sleep?" Lestra scoffed.

"A portable dome. I'd pitch it on a rock sheet, so she'd stay dry and warm during the rains."

"You'd seriously do that for it? Risk punishment and banishment? Let it live in one of Enestia's most sacred places?"

"Yes."

"But for how long? It could be months before your father grants you access to a ship—that is if he ever does."

"He will, and I will take care of her for as long as it takes."

"What is it with you and that thing? I still don't understand how can you care about it so much."

"I can't help how I feel. I can't explain it."

"I can." Lestra's face shimmered under the light in my room. Apparently she'd been applying shell powder to more than just her arms. "It's called pity. That's what you're feeling, and you're mistaking it for something else."

"It's not pity. It's…something more." But did I dare tell her what?

Lestra turned her back to me and sighed, making a whistling sound of air through shell.

Damn. The last thing I needed was a pissed off Timuary in my room. "Lestra, come on. I, I don't know how to explain it, but I feel like I have a special connection with her, like we're more similar than we are different." She crossed her arms with a clack. "We have a special connection, too, just in a different way. I care about you. I need you. You know how important you are to me."

"Yeah, well apparently my fool of a brother has some kind of stupid connection with it, too, or he wouldn't have given that pathetic creature a blanket and told me to tell you what happened between your father and the human," she said, continuing her rant. "You both make me sick!" She turned on her heels.

I caught her hand in mine and gave it a squeeze. "Look. I'm sorry, okay? I didn't know I'd end up caring for her the way I do. It just happened."

"It's not like you can have a relationship with that thing."

"I know that!" Of course I did. America and I could never be, but while she was here, we could satisfy our curiosities and fuel our lust with passion. But most importantly, I'd save her and take her home. "And that doesn't matter. I'm taking her from her cell today."

"And you'll get caught. To enter her cellblock and her cell is one thing, but to take her outside? There are monitors, and your shell will be scanned when you enter and exit the building. On top of that, my brother isn't the only guard on duty. You'll be seen by others. Your father will figure out it was you, and then you'll be exiled to another planet, and I'll never see you again."

Lestra dropped back to my bed and sat before resting the point of her elbows on the top of her thighs and putting her head in her hands.

She was right, but the urge to be with America was stronger than any threat of being disowned by my father. "I'll be careful. With the code, I'll be able to avoid the shell scans." And if I couldn't, then I'd be sent to another planet, but at least I tried to save her.

Another planet—banishment. The thought made my body lurch, and I lowered to the bed to sit next to Lestra.

"No, you can't risk it. I don't want you sent to another planet, and I'll never see you."

"I'll take the risk. It's worth it to me. I want her to live."

"So you're going to do this no matter what I say or do?" she asked without looking up.

"Yes."

"Then you'll need my help."

"I don't need your help. I don't want you involved any more than you already are. The last thing I want is you punished because of me."

"You don't understand. With my help, you won't get caught, but…" Her words were barely audible. "I'll have to break a Timuary oath."

"What do you mean?" I asked, turning toward her and rising on my palms.

"The Legend of Esquieria— You know it?" she whispered, setting her hand on my shoulder.

"Of course," I answered, puzzled.

"Then you know the ending."

"Yes, my ancestors turned into stone and disappeared, becoming one with the palace walls."

"Exactly. That's what *you're* going to do," she said.

"Have you cracked your shell? It's just a myth. They didn't really sink into the walls; it's a metaphor. 'One as the walls, they became.' It's referring to the royal army. Led by Esquier, they formed a wall—of soldiers—who forced the Vengards back to their ships where they withdrew and returned to Vengard Nine, defeated," I said, breaking out of a whisper.

"Shhh. Listen to me. It's not a metaphor. They did become 'one as the walls.' Why do you think the walls and the floors of this palace were never replaced after the invention of merilum?"

Large sheets of merilum were used to make Enestian homes, inside and out, reminiscent of our shells by creating delicately domed roofs and smooth, white walls arching into high ceilings, but the palace and lab were never refurbished like the rest of the kingdom, retaining its original curved stonework instead.

"Because this is our ancestral home. This palace was built by our ancestors. To tear it down and replace it would be a sign of disrespect and an insult to our traditions," I said, running the top of my wrist under my nose.

"No, Garran. That's not the reason. The Timuarys stopped it from happening. *You* can disappear into these walls, or I should say, inside these walls. That's why they haven't been replaced."

Maybe she was right. The exterior of our palace gleamed with a seamless sheet of merilum within months of the material's invention, but the natural interior had never been touched or modified.

"And why would you know this and I wouldn't?" I protested, a bit annoyed with her sense of supposed knowledge over mine.

"There is a simple answer, Garran." She took a breath deep enough to make her plates scrape. "I'm a Timuary," she said confidently.

"What does that have to do with anything, and how could your family halt a palace upgrade? Timuarys don't hold that kind of power."

Lestra's shell appeared gray in the dim light of my quarters. "That's where you are wrong, my prince," she beamed. "Timuarys aren't just your servants. We are also your protectors."

"What in the galaxy are you talking about? My father never told me any of this."

"Your father doesn't know."

"That's impossible. My father is privy to everything Enestian."

"Not this." The plates around Lestra's eyes dilated as her grip on my shoulder tightened. "Let me explain. Listen carefully," she said. "The royal crown has been threatened three times, has it not?"

"Yes, but those attacks happened hundreds of years ago. Now we have the strongest defensive and offensive weaponry system in the Millennius. No planet would dare — "

"Maybe no planet, but remember, the third threat was made by a family member who tried to depose King Sithel."

That was true. "But that prince was mentally unstable, suffering from wave after wave of insanity brought on by a deep crack in his head shell. Something like that would never happen again."

"Crack in his head shell?" She smiled, shaking her head. "My great, great, great, great uncle was the prince's royal adjutant. My uncle passed down the truth— That prince was no more insane than you or me. His only disability was greed."

The shell plates around my eyes buckled at Lestra's insolence, but I didn't say anything and took a deep breath instead.

"It's the Timuary's duty to serve and safeguard the royal family," she continued, "not only from their enemies but also from themselves. Five hundred years ago, the king, with the help of Maeglus Timuary, commissioned the building of tunnels within the walls of the entire palace and its adjoining buildings, creating a secret place to hide. It was done discreetly with the work being performed cautiously and at night. King Sithel trusted only the Timuarys." Lestra's hand slipped from my shoulder. "At the king's request, the Timuarys vowed to keep the tunnels a secret from everyone, including the royals. When King Sithel died, the secret of the hollow walls died with the royal family."

Was I really supposed to believe this shit? The hard sheets of my forehead felt rigid, and I started to get a headache.

"Garran, when your ancestors disappeared into the walls, it was because the Timuarys led them into the tunnels, a place where they would be safe." Lestra's shell powder twinkled. "Then, after the raid was over, the royals were taken to the lab to have their short-term memories cleansed, keeping the king's secret intact. But we Timuarys know everything. We know these passages like the backs of our hands, every entrance and exit, so we know where to hide all of you if there's ever another threat, including a threat within the royal family."

"Okay, now I'm really confused. So tell me again— My family doesn't know about this because…" The pain in my head increased.

"That's where we'd temporarily hide the rest of the family members who were not involved in a plot to overthrow the king, and the Timuarys would fight to restore order in the palace," she said in one whispered breath.

"So even my dad doesn't know about the walls?"

"No, but it's for the royal's own good," she was quick to add.

"Okay, okay, I get it. I don't want to hear any more."

The anger of knowing my great, great, great, great-something-grandfather lost faith in his royal family but continued to trust a family of the servant class, flooded my being, momentarily seizing my joints. The Timuarys were obedient but sometimes pompous. Now I knew why.

"So what am I going to do?"

"I'm going to take you into the walls, and when you reappear, you'll be inside cell fifteen. The tunnels extend through the lab and all areas of containment, just in case a disillusioned king imprisons an adversary who needs to be rescued."

America was definitely an adversary I considered needed rescuing. "Okay, so if this is all true, let's go."

"Right now? Are you even prepared to take her into the woods?"

"No. I just want to take her there and show it to her. I'll bring her back to her cell tonight, and tomorrow, I'll be ready to leave her there with a shelter and food."

"And if someone notices her cell is empty?"

"Slaine is the only guard allowed near her cell, and my father won't return for another visit."

"Okay," she said and led me from my room and into the hall. "Make sure it's clear."

I jogged to one end of the hall and then the other. As I expected at this time of day, the adjoining halls were empty. "It's clear."

Despite its recent damage, Lestra's heritage badge illuminated when she stepped toward the wall, and before I could blink, a seven-foot stone disengaged from the wall, suspended mid-air by a stream of wind.

"It's true," I said. "I can't believe my father doesn't know about this."

"Quickly," she said.

With a blast of air, the stone sucked back into its place behind us as we settled deep within the dimly lit passage.

Once inside, I traced the outline of my own badge, rubbing each jewel with the tip of my finger and noting the five symbols that defined my royal line. Over one thousand years old and hand carved from a stick of vexulum, the most sought after metal in the galaxy, I, like all Enestians, wore my badge with pride, but ours obviously didn't hold the Timuary magic.

"This is incredible," I gasped, feeling my blood pressure spike. "Now what?"

"Follow me. I was required to have these passages memorized from the turn of my eighth year. When we were younger, my cousins and I used to sneak in here and play hide-and-go-find."

I shook my head. "I still can't believe this."

The fit was snug at times, requiring us to turn to one side and shuffle to the left, and the passage grew darker with each turn, aside from a row of tiny lights in the floor for illumination. Despite an occasional gust of air, the passage smelled old and unused, its oxygen heavy and stale, giving the sensation that it was difficult to breathe. My arms hit the stone walls several times with a clatter.

"Don't worry, no one can hear us," said Lestra when my elbow made another deafening bang against the side of the stone passage. "We're getting closer. There's another turn up ahead. We'll be veering to the right soon," she said after who knows how many turns.

She came to a stop, and her heritage badge illuminated once again as a gust of cold air rippled through the passage. Caught in the developing suction, a tall stone separated itself from the others and hovered open behind us.

"We're here," she announced.

Chapter Twenty-Three

AMERICA

"What the—"

A sharp breeze cut across my cell, and a piece of the far wall began to move, pivoting on a center axis as the block twisted out of place. I bolted to my feet.

"America, it's Garran." His hand extended through the opening, and I ran to take it, still shocked by what I had just seen. "Come with me," he said, and I entered a passageway. Lestra peered at me from over Garran's shoulder. "Lestra has access through the walls, something I didn't know about until today."

"Where are you taking me? Home?" I asked, clasping my hands together so hard they hurt.

"No, that's not possible—yet."

"Then where?" I said, relaxing my hands.

"To a special place where we can be alone, to a place I

want you to see. Something beautiful."

"I already see something beautiful," I said, as our eyes met.

"And I, too." He brought his head closer to mine, his lips parted and ready, but as Lestra's shell clacked with a shift of her weight, he pulled away.

Inspecting my face, he lifted my chin with his fingers. "Are you okay? I heard about what my father did to you. I'm so sorry." He gave me a quick but strong hug.

"Yeah, I'm fine. My jaw's just a little sore."

He clasped my hand, and Lestra took the lead as we entered the wall.

"What if someone notices I'm gone?"

"The only person who could is Slaine, and he won't report it."

While we snaked between the sheets of stone, I watched Lestra walk ahead of us.

Her gait was full of grace, her rear end hard and perfectly round as it knocked side to side with each step like a beauty queen on a catwalk. I imagined her with a head of long, blond hair, whipping back and forth across the back of her beige tunic while she strode down the dim tunnel, following the lights on the floor.

My feet tingled against the cold stone floor, though my hand became warm in Garran's. Lestra and Garran exchanged a few words, and our pace quickened.

"We're almost there," said Garran.

After the next turn, we slowed to a stop. Lestra stood next to the far wall and placed her hand against it. Something on her tunic, a brooch of some sort, illuminated an eerie yellow, like a firefly, and a moment later, a section of the wall disengaged. With a creak and explosion of dust, the stone rotated, revealing the outdoors.

"Ready, America?"

"Yes," I said.

A ray of sun cut through the opening, casting a band of bright light across our faces. I squinted, holding my fanned hand across my eyes, and when Garran and I stepped from the wall, the damp, musky smell of mildew was replaced with a freshness of flowers I didn't recognize.

Garran spoke to Lestra in their language. Whatever he said made her fold her arms and retreat into the far shadow on the opposite side of the hall, and the block closed with Lestra behind it.

"She's going to wait for us. We'll need her to open the wall and lead us back to your cell," said Garran. But I was half listening.

Shades of green and purple made up the Enestian atmosphere, and where the two colors met, they burned magenta. A billowing of clouds scraped across the horizon, and though they shined too brightly to look at, the double blast of bright light made it obvious that there were two suns. "You were right. It's beautiful," I said. "Your sky and the trees—everything. And it smells so good."

"That's the jessom moss," said Garran, pointing to a patch of green beneath our feet.

It was storybook, once-upon-a-time perfect, something from a fairy tale. Tree trunks as smooth as Enestian shell dotted the land, their limbs fluffed with leaves of deep green and fuzzy drapes of moss. The soil was rich, the color and consistency of ground coffee beans. As Garran led me into a small grove, my feet padded lightly on the springy moss, and there was no worry of stepping on a stone.

Within the grove, a ring of trees, their trunks touching, enclosed a small clearing, with the exception of a two-foot gap. We squeezed through it, and I saw the weave of branches above, the limbs twisting around each other from one tree to the next like boa snakes of wood.

Garran squeezed my hand. "What do you think of this special place?" he asked.

"It's absolutely breathtaking."

A stone statue sat at the base of each tree, curving elegantly from the ground in a swirl, mirroring the turns of embroidery on Garran's shirt and ending with the busts of Enestians, some male, some female. Each wore a carved tunic, the collar extending above the back of each head like a fan of peacock feathers.

"Are they tombstones?" I asked, as I approached the closest one and ran my finger down its cheek.

"No, they're memorials—royals—my ancestors. Upon my death, my likeness is supposed to be added, and there it would stand, a permanent overseer of the Ring of Reverence."

"And your father," I said with a smirk, "he'll be memorialized here, too?"

"Yes," he said, "not that he deserves the honor, but it is tradition." He took one of my hands in his. "You know, America, no one has ever challenged my father before—verbally or physically—to the extent that you did, and you did both. Very impressive." He smiled. "Not only are you beautiful and intelligent, but you are strong-willed, determined. That's why I think you could live here, just for a while, until I can take you home."

"Here?"

"Yes. That's why I wanted to show it to you, to make sure you'd be willing to stay here. You'd be safe. I'd provide you with shelter and food, and of course, I'd come see you every day."

"I could do it," I said and thought about the tent I pitched just hours before I was abducted. It was crooked and took twice as long to set up as it should have—a pathetic attempt at camping—but with Garran's help I'd make it work. Anything was better than my cell. "This place is magical and majestic. I love it."

"And then you will be away from my father and his team. They would no longer have the opportunity to study you and then…" Garran dropped my hand and his head.

"But when they discover I'm gone, they'd look for me. Wouldn't they?"

"No, this particular grove is sacred. Only the royals are allowed to enter. My father would be the one, and on that day, I'd make sure you weren't here, and all traces of you gone."

"And if your father finds out you helped me escape? I… I'm afraid to die, but I'm also afraid of what he can do to you."

His head bent toward mine and he murmured, "I can bear any punishment. What I can't bear is you suffering under my father's will."

He kissed me, slowly at first, the delicate tip of his tongue meeting mine, his lips light and teasing, his breath warm and pleasantly sweet. I gripped his shoulders, and his kisses came harder as his hands ran the length of my torso. Everything inside me stirred in a tingly swirl of pleasure and desire, working its way down from my chest to where it settled below. I had to have more. He was covered in shell, but he was warm, and I wanted, no needed, to get even closer to him.

"I want you," he said as his shaking hands met the top of my blanket.

"Wait," I said before his fingers hit my skin.

"I'm sorry," he said and drew away. "I should have asked before I tried to…" His eyes darted to my chest. My blanket had slipped, enough to reveal most of my cleavage, but I didn't retighten the blanket against me.

He was breathing heavily, the plates under his tunic sliding with each breath.

Besides his beautiful shell, Garran was as human as any guy I'd ever met. I wanted to see him—all of him. I wanted to feel him—all of him. I wanted to let him touch me, let him take me.

Though the idea was beyond crazy—an earthling and an alien—every atom in my body ached because I needed him. Wanted to feel him inside me. Maybe Garran couldn't save me, and I'd die here, but I would have one magical experience. And it would be with my white knight.

I looked at him and said, "No, it's not that. I want you, too. It's just—"

"What?" he asked at a whisper, the tips of his fingers meeting my cheek.

"I'm a virgin. I've, I've never, you know…" I swallowed hard, and he smiled, the small plates around his eyes rising.

"And there is something you should know. I haven't, either." He interlocked his fingers with mine and brought my hands to his lips.

"Really?" Now I wanted him even more.

"I'll admit it is unusual for a male at my age, even one

slated to marry a pre-selected bride. I could have found plenty of girls who would have…" His eyes flicked from mine and then returned. "But I didn't. It was my choice to wait until now, until I found someone I truly wanted to be with, someone who makes me feel like I do right now." He kissed my hand again, and a pleasant fluttering expanded in my chest.

"Are we even, I mean, is it even possible for us…?" I asked, and tightened my loose blanket back into place when it slipped a bit farther.

"Yes, our anatomies are compatible," he said. "But I would need to be extra gentle, so I wouldn't hurt you."

Hurt me? I couldn't imagine what it looked like. If it was clad in shell, would its plates slide and pinch me? What if it exceeded the length and girth of what a human girl could handle? Were the male parts of him I hadn't seen also true to his humanoid form? Maybe they weren't, and what he had was something dangerous to humans, something that would tear my flesh if he wasn't completely mindful of what he was doing.

Shaking my head took away the thought of any pain that could go with making love to him, and I replaced it with the memory of how soft our kisses were against his firm but giving lips.

I did want him, more than any guy I'd ever had a chance with. I wanted him to be the one, this strong, exotic being, who made my heart dance and my insides throb in a way my body never had before.

I blinked and sucked in a small breath. "I know you'll be gentle. Let's try it," I said. "I'm ready. I want you, Garran."

"Are you sure?" He gulped.

"Yes," I said and kissed his fingertips.

"I want you, too, and I'm also ready," he said, and kissed a path from my lips to the base of my neck.

We melted to the ground and onto a patch of jessom moss so thick it felt like a sponge.

Still holding my blanket in place, I lay on my back with Garran on top of me, his palms at both sides of my body, supporting his weight.

"This is where I want it to happen," he said as his lips pressed against my neck and his tongue ran its length, leaving a trail of wet warmth as I shivered with desire.

I kissed the shell beneath his ear but drew away each time it overlapped with the movement of his jaw. His next kiss against my throat was hard, and I made my kisses match his, my front teeth periodically scraping against shell.

His upper body lowered against mine, chest meeting chest. "Too heavy," I said, between breaths, and when he lifted away, I unbuttoned his shirt with shaky fingers, beginning at the neck.

Pressing my lips against his tattoo, I traced it with my tongue, every twirl, spin, and turn. Garran moaned, throwing back his head and pressing his groin against mine.

"My turn," he said after shaking his shirt off. It dropped to the ground, and as Garran kissed the skin above the band of my blanket, I grasped a fistful of velvety moss, clenching tighter as he pulled the blanket down with his left hand. "Beautiful," he said, and ran the point of his tongue across my hard nipples. "So soft," he continued, cupping one of my breasts and burying his mouth against it.

I set my hands upon his shoulders and squeezed, massaging my fingers against his shell plates and trailing my palms down his chest, each of my fingertips tingling from the pressure, exploring each curve of shell as they buckled against his abdomen in unison with his heavy breathing.

His mouth returned to my neck, and I tilted my head toward him, taking in the warm, damp sweetness of his breath. Pulling my hands away when he lifted, a set of his chest plates slid under the next and his lips pressed upon mine.

The tip of his tongue brushed against the roof of my mouth, meeting the soft pallet with a delicate stroke. My heart pulsed hard, wracking my chest, and as the tip of his tongue gave a final stroke, the carnal sensation it created lingered, bathing my body in heat and uncontrollable need.

Garran brought his lips to my stomach with delicate licks as the place between my legs became warm and yearning. My blanket was gone at this point, thrown aside, and with my legs bent at the knee, he placed his hand against me, the thick leather of his fingers exploring my wet skin.

"Does this hurt?" he asked.

"No," I said.

One of his fingers entered me slowly, as he rocked it into place, and I arched my back with pleasure and let out a soft sigh. His touch was soft yet firm, teasing yet testing.

"Is this okay?" he asked in a whisper as his finger withdrew to touch me, swirling in small circles.

"Yes. Don't stop. Don't stop," I said, and his motion against me increased in speed and pressure.

"Yes! Yes!"

What was happening to me? I gasped and something erupted inside of me, something so pleasurable I thought I might scream as the feeling spread through my entire body, making me shake and hold my breath until it passed.

Chapter Twenty-Four

GARRAN

Careful not to bruise her delicate skin, I wrapped my arms around America's back and experienced something I could never feel with another Enestian due to our shells—the beating of a heart against my chest, a hard thump that quickened as I continued to hold her.

Her hair fanned across her shoulders, and a moment later, both of her thin arms were limp. Her breath was hot and steamy against my shell, making a damp place under my neck and chin. I brushed her hair from her face and kissed her moisture-beaded forehead. She closed her eyes as I ran the back of my hand against her cheek, keeping my touch light across her velvety skin.

"Look at me," I whispered. She opened her eyes, and as I hovered above her, my arms supporting my weight, our gazes locked. Even in the shade of the meelson trees, the soft, bronze-like coloring of her eyes was distinguishable from their black centers. And as we continued to stare at each other, my heart rapidly beating, I felt connected to her mentally and physically, though our lower bodies were apart.

She lifted her hand to my face and smiled, the turn of her lips sexy and seductive. I was drawn to push my lower body against hers. Shifting my weight, I caught her hand and kissed it, keeping my lips parted as my tongue slid against a trail of thin bone.

Her thumb slid to my palm, and while she caressed the tender, soft shell of my hand, I lowered to my elbow and caught the back of her thigh with my other hand, cupping my palm gently as I eased her even closer to me.

How could something so shell-less and soft be so beautiful? But she was, and as our eyes met again, and she sucked in a short breath, the tip of her tongue meeting her lips, I couldn't hold back any longer. A flickering of heat expanded under my shell, and my lower plate slid open.

I tugged at my waistband, pulling my leggings to the center of my thighs and then lower, below my knees. I was ready to experience her. But I had to be careful. I couldn't hurt her.

Yes, we were compatible in terms of connecting sexually. I'd seen enough human love scenes in Earth movies to know that—at least I thought we would be. But Enestian shell, something similar to the palms of our hands, did, in fact, extend to the external organs.

She gasped again as her eyes dropped below my waist. With eyes wide, she licked her lips once more, turned her head, and squeezed her eyes shut.

I looked down at her soft, wet place, pink and delicate

like a blooming tress flower, and as she opened her eyes, her gaze full of fear, I whispered, "Do you still want this?"

"Yes," she said softly.

It was about to happen—my innocence not taken but freely given to the girl of my choice. I would share my first intimate, exclusive experience with someone whose beauty and delicate nature made me unworthy of the honor and the privilege.

And that's when I entered her, slowly and gently, inch by inch, and she moaned as my pelvis lowered against hers.

"Yes, yes," she said again.

Every piece of my body ignited with pleasure as I continued, rocking against her in rhythmic, controlled thrusts. She sighed and clasped the shell of my buttocks with her hands, her hot breasts pressing against my upper shell.

An inexplicable, hot stirring developed inside my lower abdomen, becoming more and more intense and ripening into something that made me shake uncontrollably. For a moment, I couldn't breathe, and I threw back my head, savoring every second of this intense bliss, and my plates shook, grinding and tingling in a way I'd never experienced before.

When it was done, I pulled away, having experienced something so mind-blowing. I dropped next to her and rolled onto my back in disbelief.

Chapter Twenty-Five

America

"Something's wrong. I don't feel right," I said as we walked back toward the lab, holding each other. "It couldn't be from…"

"No, my seminal fluid cannot and will not hurt you." Garran brought his arm around my waist as we walked in unison. "If anything about us being together would've harmed you, I wouldn't have let it happen."

Garran rapped his knuckles against the secret door, and it opened a moment later. Lestra kept her arms crossed when we entered, and then dropped them with a clack when the wall resealed.

"She seems angry," I said.

"We were gone longer than I told her we'd be."

And hopefully she didn't suspect why. With the back of my hand, I wiped the perspiration from my forehead and shook my ruffled hair back into place. Garran's shirt was askew at the shoulders, and the flap of the shaft of one boot lifted.

Garran held my hand while we walked through the wall, and at one point pulled me closer to sneak a kiss when Lestra was ahead of us. Once we reached my cell, he entered with me, while Lestra stayed inside the passage, manning the secret door.

"That was amazing," said Garran softly, taking me into his arms. "I'm glad it was you—my first time to be with someone I care about, and not the girl I meet on my wedding day."

I smiled and lifted my head for him to kiss me. His touch took me back to the bed of jessom moss, and my body tightened with delight.

"It meant a lot to me, too." It was surreal. I'd just lost my virginity to an alien and on a planet three galaxies from Earth. And there were no regrets. I cared about him. I wanted him to be the one.

"I'll come for you tomorrow night. I'll have everything ready for you to stay there by then."

"Thank you," I said, giving him a kiss. "And will you be able to stay with me for a while once you take me there?"

"I will. I don't have communications class until the afternoon." And hopefully there'd be time to make love again.

His hand skated to my waist, and he pulled me against him for another hot kiss before letting me go and exiting into the wall.

Though in a state of enamored bliss, my gut wrenched, and I held my breath in an attempt to settle my stomach. A pain developed in the hollow of my belly. It was a pain I felt before when I'd had the flu, the pain that usually left my body retching over the toilet and my throat raw from bile. The pain subsided as I swallowed and drew in a long breath, but a moment later, a raw churning worked its way up my throat. I made it to the toilet, and it extended just in time for me to vomit without making a mess.

My hands trembling, I wiped my chin with the back of my hand and waited for the sink to project, so I could wash my face. Three splashes of cold water calmed the rising heat in my cheeks, but the back of my throat burned, and my stomach continued to bubble with pain.

What was wrong with me? Was it a reaction to the food cubes I'd eaten or was it some kind of allergic reaction to Garran, a species so different from me it was nature's way to keep us separated?

Slaine's shadow appeared on the other side of the wall as I held my stomach and leaned against the back wall until I heaved a second time, and I couldn't stop myself from gagging, my whole body shuddering as I remained bent at the waist above the toilet.

It was embarrassing with all the puking and choking sounds I made, but at least the water wall was up to block some of the noise and blur the image of me hanging over the metal basin. A rubber band would have been nice, so I could at least keep my hair away from the stream of spew.

It was Slaine who helped me to the far wall where I lowered myself and sat down, pulling the blanket tight around my torso. He reclaimed his post outside my cell and didn't take his eyes from me until the liquid curtain lowered back into place.

There was nothing left to puke up, but my stomach twisted and turned. I was cold, despite my blanket, and lonely. My teeth chattered uncontrollably until I pictured Garran in his deep green shirt, his face as smooth as a chunk of white wax. But it was a rugged face, a masculine face, and the body that matched it had done an amazing thing to me earlier that day.

Tomorrow, I was going to leave this cell for good. But would he return to find my dead body huddled in the corner where Slaine left me? That's what I felt like. I felt dead, and I might as well have been. My family and friends probably thought I was at this point, so what did it matter anyway?

But there was one thing for sure— I was not going to die without someone who cared for me on this planet. Someone who'd given me the most amazing experience of my life.

Chapter Twenty-Six

GARRAN

Today's lectures had left me completely drained. The last things I cared about were atmospheric studies, four-dimensional physics, primitive-life anatomy—we were currently studying the dimpled frog of Desna Ten—and dual-stage propulsion systems, especially after I received a message from my father, requesting I meet with him and his research team that afternoon, a meeting that could bring me closer to having access to a ship in the near future. And especially since I still needed to prepare the Ring of Reverence for America's arrival.

Lestra entered my room and stood at the foot of my bed where I was sitting. Her lips, which were normally curved at their corners in a natural smile, dropped, but it looked forced and rehearsed.

"I talked to my brother today. The human is sick." Lestra

couldn't have cared less.

"What?" I stood and grabbed her by the shoulders. My stomach twisted, and for a moment, I couldn't catch my breath as Lestra bobbled under my frantic grip. "Yesterday she said she felt like something was wrong, but when I left her cell, she seemed fine."

"You and my brother— I just don't get how you two can have feelings for that thing. Slaine is disobeying orders and breaking his pledge to the king. At first he did it because you ordered him to, but now!" She shook her head. "It just doesn't make sense to me. How can you and my brother care for it so much?" she asked nonchalantly, like she equated my beautiful human to an amphibian knull.

Enestians, though arrogant, which wasn't unfounded considering we were the most advanced beings in the Millennius, were known throughout the galaxy as being intelligent but sometimes overly emotional beings, or what we Enestians liked to say, passionate beings. Enestians of lesser bloodlines have been known to go insane if their feelings festered and were not shared with others. Slaine Timuary didn't just break his oath of secrecy and allegiance to my father, like me, he was the victim of having a big heart.

"I need to find out what made her sick." I couldn't have caused her illness. I mean, I'd visited her before, touched her, kissed her, but then again we had never made love until yesterday.

"I should have never told you about the walls," said Lestra. "I should have let you get caught and banished."

"The walls. Was it the walls? She was fine until—until we were outside."

My fingers couldn't work fast enough. My hypotheses

came so quickly that I pushed away my keyboard and worked the database by voice command. Lestra rolled her eyes, but she remained in my quarters with her arms folded and huffing every time I talked to myself, trying to think through each theory.

"Well, it's not the air circulatory system outside the lab. It's no different from the filtration and air acclimatizing systems on Earth," I announced and continued my research. "The food replacement cubes—it's not those or the water— I've checked and double checked their molecular structure and the mineral and vitamins they contain, none of which are harmful to humans."

Two hours passed. Thirty minutes more, and I'd need to quit and leave for my meeting with the lab team.

"Okay," said Lestra. "I don't think I can listen to your pathetic rant for a minute longer. You're going in circles. You're so consumed by this alien that you're not thinking logically. Every theory has been a dead end." She headed toward the door. "Here's my advice. Take a deep breath and ask yourself what the major differences are between Enestia and Earth. That's where I'd start."

She was right, and just as the door to my quarters slid opened, America's own words cut across my mind. "It's beautiful," she had said when she scanned our horizon.

"Two suns," I shouted. It's our atmosphere. Our cosmic radiation levels must exceed that of Earth's. "Until I took her outside, she was protected by the thick walls of her cell."

An overdose of radiation. Yes, that was it. Why didn't I think of that before? Enestia's suns dwarfed the sun in which the planet Earth revolved, and the radiation ours produced was unlike any type in Earth's galaxy. My shoulder plates relaxed with an uncomfortable clunk, and I smacked the top of my thigh with my fist.

"Then there's no question. She can't stay here—not a minute longer. She won't survive in the Ring of Reverence. I have to get her back to Earth."

Lestra snapped her lips. "You don't have a ship, and you won't have one in time. There's nothing you can do for it. Don't see it anymore. Forget about it. All you can do is let it die in your father's lab."

"That's what you want, isn't it? You want it to die." I banged my fist on my desk.

Her rigid posture softened. "Maybe, but it's more than that. All I'm thinking about right now is you and my brother. Both of you have taken great risks for that alien—you especially—you're jeopardizing your future as king. It's best you stop thinking about it, and then once it's dead and forgotten, things can go back to normal."

"Forgotten. I will never forget her. My life will never be back to normal after this. How will I ever be able to look my father in the eyes after knowing what he did to her?" I asked. The plates around my eyes and mouth locked until I took a deep breath.

I sat across from her, my chin to my chest and my head in my hands while a surge of sadness came over me. I blinked a few times, and a tear fell against my palm. What? It had been so long that I forgot what it felt like. I bit my lip and held my tears as I grieved for Lestra's anger and pain, the dead Trispian, my unwanted future as a vile king, and most of all, America's impending death.

Then I felt a light pressure on my shoulder, a hand—Lestra's hand. She sat next to me and leaned her head against my shoulder. "I'm sorry, Garran. I really am. I know you genuinely care about that alien. It's just hard for me to understand how and why."

"Yeah, I know," I said, and stood abruptly, ready to confront my father.

My father and me— How could two people be so different?

Quips, the most regarded fruit on Enestia, begin as fluffy white blossoms, identical in size, shape, and smell. After each blossom shrivels and the last petal falls, a small quip bubbles up in its place to grow red and ripe under the Enestian suns, and the once-thick trunk splits at its center, producing two vines in which to harbor its young fruit.

But quip growers lose half their harvest by the end of the season, for one vine produces a fruit so sweet you can taste its goodness radiating within your shell, but the other vine, though its quips are identical to the other, produces fruit so bitter on the tongue it is impossible to eat. That was my father and me—quips on a tree. Our bodies were grown from the same bloodline, but our scruples were twisted up two different vines.

My father's ten-member research team stood when I entered his private conference room in the research section of the lab. Huskus, the lead scientist, motioned with his finger for me to sit at the opposite end of the table across from my father, who by the way, was not obligated to stand at my presence and chose not to.

King Meallian. I could barely stand to look at him as he sat at the head of the long glass table. "Release the human,"

I wanted to say. "Send her back to Earth. How dare you pick on a poor shell-less creature."

But instead of using those icy words, my anger came out in the form of a fixed frown in my father's direction, a frown that caused him to grab my arm and whisper in my ear that I looked "sulky and tired" and not to "embarrass him" as I passed to take a seat.

He was a tall, strong man that most Enestian females considered extremely handsome. His shell was worn where the plates met and hinged around his eyes, a sign of his age, but his jaw was firm and square, giving him a certain inherent dignity that enhanced the royal title. No one dared to disobey my father.

"The prince has a sudden interest in our research," he said, once I was seated. "So I've decided to include him in our next research endeavor and relevant dissection."

Huskus Weevnil drew in a short breath. "My king, are you referring to the next specimen abduction or the one we currently—"

My father held up his hand. "That's enough." Huskus sank in his chair.

"Or the one that what?" I asked, leaning back with enough false confidence and arrogance to hide that I knew which specimen Huskus was referring to.

My father scratched his chin. "How far are you willing to go with this, my prince?"

"As far as I can and be just like you. The king of all kings in the Millennius."

The words burned my tongue, but my father was amused, taking delight in the fact that I honored him in front of his royal team, a dozen scientists and chemists he'd handpicked.

I tried to hold a smile as I nodded at the men and woman who helped my father study its enemies inside and out, in order to remain the most powerful planet.

"Huskus was referring to the specimen dissection taking place tomorrow."

"What dissection?" I tried to ask calmly as my heart thumped hard, practically knocking against the inside of my shell.

"Another irrelevant creature." He paused and his shell lips pursed. "The dissection is scheduled for tomorrow afternoon."

That meant America. The shell sections on my abdomen tensed, and for a moment, I thought I'd throw up my last meal. "What kind of creature?" I kept my back pressed against the cube's support and casually crossed my arms, though I was ready to leap across the table and fracture my father's facial shell with a right punch.

"That is none of your concern, young prince, for you will not be present during that dissection. Instead, you will be with Caskin and Alandra, participating in the next abduction." Another abduction? Another abduction required intergalactic space travel.

The two team members, one a pilot and the other a containment and quarantine specialist, gave me proud smiles and nods as my father said their names. How pathetic. As if robbing a planet of one of its residents was something respectable. I wondered which of the two, or maybe both, were responsible for capturing America.

"This abduction will be taking place…?"

"Tomorrow morning."

That's when I'd leave, taking America with me! "So the

ship has already been prepared for intergalactic flight? I mean, I assume the specimen is not from our galaxy."

"Your assumption is correct. The abduction will take place on a small planet several galaxies away."

Could it be Earth? My heart shot into my throat. Was it really going to be this easy? "And the name of the planet?" I asked, gingerly, containing my excitement.

The king leaned forward, interlacing his fingers before he set them on the table. "Terinan. Its inhabitants are half-shells. Their heads and abdomens are plated, but their appendages are completely exposed."

Damn! I knew it was too good to be true. I'd just have to reset the course.

"Your duty during the expedition will be to observe and learn, and that is all."

"But I can fly a dual propulsion intergalactic cruiser," I said a little too eagerly, biting my tongue between my lips.

"Caskin is lead pilot," he said sharply, "and will remain so for this assignment."

As lead, Caskin would preset the flight codes hours before the flight. Now I'd have to delete his codes and re-enter the codes manually, and that would take time—extra time I didn't have to spare.

I turned toward Caskin, unable to look at my father. "What time should I meet you at the ship tomorrow?" I asked politely but through tight teeth.

"At the eighth morning turn," said my father as Caskin remained mute. The king rarely let anyone else speak in his presence. If my father had the answer, he was the one to give it.

"And I should prepare to be gone for how long?"

"Four days at the most. You can't remain in Terinan's atmosphere for more than one day."

"And why is that, Father?"

"An explanation is not required. Just heed my warning. One day in their atmosphere and no longer." He snapped his fingers, warning me not to nudge for the answer. "I realize you'll be missing two days at the conservatory, but from what I've heard lately from your professors, I'm sure you won't be too disappointed." He smirked.

Not only did my father like to restrict others from speaking, he also liked to embarrass them when he could, even his own son. At this point, he could embarrass me all he wanted. All I cared about was solidifying my plan to take America back to Earth, and as my father discussed the details of the next abduction, his cheek plates grinding as he sneered with pleasure, it hardened my decision that I eventually had to put an end to his experiments.

My father ended the meeting with a boring brag session about Enestia being the most powerful and advanced planet in the Millennius, but his lengthy speech did do one thing— It gave me time to think up and finalize my additional plan, and surprisingly, moments of concern or indecision never surfaced.

When America was safely back on Earth, I'd come back to Enestia and stop him for good. How? I didn't know, and it might, in fact, take years to build up my power as the prince and ambassador to arrange and lead a coup—something I'd have to do if my father didn't step down from the throne willingly. But if I did, would the Timuarys be on my side or would they lead their wicked king into the walls in order to protect him?

My blood boiled beneath my shell and then tempered as I continued to concoct a plan to first save America and then eventually depose the king, and the meeting couldn't end fast enough for me. But when I returned to my quarters, Lestra was less than excited, to say the least, when I told her about my newfound prospect to steal a star ship and whisk America away from Enestia and back to Earth in less than half a day.

The opportunity to save America that plopped into my lap like a hot meteorite, just when I had given up hope, was a complete catastrophe to Lestra, leaving her speechless with her hands on her hips and her shell tense as she sat scowling at me. I didn't dare mention the second half of my drawn-out plan to dethrone my father and end the abductions. Right now, my focus was on helping America.

"It's too risky," Lestra said. "What if something happens, and you can't get back to Enestia after you return the human?" Now I regretted inviting her to my quarters.

"Then I won't come back — at least not right away. Why return so soon in the first place when my father will be waiting for me with a prison sentence in one of the containment campuses on Regis?" I asked while I turned on my virtual monitor.

"But you'd have to come straight home. Where would you go? You can't stay on Earth. To them, *you're* the alien." She was right.

"I'll go to Verla Three," I said boldly. "My father's powers of extradition are worthless there. I could stay as long as I wanted."

The flight codes for Earth appeared on my monitor, and I typed their sequence into a handheld communicator, one number at a time.

"Your mother's vacationing on Verla Three."

"Exactly. Why do you think she vacations there? If she ever gets up the nerve to leave my insensitive brute of a father, he wouldn't be able to force her to come back to the throne. Fifty-four, eighteen, seventeen…"

"Do you think your mother would actually help you?" She pressed her hands against the top of the sitting cube and leaned forward.

"No, of course not. I'll have to eventually get a job," I said quickly. "Shoot." I deleted the two numbers I transposed and began again.

Despite her scorn for my father, my mother would never come to my aid and risk losing her station or lavish expense account. Although she lacked my father's sense of cruelty, in many ways, she was more selfish than the king. Abandoning her children in order to avoid him was a self-seeking trade off. On Verla, she and I could never cross paths.

"A job? But you're a prince."

"Yes, I am, which means I'm highly educated with skills that surpass most Verlians." A means of income was more than necessary. I'd need Millennium credits to arm myself and those who'd join me in my fight against my father.

"But to get a job?"

"Why not? I'll need to, once my stashed credits are gone. You, of all people, should understand this. You're a Timuary. You're no stranger to hard work. You've been working your whole life."

Lestra kicked her heel against her sitting cube and gave me a look that could crack shell. "Thanks for reminding me."

"There's no reason to get angry. I'm just making the

point that you're not too proud to work, so why should I be, since I am no better than you, after all."

"Garran, you're a royal."

"And you are my protector, right?" I sat down on the cube across from her and set my hand on her knee.

"But…"

"But what? I have to save her. Seventy-one, twenty-two, eighty-eight. Please don't try to stop me, because there's nothing you can do to make me change my mind."

"I won't stop you, Garran. But I'll continue to try to talk some sense into that thick-shelled skull of yours. Do you even have a plan?"

"Of course."

Lestra's shell rattled as she folded her arms across her chest.

"I mean, kind of. We have to take America out of her cell tonight. From there, I'll go directly to the hangar, put her on the cruiser, set a course for Earth, and be gone before the suns come up."

"Do you really think it'll be that easy? We can't become one with the walls once we're outside the palace or lab. Since the ship is docked outside, taking America there will be extremely dangerous. What if someone sees us?"

"We'll dress her in a hooded tunic, leggings, and boots. We'll walk confidently with America between us and with the hood pulled over her head." We had to make it as simple as possible. The more complex, the more complications, the more complications, the bigger chance of something going wrong.

"They'll have a guard stationed by the ship."

"And I'll deal with that. I'm a prince, remember?" Lestra

groaned. "Once America and I are on the cruiser, it's only a matter of minutes before we take off and break through the Enestian atmosphere. At that point, America and I will be safe. My father wouldn't dare send a defensive fleet against a ship used for research. That would stir up suspicion in the galaxy, something he wouldn't want."

An armed Enestian vessel using tactical maneuvers in pursuit of an unarmed Enestian research ship? Yeah, right. That would never happen. Even if it meant life or death, my father would rather die than live knowing the citizens of the galaxy realized there was strife among the royals.

"Are you sure the king won't try to stop you from reaching Earth?"

"Positive. Besides, why would he go through that much trouble for a human that's destined to die in less than a day anyway? He's examined human specimens before. Remember the twenty-seven piths of human blood? He doesn't need this human; he only wants her so he can cut her up while she's alive, something he obviously enjoys doing to helpless creatures. To my father, America is expendable, and…" I dropped my gaze to the floor and shook my head. "And so am I at this point. After defying him like this, he'll never want me back."

Lestra put her hand on my shoulder, making me mistype a number. "Okay, so America and you are expendable, but what about me? You didn't mention me." Her voice tapered to a whisper. "Does that mean I'm not going with you?"

"To Earth? No, you're not going. Why would you?" I asked, even though I already knew the answer. She wanted to be with me even if that meant deserting the only way of life she knew.

"But you need my help."

"Yes, I do. I need you to open the walls for us."

"That won't be enough. You need a backup just in case something happens." When Lestra looked up at me with her blue and yellow-dotted eyes, it was like I was looking into my own lost soul.

"I'm not coming back, remember? It's not like I can drop you off at the lab and take off again. Once I'm gone, that's it until I can figure out a way to return without being sent to prison, and that may take years. You need to stay here where you belong."

Not coming back.

Until I said those words, the extent of what I was going to do swirled at the edges of my mind, teetering between reality and fantasy, a plan to save a life. But now the thought of losing everything, my title, my home, my family, tightened my chest plates and breathing became difficult.

"But isn't this where you belong, too?"

Was it? Enestia was the only home I'd ever known. My first breath, first steps, and first words took place within these palace walls. At the turn of my fifth year, my father pinned a heritage badge to my tunic in a grand inauguration, and during the royal address, I sat next to him for the first time, my head high, and my heart full of pride.

How foolish I was then, so eager to please my father, to succumb to his insidious indoctrination, and take his place on the throne. And now every bit of respect I had for him had withered and fallen away like the dried blossom of a ripe quip. I could never rule following his wicked guise, harming the innocent and intimidating the governments of lesser planets.

"No. Not anymore. Damn! You're making me mess this up," I said, deleting the last two numbers. "The codes have to be exact, and I—"

Before I could react, Lestra leaned forward and seized me around the neck with her arms, drawing herself against my body. Her hard breast pushed against my chest as she kissed first my neck and then under my chin.

"Lestra, please," I said, applying a bit of pressure against her shoulders with my palms.

"Don't do this again. You know I don't—"

"Please, let me have you before you leave. Just once," she whispered, her lips wet against my shell.

"Stop. I don't want to do this."

"But I do. I love you, Garran," she said with a sigh, her shell hot against my hands. "You know I do."

"And you know I don't feel the same way. Please. Stop before Murelle barges in here and sees us," I demanded, giving her shoulders another push.

She let go of me, her arms clacking down to her sides, a tear poised on the rim of her lower eye shell.

"Lestra, midnight. Please! Meet me here. It has to be done tonight."

"I'll be there, but only because I want that alien out of your life for good."

"One more thing. America needs clothes. You have access to the servant wardrobe, so would you please—"

"Yes, I'll find the alien something to wear," she said and shot from my room, her arms swinging stiffly at her sides.

Chapter Twenty-Seven

Blood dripped from my nose, a steady drip I caught in my hand as I ran to the sink. Was this another symptom of what-ever was wrong with me, or did the broken blood vessel in my nose simply reopen?

My stomach stopped rumbling, and although I was hun-gry, I didn't dare eat any of the nutritional food blocks that Slaine brought me an hour ago. The weakness in my knees was gone, and besides the empty feeling in my gut, I felt nor-mal again.

From one campground to another— That's where I was going. The Ring of Reverence, with its lacework of trees, springy moss, and delicate sculptures was more beautiful than the Laguna Mountains—the place I still wanted to be.

The Enestian air was warm, and it had been a bit humid. I could deal with that, along with the daily rainfall. I could handle anything as long as Garran came to see me each day, and as long as it led to me eventually going home.

When was he going to come for me? Time— I'd lost all sense of it. One hour rolled into the other, each minute ticking away as I played a guessing game at whether it was night or day. From boredom, I napped every few hours, so my sleep pattern was off, and with the same types of food blocks delivered three times a day, I couldn't predict the time based upon whether it was breakfast, lunch, or dinner.

I closed my eyes and imagined the soft carpet of jessom moss, my body naked and Garran pushing against me, filling me, taking my virginity while I took his. It was so perfect. It was making love.

Garran. I wanted him again. More than before. Like he'd awakened something inside me I didn't know was there. But as much as I loved the time I spent with him, especially now, the sooner I got home the better. The mystery, the suspicion, the panic, the pain, and the accusations my family and friends suffered would end, and the more time I spent with Garran, the more my feelings for him deepened. Breaking away sooner rather than later would be better for my mom and for Attie.

And easier on my heart.

Chapter Twenty-Eight

Garran

After packing a small bag and drinking a mug of warm quip juice and listening to the kind of music my mother listens to—something soft and smooth without vocals—I forced myself into a nap. At midnight, I awoke refreshed and ready for my life on Enestia, as I had known it, to end.

From prince to commoner—that's what I'd be in less than a day. I'd spent a good part of the morning making arrangements on Verla, opening a collection account, transferring my Millennium credits to it, and securing a small villa on the Belushire Coast under the name Yarlen Trink and far from my mother, who preferred the warmer and more affluent side of the planet.

Each finger tap against my communicator brought me closer to my new identity and unfamiliar means of existence. Doubts rose unexpectedly, and I shuffled them aside, knowing that saving America was worth more to me than saving my current persona, something I couldn't live up to anyway if I stayed on Enestia.

My nerves were on edge, biting at my confidence and producing a sick feeling deep in my abdomen, and I had to remind myself that discarding my future on this planet also meant saving America and keeping my integrity.

Lestra met me in the hall, wide awake and shining with shell powder. She smiled and appeared content, no longer angry or jealous. Like a dutiful Timuary, she offered to carry my bag, but I refused, giving her a pat on the shoulder that made her smile even more. But there was something about that smile. Her cheek shells locked like she was keeping a secret that she wanted to tell.

"You're in a pleasant mood," I said as we started toward the wall.

"Yeah, so?"

"So, it just seems a bit unusual, considering how you were acting earlier. I mean—"

"I knew you two were up to something," Murelle accused after she came around the corner.

Fuck! The last thing we needed was my sister trying to screw things up. "What are you talking about?" I asked, setting my bag of supplies on the floor behind me.

"What in the galaxy are the two of you doing out here in the hall? It's after midnight." Murelle's lurch bird, Bell, sat on her shoulder, studying me with its beady, red eyes.

"Why do you care?" I retorted. "And why are *you* out here in the hall at midnight? Don't you have anything better to do than spy on Lestra and me?"

"No, not really. I told you I'd be keeping my eyes on

both of you, that I'd find out what you two have been up to." Bell squawked and gave a light flap of her shelled wings when Murelle reached forward to stick her finger in my face and then Lestra's. Lestra took a step backward.

"Well, you're wasting your time, because we aren't up to anything. Tomorrow is my first day working with the research team. I couldn't sleep, so I decided to make some last-minute preparations and pack for my trip tonight instead of tomorrow morning. I asked Lestra to help me."

Murelle crossed her arms. Without her treasured shell powder, she looked dull and ashen compared to the opulent palace floor. "You are such a liar!" Her black eyes sparkled. "I know exactly why you two are sneaking around. I know what you've been doing. You can't keep something like this a secret from me. How dare you, Garran. Just wait until our father finds out about this. You're a disgrace to the entire family."

"Shhh. You're going to wake up everyone in this wing of the palace. Now get out of my way and take your stupid bird with you. You don't know anything," I said in a harsh whisper.

Murelle pulled a nut from a pocket on her robe and handed it to Bell. The bird grasped it with her right claw and lifted it to her hooked beak. "Oh, yes I do. I know everything."

"You, do, huh? Then tell us, my noble princess," I said sarcastically. "Just what *are* Lestra and I up to?"

"You're sneaking off to have sex somewhere."

That's the last thing I expected her to say. "What? You're crazy. What have you been doing, sniffing shell epoxy?"

"Hardly. There's no other explanation. Brother, you

have lowered yourself to a level even I thought you wouldn't dare go."

"Yeah, what about you wanting to fuck Slaine?"

Lestra gasped. Yeah, I guess I forgot to tell her about that one.

"Shut the fuck up."

"Look, sis. If I was going to screw Lestra, I'd do it in my room. We wouldn't have to sneak off anywhere. I told you, I wanted to pack tonight and—"

"Garran," Lestra said abruptly, setting her hand on my shoulder. "She knows, so there's no point denying it anymore." Her grip on my shoulder tightened with each word.

What the…?

"It's true," Lestra continued, hooking her arm around mine. "We've been doing it for the last week, but we've decided to end it with one last kinky fuck. Tonight we're going to do it on one of the dissection tables in the lab, and then we'll pretend like we've never done it in the first place."

More than shocked, my face plates seized in place, and I couldn't say anything.

"And we'd appreciate you pretending like this never happened, either," Lestra continued. I straightened my posture in agreement but kept my eyes away from Murelle.

"And why would I do that?" asked my sister.

Lestra bent her arm hard against mine.

"Because if you don't and you tell, I'll deny it and so will Lestra."

"So?"

"So, think about it, sis, our father would rather believe your accusation is false, and even if he did suspect it, he'd push it under the palace rug and order you to quell the rumor. I am a prince. Do you really think this palace maid is the first girl I've ever fucked? I have to put in some kind of practice before I meet my bride, and I'm sure Father understands that and will look the other way."

Lestra tried to pull her arm away, but I kept it pinned against my shell plates in the crook of my arm. If she wanted me to go along with this lie, then I would do it justice, even if it made me out to be an insensitive user.

"You make me sick!" Murelle turned on her heels so quickly I thought Bell would fall from her shoulder and crack a wing on the stone floor.

We watched Murelle storm off into her quarters, and then I backed up against the wall and secretly slipped into its interior when Lestra's badge illuminated.

"What the hell were you thinking?" I asked Lestra once we were safely inside the tunnel.

"I was thinking that we better think of something she'd believe."

"But…"

"Don't give me any shit," she snapped. "You enjoyed that."

"Enjoyed what?"

"Talking about me like I was just a casual lay and then telling your sister you've been screwing a bunch of other girls, too." In the glow from the tiny lights on the floor, Lestra's scowl shadowed.

"Hey, you started it, and you made me finish it."

"I told her that in order to protect you. We had to go along with her hunch about us."

"Yeah, and you enjoyed letting her think we were sleeping together." She didn't answer. "I didn't like saying what

I did. I have more respect for you than that. I was going to stick to the first lie we told her. Now she thinks I don't have any respect for myself."

"And she thinks I'm a slut."

"Again, your fault."

"Yeah, but unlike you, after you leave this planet, I'll still be here with your sister thinking I was nothing more than a pathetic practice lay for the prince."

"Who cares what my sister thinks? I don't." My elbow rapped against the stone wall with our next turn.

"I do. I'll still have to see her every day," she huffed.

"I'm sorry. My sister threw us off guard. We said what we had to say, so let's just forget about it." What was the point? Lestra was pissed off about something that never happened between us in the first place.

Chapter Twenty-Nine

A block of the wall pivoted open, and a chilly blast of air lifted the edge of my blanket as I sat in the corner of my dim cell.

"America," a welcomed voice whispered. "How are you feeling? Are you okay? Slaine told me you were sick." When he spoke, his lower shell lip quivered.

"Yeah, I'm fine now. It was really weird. I was sick for a few hours, and then it just went away."

When I reached to hug him, he caught my hands and held them. "Lestra's here, too. She doesn't know, and I don't want her to suspect anything's happened between us. It's just that…" The shell plates above his eyes overlapped.

"It's okay, Garran. I understand. I know she wouldn't approve." Lestra folded her arms and rocked her head upward to stare at the ceiling, obviously avoiding eye contact with me. "She doesn't even approve of this, does she—you being here?"

"No, she doesn't. Being a palace maid, her opinion shouldn't matter, but she and I have grown to be friends." Lestra's foot tapped against the floor like seconds ticking on a clock. "I, um, have something for you. Clothes. They're from the servant's wardrobe. Lestra picked them out."

"Then I'm sure they'll be especially flattering," I said sarcastically. "As long as they keep me warm when I'm at the Ring of Reverence."

"Were not going to the Ring of Reverence. If I take you there, you'll get sick again." The soft plates between his eyes wrinkled. "I found out that the cosmic radiation in our galaxy is higher than that of yours. In addition, the molecular structure of our radiation is also different than that of Earth's. You were sick because you were exposed to too much radiation."

"Radiation poisoning," I said. No wonder I felt like shit. "Two suns." My throat tightened with the thought of gagging again.

"Until I took you outside, the thick wall of this cell and the lab had protected you from our suns. The palace wall might not even be thick enough to do so, but in time…" He shook his head, and every muscle in my body become cold and trembled. "I need to get you away from Enestia as soon as possible." His eyes widened, and the gold flecks in his irises sparkled. "So I'm taking you home tonight."

"Oh my God!"

He set his hand on my shoulder, and its warmth, in contrast to the sudden chill I was experiencing, made my skin prickle.

"We got lucky. Just this afternoon, my father granted me access to a ship."

"So we're going right now?"

"Yes. Your absence will be discovered in the morning, but by then, we'll be in the next galaxy."

There was no question I had to leave Enestia, but what about Garran? "But if you take me…your father… He'll figure out that you're the one who helped me?"

"Yes," he said, looking down at the floor.

"And what will happen to you when you return?"

"*If* I return, I'd lose my inheritance of the throne, along with my title as prince, and my father will probably send me to one of the containment campuses on Regis Seven."

"You mean a prison?"

"Yes, it's a prison for those who commit treason, those who are disloyal to the throne." The shell plates where his eyebrows would be tightened.

"Your father would actually send you to a prison camp?"

"Yes, and I would go willingly rather than spend the rest of my pre-planned life following in my father's footsteps and mastering his cruel ways. But that's not going to happen. I'm not coming back to Enestia—at least not right away."

"Where will you go? Do you even have a plan?"

"I do, but what happens to me and what I'm going to do doesn't matter. My only concern right now is you."

But what was his current plan? It wasn't as simple as putting me on a ship and taking me back to Earth. Taking me home would impact him for the rest of his life. As much as I wanted the details, I decided not to push.

There was something different about him tonight. His eyes were dull and as the dim light of my cell accentuated the shadows cast by one face plate overlapping the next, his shell looked faded, like he was washed out by the sun. Poor Garran was beat down, exhausted with the weight of my fate on his shoulders.

"Are you sure you want to do this?"

He smiled. I caught a glimmer of anticipation but also fear in his eyes. "Yes," he said. "More than anything. I'd rather spend the rest of my life on Regis Seven with you alive and well on planet Earth than continue to be a slave to my father and the crown. I've only made two major choices on my own," Garran continued. "The first—learning how to fly an intergalactic star ship and navigate star systems, which my father still thinks was a waste of my time, and the second—taking you away from here."

"Thank you, Garran." My heart blossomed with his touch, his words, and his kind, unselfish ways.

Now I was the one being selfish. I didn't have to go along with his plan. I could refuse to go, tell him I wouldn't allow him to throw away his life on Enestia for me.

But I also had my friends to think of, Attie, Logan, and Kevin. People didn't just disappear without someone held liable. And my mother had no one but me. I could only imagine her grief.

I was so torn, but I had to have faith. If Garran was resourceful enough to get me home, he was resourceful enough to find a way to save himself from prison— I hoped.

"But—"

"No, America," he said as if he could read my thoughts. He shook his head, and as the plates beneath the hollows of his eyes dropped, I thought I saw tears forming. "You're going home, and I'm taking you there. My father was responsible, and I must pay for his arrogance."

"I understand why you're doing this, but I still want to know," I said after a long pause. "If you're not going back to Enestia, where will you go?"

Garran sighed, and said almost at a whisper, "To Verla Three, a planet in my galaxy. I can make do there until I can eventually return home. Now please, no more questions. We need to leave as soon as possible."

He handed me a black cloth bag, and while I changed, he retreated back into the tunnel where Lestra had been waiting.

I dumped the bag of clothes on the ground and dug through them. There were no undergarments, only a pair of black leggings, hooded gray tunic, and pair of flat shoes that conformed perfectly to my feet when I slipped them on.

The tunic was itchy and the fabric paper thin. I wished I had a bra to not only support my Cs but to keep the skin of my breasts from showing through. As awkward as I felt in the strange clothing, anything was better than a blanket, and the soles of my feet were warm for the first time in I didn't know how many days.

I entered the wall and grabbed Garran's hand. He turned to Lestra and spoke, his foreign words first bitter and then strangely sweet against my ears. She rocked slightly to one side like she was soothing a baby in her arms. While focused on Garran, her natural smile elongated until I could see not only her top teeth but a set of pink gums, but when she brought her eyes to meet mine, her smile vanished and her eyes narrowed.

"What did you say to her?"

"I thanked her again for bringing me to you. She is

taking a great risk in doing so. She broke a family oath and tradition. If anyone finds out about it, she will probably be dismissed from her position at the palace and disowned."

"Why is she willing to jeopardize so much for me?" I asked.

"She's not doing this for you; she's doing it for me." Garran shifted his eyes to Lestra and then back to me. "I recently learned that she's not only my servant, she's also my protector."

Protector? Lestra was half his weight and at least six inches shorter when it came to height. She couldn't protect him anymore than I could. Maybe there was more going on, but if there was, I didn't care. I was going home!

"So, um, how long will it take to get there?" I asked as my heart leaped.

"About thirty-six Earth hours, but first we have to make it to the ship without getting caught."

We entered the wall, the block of stone locking back in place behind us with a thud. Taking the lead, Lestra jogged ahead of us, and Garran and I matched her pace, only slowing when the passage thinned at each turn, and we had to sidestep to make it through.

"How much farther?" I asked.

"I'm not sure. I haven't gone this way through the walls before. Lestra's taking us to the other side of the lab where a cruiser's parked outside."

"So we're going outside?"

"Yes, we have to, but you're exposure to Enestia's radiation will be minimal. The suns are down, and we'll be free from Enestia's atmosphere within minutes after takeoff."

As we came to a stop two turns later, the toe of my right

foot hit the wall, and Garran caught me by the waist mid-stumble while I regained my balance. Lestra spun around, the hair I imagined on her head, flipping over one shoulder. She said something to Garran, and a moment later, her badge illuminated, a swirl of wind whipped through the tunnel walls, and the hidden door started to open.

"Does yours do that, too?" I said, while the block of wall disengaged and slowly turned. I ran my fingertips across the pattern of jewels on Garran's brooch, a design that closely mirrored the turns of gold thread on his tunic and of his tattoo.

"No, mine is not a key to the tunnels. It holds no magic." The jewels sparkled in the soft light radiating up from the floor. "I should have left it in my quarters."

"Why?"

"I'm not very proud of my heritage right now," said Garran, his eyes fixed straight ahead as the wall wedged open just enough for Lestra to hook it with her hand.

A spattering of rain hit the floor at Lestra's feet as she peered through the opening and whispered to Garran. I laid my hand against the center of Garran's warm chest. There was no heartbeat to detect, just the expansion of shell with each breath, the air escaping his nostrils making a pleasant sound, a deep, almost inaudible whistle.

"There's one guard by the cruiser," he translated, bringing his lips to my ear.

I pulled the hood of my tunic onto my head, tucking my hair away until it disappeared into the back of it.

"Do I look like an Enestian?" I smiled.

"No, you are too beautiful to be an Enestian," he answered, adjusting his own hood. In the soft light of the tunnel, he could have been mistaken for a human, though his knight's eyes glimmered bright blue with dots of fiery yellow.

"Ready?" asked Garran.

"Ready," I answered with a deep, anxious breath.

Lestra released the door, and it opened completely, teetering in its frame, my vision blurred by a blast of air when I looked over my shoulder as the door released behind us. Garran locked his arm with mine, and we stepped into the gusty night air.

Rain fell in angled ropes in a barrage of water globules bigger than I'd ever seen, and when I lifted my head to peek at the Enestian landscape, my face stung with the smack of a dozen heavy drops.

Three buildings loomed before us, all bright white and smooth with domed roofs, their exteriors covered with large sheets of thick material reminding me of an Enestian's shell. A fringe of magnificent trees towered beyond and above, rows and rows of thick greenery, a tapestry of botanical magic.

"There's the ship." Garran pointed to a black, angular object in the distance. A tall figure stood next to it with his back to the lab. "Don't worry. I have a plan," he said, interlacing his fingers with mine.

We crept toward the ship, my shoes sinking into soft pads of jessom moss that dotted the ground. "But I don't want the guard to see us yet," Garran whispered with breath as sweet as the moss itself.

We approached, the patter of rain drowning the sound of our footsteps. The guard remained still and unsuspecting, but just as Garran was about to announce our presence, another figure emerged from the lab.

Chapter Thirty

GARRAN

"What are you doing out here?" said Murelle, appearing from a side exit of the lab.

Not again. Damn her. "None of your business." I brought America's hand of skin down to my side and behind my legs to hide it. America lowered her head to hide her face in the folds of her hood. "But I have a better question. What are *you* doing out here, Murelle?"

"Spying on you again," she answered proudly. "You and Lestra are up to something, and it's not just screwing around. I think it has something to do with our father's research. Why are you suddenly interested in the lab, and who's that?" She pointed at America. America's head was lowered, hidden by shadow and a curtain of heavy rain.

"It's none of your concern. Go back to bed, Murelle, and take that stupid bird with you!"

A squawk came next. Murelle gave her bird's shell a stroke, and it settled down, sidestepping on her shoulder to wedge under her tunic hood and get closer to her neck.

"Actually, I don't have anything better to do, so why don't you just go ahead and explain yourself to me," she answered, her foot tapping against a patch of spongy moss.

Murelle's face flashed purple in the outdoor lights as their beams expanded from the corners of the lab and stretched to illuminate our path to the cruiser. Wearing shell powder at one in the morning? What was *she* up to?

"Get out of my way!" I said under my breath, knocking her shoulder with mine as I passed.

"You are in such a hurry to go where?" Murelle ran up behind me, and her bird gave another ear-breaking call.

Now there were two obstacles facing America, me, and our freedom: Murelle, and the stationed guard, who finally turned in our direction but oddly remained at his post. Even if Lestra and I could trick the guard into letting us take the ship as planned, Murelle would put a stop to it by calling our father.

"So," continued Murelle, racing up behind us. "What are *you* doing out here, palace maid? My brother won't answer me, but you better explain yourself to me right now."

Lestra's response was to keep walking briskly and drop her head.

"I think I'll just call our father right now and let him know where you're at, big brother." In a cruel tease, she motioned like she was going to activate her communication cuff. She had me. Wrestling her to the ground and deactivating her cuff wasn't an option — at least not with the guard only yards away.

"Well, you got me, Murelle. I have no choice but to finally tell you what we're up to, and maybe if there's a bit of sympathy in your heart, a little speck somewhere hidden deep within, you'll walk away from here quietly and go back to bed without telling anyone that you saw us tonight."

The shell around her mouth twisted, and her foot tapping stopped. With my left hand, I put my fingers under America's chin and gently lifted her head, revealing a face of skin that shone light blue through the artificial light and heavy rain. America smiled, looking up from under her eyelashes.

"Who is that?" asked America, blinking away the rain spattering toward her face.

"Princess Murelle."

"She's beautiful," said America.

Murelle's lightly glittered face, a pale purple, matched the trail of jewels epoxied to the top of her hand, gems that sparkled despite the rain as she gathered the fabric of her hood under her chin and held it there.

"Your sister," America continued. "So she speaks…"

"Yes," I said.

The clouds shifted and the rain quickly petered to a light sprinkle that was refreshing rather than annoying. America pulled her hood back just enough for her entire face to show.

"Hello, my name is America."

"She's a…" Murelle choked in English.

"A human. She's our father's last abduction. I need to take her back to Earth where she belongs. I'm taking the cruiser."

Murelle took a step toward America and reached out her hand. "Skin," she said.

"Yes, skin instead of shell," said America. Her soft lips

curved to a smile, and Murelle's hard lips turned upward in a grin of wonder and curiosity.

"Other than that, she is no different than you, me, or any other Enestian, for that matter," I said.

Murelle brought her index finger to America's cheek, but when her finger met its mark, Murelle flinched and withdrew.

"Don't be afraid of me," said America.

"She's no longer under quarantine. Father has already examined her twice," I added. "And that's why I need to take her from here. The next time he will" — I gulped — "she will not survive the next time."

America took Murelle's hand, and Bell jumped from Murelle's shoulder to America's and buried herself in the folds of America's hood.

"Bell," said Murelle. "She never does that. She doesn't like anyone except…"

"Bell, what a cute name," said America. She stroked Bell's layers of shells. "They are like the scales on a fish." The skin between her eyes wrinkled as she studied Murelle's pet.

And at that moment, Bell caressed its wet head under America's jaw, nuzzling her beak against America's neck.

"See, sis," I said, breaking back into Enestian. "America is an upper life form. I can't let her die under father's cruel hand. Please understand that," I said sternly. "We've become friends." America held out her hand, and Bell jumped to America's extended finger. "More than friends," I continued at a volume too low for Murelle to hear.

"But if father finds out, you'll be banished." Murelle's English wasn't as good as mine, her accent thick as America tilted her head and wrinkled her brow in an effort to understand.

"I know, but if she stays here, she'll be tortured. Dissected live. I've been meeting with her for days to learn about her culture, and I can't let her suffer like that. I care about her. What our father did to her was wrong, so I am going to make it right. Please don't try to stop me." America's fingers tightened against my waist.

"If I let you go, and father discovers I'd allowed it, he'll…"

"He won't. He'll never know because once I'm gone, I'm not coming back," I lied. "Then *you* will take my place as ambassador at the turn of your twenty-second year, and when our father dies, *you* will become queen."

"You're not coming back, ever?" Murelle pulled at the folds of her hood, and her bottom shell lip trembled.

"No," I said, continuing the fib, knowing I'd return to unseat my father once I was able to do so, even if that took years. "Why return to a life in a prison camp? But why do you care? You despise me anyway."

"I-it's not that. I don't despise you," she stuttered and switched back to Enestian. "I just despise the fact that our father loves you more than he loves me."

"What are you talking about? Our father doesn't know how to love. What he shows us isn't love. It's pride, selfish pride. Don't you get it?"

The light spattering of rain intensified. A flash of lightning danced across the clouds followed by a double clap of thunder. Murelle's lower lip dropped, and Bell made a squawk barely audible against the increasing rain as she leaped back to Murelle's shoulder.

"We're extensions of him," I continued. "He made us, so he controls us. When we accomplish something, it's like he's

accomplished it, too. If we do something to humiliate ourselves, then we're humiliating him, too. If we fail, he's failed.
He can't handle or face that kind of outcome, so instead,
he'd rather break all ties and disown his own kin."

"But—"

"There's no but. That's what's going to happen to me. I'll
be disowned for this, but I don't care. Being a prince doesn't
matter to me anymore. I don't want to be like our father,
participating in his morbid experiments and continuing his
selfish legacy when he's gone. The only thing I care about is
saving this girl."

Murelle stroked her heritage badge. In the waning light,
it glowed as if it held the Timuary enchantment.

"But I know ruling Enestia means something to you. It
means a lot, so please, sis, let us walk away from here and
take the cruiser. And don't tell anyone what happened until
morning, when we'll be far from this galaxy."

"A human," Murelle said. "I never thought I'd ever see
one. So different than what I imagined. So expressive. So
emotional."

"And intelligent like us," I said.

"You are beautiful, too," said Murelle in English, and
grazed the tips of her fingers across the side of America's
face. "I would have liked more time to study you, to know
you," she said, her accent so strong I wasn't sure America
understood what she said.

But that didn't matter. Murelle peered deeply into
America's eyes, her lips parted, her eyes mere slits, and the
two returned smiles, so warm I couldn't believe the Enestian
was actually my sister.

"What about the guard?" she asked with stiff lips.

"I'll take care of the guard. I'm going to convince him that we have permission to leave, and if that doesn't work, I'll order him to let us take the cruiser. He'll stand down. As of this moment, I'm still the prince after all."

"And I'm the princess." She smiled. "Two royals will be more convincing than one. Come on."

Whether it was a speck of hidden sympathy emerging from Murelle's soul or the knowledge that she'll be made queen, it didn't matter, though I believed my sister's heart warmed while she made a brief, yet unique, connection with a species that she studied. My sister had actually come to her senses for once, bringing me one step closer to getting America home.

"Slaine Timuary!" exclaimed Lestra when we were close enough to the guard to see his face through the rain. "Why are you here?"

"I requested this post. As soon as I found out the prince was scheduled to leave tomorrow, I could only assume he planned to 'borrow' this star ship. And I wanted to make sure he'd be able to do it." He winked. "You should be safe for now."

"Thank you, Slaine." I put my hand on his shoulder.

"He's letting us leave?" asked America.

"Yes," I told her.

"Thank you, Slaine," she said and held out her hand.

Slaine took her hand, bent forward, and peered at America's face under the hood.

"So you know all about this, Slaine!" Murelle exclaimed over the splash of rain, pulling the edge of her hood to cradle her wet bird.

"I do, my royal," he answered, without a hint of regret

in his tone.

"But only because he was under my direct orders," I lied again. "I threatened disciplinary action if he didn't obey me. Slaine hasn't done anything wrong. Please, Murelle, whatever you do, don't implicate him in these matters or Lestra, either. They only helped me because I forced them to. The only one who's guilty of defying the king is me, only me, and I will willingly pay the price."

Murelle folded her arms, surveying Slaine Timuary as he stood, his hands at his sides, his feet slightly apart, his wet tunic and leggings artfully defining the bulging shell of his arms and thighs.

"Go! Go, now. Go, Brother, before I change my mind," she shouted, turning away, her soaked tunic tight against her body.

"Okay, this is it, America. We're going to board the ship."

I nodded for Slaine and Lestra to follow us to the cruiser. It unlocked with my shell scan, the door lowering to the ground as the exterior lit with rows of tiny lights.

"Slaine, thank you for your kindness and sympathy."

"You're welcome, my prince," he said as we clasped each other's opposite shoulders simultaneously in a sign of genuine Enestian friendship and respect. "And please tell the human girl that I wish her only happiness back on the planet where she belongs."

"I will, my friend."

"Thank you, Lestra—for everything. You've been such an important person in my life for so long," I said, swallowing hard and feeling the shell pressure increase under my eyes. "You know how much you mean to me and how much I will miss you."

I wanted to say more to my best friend, but the words didn't come. With the strengthening rain, I needed to leave as quickly as possible while I had the chance.

"Murelle," I said, turning to face her. She turned in my direction but kept her head lowered. "I've never asked you for anything before, but I'm asking you for one thing now, not as the prince but as your brother. Please, please help the Timuarys shed their reputations of this. Please make things right after I leave. That's all I ask and will ever ask of you again."

She lifted her head and looked up at me with her black and purple eyes, eyes wet with rain, or wet maybe with tears. I could only hope they were tears, that single drop of compassion working its way to the surface of her cold heart. A bit of a nod was all I received in return, but her softened eyes told me she'd abide, and I didn't need to worry.

America and I hastened up the ramp. I positioned myself behind the helm, and America sat directly behind me on the captain's bench. The door lifted and closed, and America gasped when her automatic restraint belt projected from the seat, slithered across her lap and chest in a crisscross pattern, and locked against her.

Without the flight codes, I had to program our course manually, Caskin having set the codes just hours before. From my bag, I withdrew my handheld communicator, and its screen flashed a bright white with the sweep of my finger.

Typing in the codes manually was laborious. If my father had chosen me as lead, the task would have taken less than a second, with the touch of my communicator against the helm's up-loader. But without Caskin's clearance, I had to program our course one number at a time, and I did so as quickly as I could.

Seventy-seven, forty-three, one, thirty— Each tap echoed through the bridge. Eighty-eight, sixty-one, thirty-nine. No, I left out a number—eighty-eight, twelve, sixty-one, thirty-nine. My eyes shifted back and forth from the communicator to the helm's operating system as I repeated the numbers in my head and tapped the control panel in unison.

Tap. Tap. Tap, and then a louder tap, a rap against the nose of the ship, reverberation through the bridge, sending a chill up my spine. From the window, I saw Murelle pointing to her left, her eye plates wide as she signaled me to raise the ship.

I dashed to the ship's door and rose onto my toes to peer out the tiny window above, America coming up behind me.

"What's wrong?" she asked.

"I'm not sure."

Slaine was talking to another guard, a Timuary no doubt. But allegiance to the king was thicker than Timuary blood, with the exception of Lestra and her brother.

Slaine shook his head as the other spoke, gesticulating with both arms wildly enough to make a clack that I was sure Murelle could hear above the rain. The guard turned on his heels, his hands behind his back, and headed toward the lab in a stride verging on a jog.

"Damn it," I whispered, and raced back to the helm. "There's another guard." Fifty-three, seven, nineteen, eighty-one. The plates on my fingers buckled, and I held my breath, hoping I wouldn't experience a premature case of shell lock.

"Hurry, Garran."

"Just a few more." Thirty-six, seventy-one, twenty, forty-four, and after what seemed like hours instead of seconds, I entered the last number.

Murelle kept her post at the nose of the ship. I engaged the engines. Her lips flexed into a smile, Bell's wings poked from the folds of her hood, and the sweet hum of the ship cut through the gusts of rain.

Murelle and Slaine stood in the mud before the cruiser, Murelle clinging on to her hood to keep it and her bird in place, while Slaine let the wind take his, shielding his eyes with his hand instead as I gave them both a final wave from the bridge window.

The dual-propulsion galaxy cruiser lifted above the lab as I took the controls and guided it into the open sky. America was on her way home, and I could only hope that Murelle and Slaine could talk themselves out of disciplinary action.

My sister— Yesterday, I couldn't have cared less about her fate, but after helping America and me escape, my disgust for her shattered like a fragment of broken shell.

Chapter Thirty-One

AMERICA

"Is it safe to fly in this weather?"

The whip of rain was violent, each drop like the hit of a tiny hammer against the ship's exterior. We shifted left, and I held my breath as the ship dipped and my stomach dropped.

"Yes, very safe. Are you okay?" asked Garran, reaching behind to set his hand on the top of my thigh.

"Yeah, I'm just. I mean. We're going into space, so I'm a little freaked out. I was unconscious the first time, so this time—" The cruiser began to shake, a rhythmic rattle that vibrated into my bones. "What's that?" I asked, my heart pounding as rapidly as the ship's quaking.

"We're breaking through Enestia's atmosphere. It will stop once we're through."

I gripped the sides of the padded bench and took deep,

controlled breaths. "And this is the same kind of ship that brought me to Enestia?" I asked, while secretly praying this tiny vessel wouldn't break into pieces and burn up while we took orbit.

"Yes, it is. There is no need to worry. We're almost through," he said.

The ship steadied, and I peered through the front window at the expanse of stars, and from the window to my right I saw Enestia, a ball of green and blue. Whew!

"So do you think the other guard reported us?" I asked once my pulse slowed.

"Most likely. I'm sure my father knows by now."

"Do you think he'll send someone after us?"

"No. He wouldn't want anyone to know that I betrayed him. He'll probably explain the situation by saying that I'm attending military training on Mencius Eleven." Garran chuckled but a moment later his reflection in the front window changed. He blinked several times, and his nose plates lifted in what I believed was a sniffle.

His hand was still on my thigh. I placed mine over it and gave his a light squeeze. He turned his head to look at me and smiled.

"Thank you," I said.

"You're welcome."

I brought his hand to my lips and kissed each of his fingertips the way he did mine when we were in the Ring of Reverence.

"Once we're past the meteor belt, I'll switch to—"

"Meteor belt? That sounds dangerous." I gripped his hand hard, forcing his fingers to overlap.

"It's not." He laughed again. "This cruiser is equipped

with instinctive laser assistance and spontaneous course tri-
angulation. If I misjudge a distance, the ship will either compensate or disintegrate the intrusive space matter." He threw
me another smile over his shoulder. "But that won't have to
happen because I'm, um, what's the word? Awesome. I'm
an awesome pilot—class five—very rare for someone at my
age and with my inexperience. There's only one other person who ranks with me, and that's Slaine Timuary. Last year,
he demonstrated an aptitude for flying, so my father actually
allowed him to—"

"Wait. Wait. Wait. Back up. You said *you* were inex-
perienced?"

"Only because most of my training was on a simulator,
but—"

A simulator? That was basically like playing a video
game, one of those fancy types found in arcades. "But that's
not the same...I mean—" The ship bobbled, and the words
froze in my throat. "What was that?"

"We hit a band of solar wind. It's okay. It's completely
normal for the cruiser to react like it did. In the simulator,
I've tackled bigger bands than that one."

I closed my eyes and inhaled deeply, breathing in
through my nose and out my mouth, hoping my blood pressure would drop. "But still, a simulator? What I need is a
shot of tequila."

"You told me my English was awesome, and most of my
learning took place communicating with a simulator," he
teased, his eye shells coming together on one eye in a wink.

"You remember I said that?"

"Of course. I remember everything you've ever said."
He flexed his fingers to relax my grip, and then re-took my

hand so gently his palm felt like skin instead of leathery shell. "Tequila—a distilled beverage made from the blue agave plant." He smiled. "There should be some quip wine in the food stores. I'll get you a glass as soon as we pass the asteroid belt."

"You can leave the controls?"

"Yes, all coordinates have been locked. The ship's computer will do most of the flying."

"Automatic pilot."

"Yes, that's one way of putting it. Are you feeling any affects from Enestia's atmosphere?"

"No. Besides being nervous about flying through space, I'm fine."

The bridge's design was angular, metallic, and black, mimicking the ship's triangular exterior. In front of the control panel, Garran sat upon an upholstered seat with a high back. Each side of the ship was flanked with a short row of windows, the largest centered with the control panel, overlooking the nose of the ship. Through those windows lay total darkness, dotted with pinholes of bright light. Space. My stomach dropped. A chill spiked at my spine.

A dashboard stretched below the length of the cruiser's windshield, and across it ran a strip of illuminated colored squares, slightly bigger than the keys on a computer. In the place where a steering wheel would be, a white Frisbee-sized disk sat flush with the control panel. Using the tips of his fingers, or one or both palms, Garran maneuvered the ship by touching the circular control as if it were the touchpad on a laptop.

Almost everything about the ship was dark—black floor, black seating, black walls—contrasting sharply with

Garran's exposed shell. A large window wrapped around the ship's nose from the ceiling to the floor. Next to the thickly padded anchored cube where Garran sat at the controls, a smaller panel jutted up from the floor on a black pedestal.

Backlit with bright blue, the angular panel burst with an array of colored buttons, from ruby red to a deep purple that was similar to the eyes of Garran's sister. Garran sat forward and his fingers danced across the panel, the buttons eclipsing as they morphed from one color to the next in a magical language between the Enestian pilot and his ship.

The cruiser trembled, matching my already unsteady nerves, and Garran pulled his hand from mine to steer the ship with both hands.

"Now what?" I asked, and as I leaned forward to place my hand on Garran's shoulder, the seat belts tightened, snapping me back into place.

"Space dust. The particles are too small and close together to avoid, so all intergalactic cruisers are fitted with a metrium exterior."

Asteroids, hundreds, maybe thousands of them, lay ahead of us. Their sizes and shapes varied, but each one scared the crap out of me as they spun in slow motion, floating weightlessly against the expanse of space.

"And that will protect us if we hit them?"

"Most of them, but not all. That's why manual steering is required until we've cleared the belt."

"Can't we just go around it?"

"We could, but it would add three days to our travel time, and then we'd encounter another belt even larger than this one."

"When you go to Verla, will you have to come back this

way? I mean, back through these meteors and solar bands?" What if this ship couldn't take a second beating? What if Garran miscalculated and maneuvered toward danger?

The cruiser veered right, left, up, or down as Garran navigated through the field of meteors, and when dust particles made contact with the ship, I closed my eyes until the cruiser stopped shaking.

I screamed when we snuck between two asteroids.

"Yes, I will need to take the same route. But don't worry. The meteors are not as close as they look, but if I did accidently come near one, this would happen," said Garran.

He steered the cruiser toward what appeared to be a baseball-sized meteor, and just when I thought we'd make contact, the ship hummed, a bright light exploded against the windshield, and the ship rocked violently.

"What the hell was that?" I blurted, as the restraint against my chest puffed, keeping me securely pinned within my seat.

"I don't know the translation, something more advanced and powerful than the light amplification process used on Earth."

"Light amplification. You mean a laser." The cruiser vibrated, and a barrage of space particles pattered against the ship's metrium shell.

"Yes, the ship's laser destroyed and redirected the space matter, but now we're passing through what's left of it, a dust cloud, more concentrated than the one we passed through before."

My heart kicked into high gear as I frantically gripped the sides of my seat once again.

"I'm sorry. I shouldn't have done that. I didn't realize

how afraid you were." He smiled, and the calm in his voice extinguished my panic.

"How much longer before we're through?"

"We're almost there. Close your eyes, and when I tell you to open them, we'll be at the edge of the galaxy."

I closed my eyes and forced my fingers to uncurl from the sides of the seat. I counted slowly, and as the ship's ride gentled from a series of jerks into a mode that felt like we weren't moving at all, my body relaxed and the pulse in my neck became undetectable.

"Open your eyes, America."

Garran stood before me, bent slightly at the waist, one hand behind his back and his face close to mine. He lowered to his knees to meet me at eye level. Under the harsh ceiling lights, the shadows between his overlapping shell plates disappeared.

"Don't worry. Everything's okay," he said, his face plates as relaxed and milky as the light above the helm.

"Automatic pilot," I gasped, eyeing the empty, high-back chair. The bridge was bare, and no sound stirred the room other than a soft, steady swishing of engine noise.

"Yes, and for you," he said, presenting a tall, skinny glass filled with blood-red liquid. "Quip wine."

He smiled and I blinked, my eyes brimming with tears as my heart took residence in my throat—again. Through the blur, Garran's face plates almost seemed to disappear, melting away into one pale sheet of skin.

"Quip?"

"It's a special fruit that grows on Enestia. I think its taste will please you."

"Thank you."

Garran slipped his hand into mine and gave it a squeeze. "There's no need to worry, I promise. Our technology is well beyond that of Earth's. This ship is incapable of an engine failure, and besides, my piloting skills are, like I said before, awesome."

The temperate coloring of his eyes, his gentle tone, and the placidity of his shell plates were almost enough to put me at ease. "I'll try not to," I said with a return squeeze and scanning left and right.

I took the glass and lifted it to my lips. As the red liquid hit my tongue, I braced myself for something bitter and foreign. It was surprisingly sweet and acrid at the same time. My throat warmed as it spilled down to my stomach, and within seconds, the tightness in my muscles eased and the spread of space through the window became beautiful—awe inspiring—instead of menacing.

The sense of urgency I felt on Enestia was suddenly gone. Garran's plan was no longer just in place, it was in progress. Space was not my enemy, it was my friend, its silent, unending miles of nothingness a cushion of comfort, protecting me from the fear of being recaptured and taken back to the Enestian king.

Though the cruiser was probably traveling faster than I could fathom, I felt a strange sense of calm. Garran and I could finally take a deep breath, relax, and stop looking over our shoulders for trouble at our heels. The anxiety was still there, my body revving a hundred miles a minute, but the unexplainable peace kept my thoughts steady. A deep breath, followed by another sip of quip wine, settled my stomach. Our mission was almost complete.

Arching my back, the restraints against my chest

loosening, I gave my shoulders a stretch and examined my fingernails, the red polish a mere memory, having almost completely chipped away.

I smiled and licked my lips, and Garran smiled back, his knight's eyes lit with an eternal fire than made me want to kiss him. Moving forward, my restraints released and then sucked back into my seat's interior.

His heritage badge caught the light when he came closer, flashing an array of colors—yellow, blue, purple, and red—as the largest stone centered among the rest sparkled deep green, the same rich color as his tunic. I took another sip of wine and admired the tunic's filigreed pattern of gold as it curled and turned with soft but masculine lines between the setting of stones.

He set his gaze on the metallic floor of the ship, and the plates in his face and neck froze like a statue. What thoughts loomed within the smooth shell of his head I didn't know, but his eyes turned lost and scared.

"You've heard from Enestia," I stated.

"Yes, my father signaled the ship and my communication cuff several times while we were in the meteor field, but I didn't answer and aborted all channels of communication between this ship and my home planet, so they couldn't track our course."

"I'm sorry."

"There's no need to be sorry."

Garran pulled me to my feet and brought his arm firmly about my waist, making me practically weightless under his power, and I slid my palm against his chest and felt his breast plates, hard and defined, where thick muscle was hidden underneath.

"I want to show you something." His shoulder pressed tightly against mine, Garran led me to the largest window to the left of the helm.

He stood behind me, wrapping his arms about my waist and resting his chin upon my shoulder.

"The glass is cold," I said when I leaned forward, and my breath fogged against it.

"Space is cold," said Garran, his words warm against my neck. "Do you see that?" He pointed.

A swirl of purple and pink enveloped a pocket of stars, churning the void into a carousel of light and color. "What is it?"

"I'm not sure of the English translation, but it's incredibly dangerous, despite its beauty."

I tried to suppress a shiver, but Garran's sensitive shell detected my movement and held me tighter.

"There's no need to worry. It's farther away than it looks."

"What would happen if we got too close?"

"We would join that whirlpool of space matter, and our engines and life support capabilities would be thrown off-line." As I turned in his arms to face him, he smiled slyly, his left cheek plate rising.

Spinning in a whirlpool—that's what I was—detached from the planet and people I loved, and the farther we moved away from Enestia, Garran joined that same maelstrom of uncertainty where I was already a member.

Was he having second thoughts about his decision to take me home? And what if something happened to Garran in the process? Was I prepared to live with that guilt?

"Garran, you shouldn't have done this. You're giving up

everything for me."

"And it was my choice to do so."

His answer wasn't enough. Another wave of guilt made my stomach sour. He blinked and inched forward until he was close enough for me to count the golden dots on his irises.

"Earth is where you belong, where you will be away from my father."

His chest first brushed and then pressed against mine as he moved closer, his arms dropping to my hips. I stroked his cheek with the back of my hand, and he kissed the top of my shoulder, the rub of tunic fabric under his warm lips making me shiver.

"And there's something else... *Nes tesilin avor.*"

"What?" I asked, mesmerized by the shimmer in his eyes and the melody of his words.

"It means that I care about you very much."

And I cared about him deeply, too—this brave prince in a shiny tunic. My heart wavered, each breath heavy, making me light-headed. I took another sip of wine.

Garran's hands, leathery and strong, held me delicately at the waist, each fingertip like a spark against my skin, and I tilted my head toward him until our foreheads and noses rested against each other.

I wanted Garran to hold me, his hands firm against my back while I nuzzled my head under his chin. As I tossed my head, a strand of hair stuck to my lips, and he caressed them with his fingertip, sweeping my hair away from my face. I placed my hand against his warm cheek and navigated his facial shell, running my fingers across his lip plates, then tracing the ovals of his eyes when he closed them and sighed.

"How much longer until we reach Earth?"

"Not long. A time equivalent to eighteen Earth hours."

"And then we'll never see each other again." The thought of not seeing Garran again brought a pain to the pit of my stomach—an uncomfortable emptiness—something I couldn't fill without having him in my life.

"Yes." Garran lowered his head. "But I wish that were not the case. If only there was…"

"Was what? Tell me."

"A way for us to be together, but the radiation would be too strong for you on Verla as well, like it would be on any planet in my galaxy or even the next sector closest to your planet. The only life-sustainable planet in your own galaxy is Earth, and we both know I couldn't live there with you. Not like this," He forced a chuckle and rapped his fist against the shell on his forearm.

"Are you sure you can't go home? Maybe your father will be more lenient than you think, and he'll understand and forgive you."

"No, my father would never forgive me for this, but it doesn't matter." He lowered his chin to his chest, and I watched the shell panels of his abdomen rise under his tunic with his next long breath. "Enestia is no longer my home, not while my father is king." There was a flash of sadness in his eyes. "When I can put an end to my father's evil? I'll return and take the throne."

"But until then, are you sure you'll be safe on Verla Three? How will you—?"

He put his finger across my lips. "Don't let my problems become yours. You're the only thing that matters to me right now."

"But my problems are yours."

"And we only have eighteen hours left to be together. Let's not waste them."

Still holding my hand, he kissed my cheek, stoking the fire in my heart. I set down my glass of wine and reciprocated with a soft kiss that became harder when his hands wrapped around my back.

Chapter Thirty-Two

GARRAN

America thrust her hands under my shirt, the tips of her fingers raking my shoulders. I brought her to the floor of the cruiser, my hand against her back, lowering her slowly while her lips and tongue were hot and twisting with mine.

Her kisses were powerful, filled with the same urgency I felt, knowing that this was our last time to be together. Every stroke of her tongue kindled my burning desire to explore her soft body and enter her again.

"You are the most beautiful, amazing creature I've ever known," I told her as her lips worked against mine in sweet rhythm, mimicking the cadence in which I rocked my lower body against hers. "I will miss you more than you know."

"Things happen for a reason," she said through a soft breath against my ear. "I believe that. I always have. You were meant to be my first."

While she fumbled with the buttons of my tunic, I pushed hers toward her chin, exposing, once again, the most beautiful breasts I had ever seen—soft with pink, firm centers—unlike the hard, bulbous shell of Enestian women.

She sighed and licked her lips when my tunic fell open with the last button. Her warm hands ran the length of my chest, and when they reached the top of my leggings, the pressure below became almost unbearable.

I helped her slip from her leggings, my hands trembling as each inch of her exposed skin added to the fire pulsing deep within my shell.

"I will miss you so much," she said and ran her tongue along my chest, the pressure of her lips just enough to make every inch of my body tingle.

She bent her legs, and I caught one of her knees in my hand and massaged it lightly, tracing the cap beneath skin and then gliding my fingers to her inner thigh, squeezing its yielding but tight muscle.

"Ah," she said with a sigh, and clasped my buttocks, her fingers hard against my shell, massaging, working their way to my front plate.

"Not yet," I said and touched her most delicate place. She tilted back her head, and I kissed her throat, holding back the urge to catch her bottom lip with my shell and give it a soft bite.

"Am I hurting you?" I said through a string of kisses beneath her ear.

"No. Keep doing that," she said, her breath heavy against me.

I continued, touching her delicately. She blinked, her eyes glinting in the overhead light, and the skin on her chest sparkled with perspiration. A moment later, her back arched, and she moaned with pleasure while pushing herself against my hand.

"More. I want more." She pushed me upward with her palms.

"Too heavy?" I asked.

"No." She smiled. "You're just too hot for me not to do this."

"Do what?"

"On your back, alien."

I shifted, and she straddled me, her pelvis against mine, her palms on my shoulders. Beginning at my lips, she kissed my shell tenderly, guiding her tongue along the contours of each plate.

"Don't move," she teased, "or you'll pinch me."

Keeping still was pleasurable yet torturous at the same time. My hands ached to fondle her soft breasts and re-explore her other places, and each time the sweet tip of her tongue ran between the sections of my chest, the tingling in my extremities shot below.

Her fingers dug at my waistband, exposing more shell. My lower plate was still intact, but it burned with the desire to be touched as she continued to inch my pants downward. Once it was uncovered, she cupped my bulge of shell, massaging her fingers against it, as I feverishly stripped off my leggings.

The pressure was too intense. America gasped as my plate slid away violently, and I was exposed. On her knees, she moved backward and lowered her head, coming down upon me in an act of passion I'd never heard of, or would ever expect. The plates on my stomach tightened as my body tingled, and the pleasure I was experiencing spread through my chest.

Her hair swung forward, brushing the casing at my hips and waist, sending the scent of something herbal and fresh in my direction. She released her mouth from mine and rose, then positioned herself on me, easing down slowly with her knees on either side of my pelvis until I was completely inside.

"Are you okay?" I asked her when she closed her eyes, bit her bottom lip, and held her breath.

Chapter Thirty-Three

Sinking gently, I took him inside me more easily than I did the first time. With my palms against his chest, I moved slowly. He reached for me, and I leaned forward, my speed increasing and becoming more rhythmic.

A wave of heat and pleasure erupted in a spasm of sweet delight that radiated up to my neck. Every inch of my body danced with something so powerful my heart beat wildly and my breathing turned shallow.

"Yes, Yes," I screamed. "Garran. Yes."

He moaned and slammed the palms of his hands against the metal floor, the sound it made echoing with a sigh as he took a deep breath and groaned, and I could feel him spasm. The rings of shell at his neck overlapped as he brought his chin to his chest to look at the place where we were connected. His gaze, passionate and penetrating, concentrated

on mine, and we stared at each other unblinking, still in awe
with what we'd just done for a second time.

I lifted away, he withdrew, and I fell against him, the hot
skin of my chest against his warmth. He smelled so good. I
took a deep breath, enjoying the fragrant blend of honeyed
moss and hot shell. I nuzzled against him, his heavy breathing against my ear, the top of my head under his chin.

"For humans, is that customary while lovemaking?" he
asked softly.

"What?"

"What you did, using your mouth?"

"Oh, that." I laughed. "Yeah, so Enestians don't?"

"No, at least not that I know of. I've never heard of that
form of lovemaking before."

"On Earth a lot of couples do that to each other."

"Each other? So the male puts his mouth on the female,
too?"

"Yeah."

"I'm sorry. I didn't know or I would have."

"No, that's okay." I kissed his cheek. "I'm not sure I'd
want those shell lips of yours anywhere near there," I joked.

I rolled onto the floor next to him, the cold metal against
my warm shoulders giving me a welcomed shiver before I
turned onto my side and snuggled against him with my head
on his chest. And while my body lifted and settled with his
steady breathing, I studied his alien body, the curves and
contours where muscle bulged beneath it and the plates of
shell defining a silhouette identical to that of a human.

"I don't want to leave you," he said.

"And I don't want you to."

Chapter Thirty-Four

GARRAN

"I'm taking you to the same location where you were abducted," I told America while I fastened the last button on my tunic, and she pulled her shirt over her head. "Is that far from your dwelling?"

"Yeah, it's pretty far, but that's not a problem. Just don't drop me off in the middle of the Sierra Desert or the top of Mount Everest." She laughed. "I'd die before I could find someone to help me."

"I'm sorry. I wish I could get you closer to your home, but it's too risky. The location of your abduction was selected by the research team based on the cruiser's ability to arrive and depart undetected. Taking that exact route is the only way we can reach your home city without being seen by your planet. Any deviations could trigger an attack or interception by your country's armed forces."

"Not a problem," she said.

But to leave her alone to seek help under her own devices was something I didn't want to do. I couldn't risk leaving the ship, but I needed to be sure she found a way to her home.

"No communication device, no monetary means, and no transportation other than your own two legs. I fear for your safety and your ability to find sufficient aid."

"I'll find a phone and call Attie. And after that everything will fall into place. I'm not worried about making it back to San Diego. There are plenty of camping grounds in the Lagunas, and many people live there as well. I'll easily find someone to help me, and I'll be home in no time."

"Are you sure?" I asked, filling my chest with a lungful of air in order to relax my tightened plates.

"Positive." She smiled. "I am a little hungry, though."

"I'll get us something to eat."

The ship's stores were stocked with enough nutritional food replacements and non-perishable goods for two people for three, maybe four, days. I might need more, depending on how welcome I would be on Verla. My mother had probably already been informed of my disloyalty to Enestia and its king, and depending on the story my father tells our people when it comes to my disappearance, I may or may not have any clout on Verla Three as the prince of Enestia. Good thing I had decided to arrive and live there using the name Yarlen Trink.

Using the set of plates and utensils reserved for the royals, I arranged a selection of food replacements, a cup of hot water, container of tarla beans, and dried fruit on a tray and presented it to America. She sat across from me at the captain's table, sipping quip wine and eyeing the plate of unappetizing cubes.

"I'm sorry. This is all we have. The cold unit isn't stocked until an hour before lift-off, so we missed getting any non-perishables. But we do have this. I think it's something you'd like to see."

I scooped a palm full of tarla from their container and dropped them into the glass of steaming water. Each bean descended slowly, releasing a trail of tiny bubbles from a pinhole in its seed coat.

"You've told me about this," said America, her eyes fixed upon the glass.

"Yes," I said as each bean casing wrinkled.

Within seconds, a tiny tendril of white root poked from one end of the seed while a green splinter of curled leaf pushed through the casing. The leaf unrolled, its tiny weave of fibers taking shape in the form of an ellipse, and as it did so, the essence of each bean released, turning the water amber.

"Hold out your hand," I told America.

She held out her cupped palm, and using a spoon, I fished out the beans and their sprouts, then deposited the tiny shoots in her hand.

"So beautiful," she said as a bud sprang from each bean and opened, exposing a tiny pink blossom the size of America's thumbnail.

"But not as beautiful as you," I said, and gave her a small kiss that made her smile even wider.

"We don't have anything like this on Earth. Nothing can bud and bloom this quickly."

"And taste," I said, raising the glass to her lips.

"Delicious," she said. "Like a sweetened herbal tea. But what do I do with…?" She looked down at the tiny bouquet in her palm. "They need to be planted, but—"

"But they only grow within a blanket of jessom moss, which only grows in one place, Enestia. Jessom can't be transplanted or transported."

"So they will die?"

"Eventually, but that means you can also take the rest with you, and there is no worry of the beans taking root and upsetting the balance of your planet's indigenous species."

She gently placed the handful of miniature flowers in the center of the table, and I handed her the half-full container of tarla. She slipped it into a pocket on her tunic and patted the outside of the fabric once the beans had settled.

"And every time I enjoy a cup of tarla, I will think about you," she said and took a deep breath, her eyes becoming teary. "This looks good. What is it?" she asked, holding up a wrinkled slice of quip.

"It's a quip, but all the moisture has been taken from it."

"Oh, it's dehydrated." She took a bite and smiled. "It's delicious."

The way she held the piece of quip delicately to her lips and took a nibble, the way she stared at the cubes of food and her lips curved downward before taking a bite, the way she held her cup of quip wine, her fingertips so light upon the glass— Everything about America made me smile, and my body pleasantly stirred under my shell.

Could an Enestian girl have this same effect on me? Would I find a mate on Verla Three? I had my doubts.

"I'm not a fan of this one," said America. She set a half-eaten cube back onto her plate, and I watched the soft flesh of her throat move as she swallowed a mouthful of wine.

No, I didn't want to meet anyone else. The only girl I wanted was America, but being shell-less, she wouldn't survive beyond Earth, and on Earth, I'd be discovered, captured, and treated like one of my father's specimens.

Besides, I had to dethrone my father as soon as I had the resources to do so. His abductions and experiments needed to end, and I was the only one with the drive and ability to make that happen.

I couldn't count on Murelle to challenge the king, even with her newly softened heart for humans. How long would her sympathy last, let alone stretch beyond the intellectual shell-less and extend to the lesser shelled creatures that continued to die in my father's lab? If she took the throne before I could overthrow my father, would she be any different than him? I didn't know, but I couldn't take the chance that she'd change things.

America yawned against her palm and rotated her shoulders in a sexy stretch that amplified her breasts.

"Tired? Quip wine always makes me sleepy," I said.

"Yeah." She stood, came up behind me, draped her arms over my shoulders, and kissed my cheek. My heart leaped with her touch, the sensation descending to my lower plate.

Minutes later we were nuzzled next to each other on the captain's bench, and when her breathing became soft and her eyes closed, I knew she was asleep.

No, I didn't want anyone else, but we could never make this work.

Chapter Thirty-Five

AMERICA

I screamed and gripped the table, my fingers curling against what I thought would be metal, but instead was soft and billowy against my palms.

"America!" said Garran. I blinked against the bright lights above me. "Are you okay?" He leaned over me and ran the back of his hand across my cheek.

"Yeah, I'm fine," I said, and sat up from the captain's bench, my heart still beating rapidly. "It's just that for a minute, I, I thought I was back in the lab on an examination table. Your father was there. I couldn't move, and…" I sighed. "Thank God it was only a dream."

"Yes, only a dream. Eating a quip before bedtime is supposed to bring pleasant dreams." He smiled. "At least, on Enestia, that's what mothers tell their children."

"Then it's either an old wives' tale, a sort of superstition, or it doesn't work on humans. Although the first dream I had was rather pleasant." And it was. It was a dream that flooded my heart with the ultimate satisfaction. Unfortunately, it was also a dream that could never come true.

"Tell it to me," said Garran as he sat down next to me.

"Well, you took me back to Earth. I said a final good-bye to my family and friends, and then you and I traveled the galaxy together in this ship, avoiding the areas with high radiation levels until it was time for you to take your father's place on the throne." Retelling my dream left a warm spot in my chest, and I had to stop and take a quick breath.

"If only that were possible," said Garran. "But this ship— We'd run out of supplies, and once I returned to Enestia, you'd become sick again."

"I know, but it was nice to experience it, even if it was just in a dream," I said. The sad emptiness in my gut returned. "So how long was I asleep?" I asked and patted my bedhead hair back into place.

"About six hours. I slept for a while, too, and then I rechecked our coordinates, and…"

"And were they okay? Are we headed in the right direction?"

But Garran only smiled, stood, and offered his hand to me.

"What?" I asked as he pulled me up next to him.

"There's something I want to show you." He leaned toward me, the yellow specs in his eyes dancing under the light above.

"A star?" I asked when he led me to the window. It was larger and brighter than the others, though it didn't twinkle.

Garran ran his index finger across a blue button on the

control panel, and what once appeared a star became a planet as it magnified — my planet.

"Earth," I gasped.

There it was, the big, blue marble we call Earth, its spin of land, ocean, and cloud like the swirl of a blue and white lollipop. "It's so beautiful," I said, my breath hot against the window. "From here it looks just like Enestia."

Placing his hand against the window, Garran leaned forward until his forehead pressed lightly against the glass. But he wasn't looking at my Earth. His gaze was beyond, to the right, and through the abyss of twinkling stars.

"You miss Enestia already, don't you?"

"I'll miss the planet, but not its people."

I didn't say more. What words could comfort his alien soul? Instead, I placed my hand on the center of his back and tipped my head until my cheek was against his shoulder. The shell under his tunic flexed.

"We're in your territory now," he announced and kissed the top of my head as he turned to take the helm and readjust the magnified screen. Earth shrunk to the size of an orange and then grew as we continued to come closer.

He ran his fingertips across the lighted panel, and I sat behind him, waiting for the safety restraints to snake over my body.

"Are you ready to pierce Earth's exosphere?" he asked over his shoulder. "This is where it gets tricky." I straightened my back, and as I clutched the armrests, the seat belts locked against me. "I have to follow the flight path manually in order to avoid your country's radar and satellite systems. One mistake and the cruiser will be detected."

"I'm scared," I said. "I'm not sure what our defense

systems will do if it picks up your ship." Hopefully automatic missiles wouldn't be triggered.

"Don't be scared. Nothing will happen, I promise."

The light swishing sound of the cruiser heightened as the ship rumbled into a vibration similar to the one we had when we left Enestia. I flattened my back against the cushion of the chair, but Garran was unaffected, continuing to work the controls, which now included several levers and a virtual screen that was projected from above.

My fingers sank into the arm of the chair, and my muscles tensed until they hurt. Home! I was coming home! Hell, yeah!

The ship rotated, the bow closing on the Earth until my planet was dead center with the helm. A fuzzy ring of blue, the Earth's atmosphere, rimmed the Earth's crust. My nerves started to settle.

"Space: the final frontier," I said to ease my anxiety. My words were barely audible, but Garran caught them and responded with a laugh.

"Yes, I'm familiar with your Captain Kirk." How cool was that? Not that I was a Trekkie, but I was a huge fan nonetheless.

"Oh my God. There's Africa, Asia, South America, North America!" I exclaimed.

My jaw tightened, and my fingernails continued to bite into the chair. Garran's fingers feverishly worked the controls, unaffected by the ship's erratic tremble.

"It's dark," I said when the shaking ceased, and I expected to see Earth's blue sky.

"Yes, when I plotted our course, I regulated our speed, so we'd arrive at night," said Garran, as he powered down the virtual monitor.

"So no one can see us?" I said, noting the flashing lights of a jet from the right-side window.

"Yes, no one. I engaged our defense screens some time ago. Right now we're invisible to human eyes and artificial ones—telescopes, radars, heat-sensing technology."

"Then why was I able to see the ship that abducted me?"

"In order to enter or exit the cruiser, we must drop our screens. We're vulnerable, but only for a short time. That's why leaving and boarding the ship must take place quickly," said Garran, his eyes fixed on the windshield as he tapped the controls.

Millions of tiny lights dotted the landscape below, none of which were recognizable at this point, but it didn't matter. This was Earth. My home! But how would I explain my disappearance?

"Ready to see where we are, America?"

I nodded, and the surface below ignited with gentle colors.

"Night vision and still nobody can see us?"

"No, they cannot."

"But can they hear us? I heard the ship take me."

The memory of the mysterious hum sent chills into my arms. My head spun, adrenaline eaten up by my anxiety. From the window, I saw trees—lots of them—great pines splintering the airspace, mountains, some jagged and some smooth with exposed speckled boulders of granite. Yes! The Laguna Mountains.

"That was the propulsion system and the gravity capture beam that brought you aboard. Once the engines are set to neutral and you've met the ground, the ship will become silent."

The cruiser bobbed several yards from the ground until it became still, floating effortlessly, and I knew that within minutes, I'd never see Garran again.

He stepped from the helm and took my hand. He was so human in so many ways except for one; no human guy would have ever sacrificed this much for me. How could I bear leaving this amazing being, this alien covered in shell, his knight's eyes batting with tears as he kissed my hand tenderly?

But I had to. We had no other choice.

Chapter Thirty-Six

GARRAN

The pressure behind my eyes was almost unbearable, and locking every face plate didn't help. A tear fell from my eye, and I rubbed it away with the back of my hand.

America's delicate lips trembled, crumpling like the bud of a pink waysum flower, and a barrage of sweet tears dripped from her lashes and pooled under her eyes and against the side of her nose.

"What did you say earlier to me in Enestian?" she asked.

"*Nes tesilin avor*," I answered and rubbed away her tears with the pads of my thumbs as I took her head in my hands.

"*Nes tesilin avor*," she said, her lips continuing to tremble, and her eyes fixed on mine.

She fell against me, holding me tightly and crying on my shoulder, and I held her, savoring my last moments with this amazing human female.

"You gave up so much for me, and I haven't done the same for you," she sobbed.

"Just having you in my life, even for a short time, is enough," I told her.

"Thank you for saving me. I would have died without your help," she choked out. She released me, sniffled, kissed my wet cheeks, and I turned my head, so our lips would meet.

Our last kiss was explosive, our hands touching with such hard, feverish passion it was as if we were trying to imprint the memory of each other's bodies on our fingertips before we let go.

A soft buzz sounded at my touch, and the door opened, followed by a ray of light with suspended particles ready to grab America's body and take her to the ground.

"I'm back. I can't believe it." She beamed as she stood in the doorframe.

"This is it—the place where you were taken from?"

"Yeah, this is it. There's the clearing where we had our campfire," she said, her words strung together so closely I had trouble understanding her. "Isn't it beautiful?" she said, looking up on the full moon. "I was over there when the ship... What the hell?"

Her shoulders slumped, and she pointed below at a piece of thin, yellow band wrapped around one of the trees.

"What's wrong?"

"That's crime tape. This was a crime scene. My crime scene," she whimpered. Caught by a gentle wind, the fragment of tape fluttered, flapped, and snapped against the tree trunks.

America drew me in for a hug so tight I thought my neck would split, and when she studied the thick, cylindrical ray of the gravity capture beam, the skin on her forehead wrinkled.

"I'm so sorry you can't go back to Enestia," she sobbed, and a new set of tears fell to her cheeks. "I'm so sorry, Garran."

"There's no reason to be sorry. This was my choice."

"I'll never forget you, Garran."

"And no matter where I am in the Millennius, my memories of you will be with me for the rest of my life."

I squeezed her hand, and a whip of panic rose through my chest. "Are you sure you will be safe? That you'll find someone to help you? Just in case, you can take some supplies from the ship, some food, some water, some…"

"I'll be fine," she said confidently and with a gentle laugh. "I don't need any supplies. I'll be home within the next couple of hours."

She returned the squeeze, let go of me, and stepped through the doorway with one foot, but didn't step with the other until her first leg was caught and stationary within the beam. Suspended momentarily above the forest floor, she smiled and waved until the particles shifted downward. The natural satellite humans refer to as the moon reflected just enough light to see where she landed.

When both her feet were firmly planted on the ground below me, the beam sucked back into the ship, and she looked up at me and said, "I care so much about you, Garran. I always will. I, I…"

"I love you, America," I said confidently. Yes, I loved her—an alien female I'd never see again.

"And I love you, too," she shouted up at me. My body warmed beneath my shell, and the urge to leap from the cruiser and follow her were so strong that I gripped the inside of the doorframe in order to keep my body still.

A small path cut away from the clearing below, and America jogged toward it. Where the shrubbery met the path, she stopped to face me and give a final wave. I waved back, and the cruiser door slowly closed as she disappeared down the trail.

But what was that? A scream?

"America!" I shouted and commanded the door to retract and the ship to become invisible.

With a running start, I jumped from the ship, almost falling when my boots hit the hard earth. Leaves cracked and twigs snapped under my weight as I cranked my arms and sprinted down the path. My soft boots were no match for this hard alien terrain. Broken sticks stabbed at my ankles, and sharp stones cut into my soles. Stray branches jutted into the trail from the left and right, and I batted them away with my open hand as they poked and scratched hard against my shell.

"Stop. Garran. Don't move," America ordered. She stood in the center of the dirt path as still as one of the statues in the Ring of Reverence. "Don't speak."

The air was thick with the odor of the towering trees lining the trail, arborous giants with needles for leaves and the knobby, brown balls they dropped to cover the floor of the forest. I longed for the sweet smell of jessom moss as my lungs continued to feed upon the strange alien air.

A breeze caught America's hair, and a strand danced in the wind like the broken yellow crime tape behind us, but she remained frozen, her eyes fixed on something to her right, something I couldn't see.

There was a sound, something to my left, a crunch of leaves, the snap of twigs. Our light source, the alien moon above our heads, was just a sliver now, shining between the thick canopies of trees, making it almost impossible to see.

The noise came again, the same crisp gnawing against the forest floor. What was it? Why was America's face full of fear?

"Garran," she whispered. "Go back to your ship. You shouldn't have followed me. Don't turn around. Take each step backward slowly."

"I don't understand—"

Something sprang from America's right, a flash of yellowy brown. She fell to the forest floor, and I rushed forward and threw myself upon a furred creature. It twisted and clamped the back of my neck with something pointed and penetrating. America rolled, screaming among the dead leaves, and I collapsed, falling forward with the weight of the heavy, menacing beast upon my back.

After jabbing my elbow behind me and pushing up onto my knees, I turned to face my foe, but became momentarily blinded by a swipe against my head, a paw knocking me back to the ground.

The beast's claws reached for my neck. I heard the crack of shell before I felt the claustrophobic sensation of its shattered pieces pressing against my raw, vulnerable muscles underneath.

America? Where was America?

The creature's teeth embedded in my shoulder and yanked its jaw away, ripping my tunic and taking bits of shell with it. Through the blur of a great paw ready to make another blow, I saw the flash of America's face in the moonlight, her eyes wide, her lips curled and showing teeth.

"No, stay down, America," I ordered.

She rose, wielding a tree limb above her head, bringing it down upon the beast's back. The branch flaked into two pieces as the animal shrugged it from its shoulders and crouched down on its raised haunches. Turning its attention to the thin-figured girl who crumpled to the ground, having used any last bit of strength she had, the cat readied for a pounce.

"No!" I shouted, waving my crippled arm.

In the moonlight, its fur casting a pale yellow, the great beast changed its mind and made its strike, leaping in my direction. Catching it by its thick neck, I planted my foot against the mighty cat's chest. One push knocked it aside where I made my final attack, hurling myself onto the animal's back.

Bringing my forearm around its neck, I locked its wide head against my chest and squeezed. Another crack came, the splitting of shell at my torso, each plate disengaging from its socket at the joint, but it didn't stop me from increasing the pressure I put upon the animal's throat.

The creature kicked and pawed, jerking left and right until its massive body became limp and all was still. As I straightened my arm to release the alien beast, the shell on the inside of my elbow bowed and split, biting into the exposed muscle underneath.

I sank to my knees in pain as the beast fell with a thud against a cushion of dried leaves at the edge of the trail. I watched as the released dust and minute particles of plant material rose from the forest floor to dance in the moon's weak glow, where they remained suspended mid-air by a light breeze.

My eye plates heavy, flickering opened and closed, the trees swirled in the distance as my head lolled from one side to the other. Every part under my shell burned, and I became aware of a widespread pain working its way through my limbs and into my chest.

"Garran?" said America, her voice faltering.

"I'm here. The creature is dead," I huffed.

And what a creature it was, so soft, yet so brutal. So innocent it looked now with its legs wilted and its mouth slightly ajar.

"It's never my desire to kill," I said, with shortened breaths, "even an alien animal such as this. But I had no choice."

"You had to do it." America's sweet voice fell flat against the night air. "It was a mountain lion. They're known to attack and kill humans."

"I still am not proud of it," I gasped, lowering to the ground with a clatter of bloody shell.

America's delicate hand came first, her fingertips gliding over the fragmented plates on my face before she spoke again.

"Your shell," she cried with a voice that trembled.

"I know. It is far beyond repair."

America winced, and I saw that she was broken, too, at the shoulder, the skin ripped and hanging in shreds. Her arm thick with blood, she bit her bottom lip and clasped her other hand against the wound.

"I need to get you back to the ship. You can call for help." Her words were desperate, full of hard swallows and sobs. "Someone can come for you and take you back to Enestia. They can try to fix your shell."

"I, I can't walk. The sharp edges of my broken shell will cut into my muscles and internal organs if I move. I have to stay as still as possible." I knew the drill. Something Enestian's learned from the day they could walk.

"Then I'll go to the cruiser. I'll call for help. Just tell me what to do."

"I made it invisible. You won't be able to find it, and even if you did, you wouldn't be able to reach it."

"I can do it. I'll find a way. How do I get inside?"

"The door— It should still be open, but its interior is invisible, too. You won't—"

"Yes, I will. I've got to. I have to," she cried. "And once I'm inside, what do I do? Tell me," she pleaded.

"You'd need to send an alert to Enestia. The round, red key below the left panel. It will signal my location, and then someone may or may not come after me. It's not worth you risking your own health."

"Yes, it is! I can't leave you like this. I won't do it!" She broke into a cry that clipped the dry air, each sob and deep draw of breath almost Enestian in nature.

"But you're injured. Leave me here and find help for yourself first."

"No, I'm going to your ship to signal for help. I'll hide you, here in the brush, so no one will find you when I'm gone."

"But you need to get to a hospital. You're still bleeding. It hasn't stopped. Humans can only lose a certain amount of blood."

"I know, but I'm okay. Don't talk and try not to move."

My eye plates closed. I had no strength left to hold them open, so I used my ears to visualize America's strained movements. Scraping sounds, pulling sounds, and the huff and puff of America bringing a collection of shrubbery to cover my faulty shell. Thick, dusty twigs strategically woven into a camouflage of foliage by her hands in order to conceal my broken body.

"America? Are you still there?" I asked when the last handful of leaves settled against my torso.

"Yes, I'm here. No one should be able to see you now. Try not to move or make any noise. I'll be back for you as soon as I can."

Straining to open my eyes against a knitting of twigs against my face, I saw the glint of her tunic as she disappeared down the trail.

Chapter Thirty-Seven

"Where the fuck are you?" I whispered into the night and looked up at where I thought the ship was floating.

I threw another rock into the void, hoping to hear a *ting* this time. No *ting*. Still holding my torn shoulder, I picked up another rock and gave it a hurl. Using my left hand made it difficult, and the pain in my right shoulder was to the point of being almost unbearable. Blood continued to drip, running first down my arm and then to the tips of my fingers. As I wound up and made the throw, I felt a pulse in my shoulder and the patter of blood on the dirt at my feet increased.

Ting.

"Yes, I found you, you son of a bitch."

I fell to my knees and loaded my left hand with a barrage of pebbles, and pelted them one at a time, up and down, left and right, to get a sense of the ship's exact size and location.

There were two trees next to where I predicted the open door was located, and with a quick scan of the tree's limbs, I determined the tree on the left would be the better climb.

But could I do it with only one arm? I had to. I couldn't let him die.

Keeping my right arm bent and pressed across my stomach, I grabbed the lowest branch with my left hand and pulled as I set one foot against the trunk and pushed off from the ground with the other. Every muscle ached with the strain. My head spun and my vision blurred, but I made it to the next branch and bent over it at my stomach, then caught another limb with my toe.

But as I reached for the branch above me, my toe gave and I dropped the ten feet I had climbed, landing on my back and shoulders. A shower of pine needles with a Christmasy scent settled around me, a cloud of stale dustiness. I rolled onto my knees, still holding the rags of flesh on my shoulder, and crawled back to the tree, determined to try again.

"America?" came a male voice from behind me. "Is that you? Oh my God. I can't believe it! What a relief!"

Was that Attie's boyfriend? "Logan?"

"Yeah, it's me."

"What, what are you doing here?"

"I've been coming here every day at midnight ever since you disappeared, hoping that thing we saw would bring you back to the same spot where… You're bleeding! What happened?"

"A mountain lion. It just attacked me."

"I need to get you to a hospital right away. And call the police. Everyone's been looking for you."

"No, not yet. I need to help…" I tried to explain, but I

was so lightheaded the words didn't come.

"My truck is parked where it was that night. It's not far." He took me by my good arm and steadied me.

"No, you can't! Don't take me away from here. I have to do something first. You don't understand. Please. I need to get to the—"

"Leave you here? No way! You need help, and I need to call the police ASAP."

"No!" I screamed, my hurt arm dangling as Logan held me against his side, forcing me to cut through the clearing with him. When we reached the remaining crime-scene tape, he ripped it from the tree, and we entered the thick woods.

His flashlight, held awkwardly while having me in his grip, was practically useless, its beam hitting everywhere except the ground beneath his feet. He stumbled twice, the second time as his tennis shoes met a blackened log at the center of the campfire, a branch that was probably left from our own makeshift fire on the night I disappeared.

"You're not thinking clearly. You've lost a lot of blood. I'm not leaving you here."

"No! No! I don't want to go with you," I cried and swung my good arm, landing a punch on the side of Logan's face.

"What the fuck," he shouted, and with a jab of my knee to his groin, he doubled over, and I sent him to the ground with another fiery kick to his ribs.

He scrambled to get up, but I was on top of him, my injured arm dangling while I hammered blow after blow into his back with my other fist.

"Stop it, America. You don't know what you're doing. Too much blood loss. I don't want to hurt you, but I will if I have to."

He grabbed my fist and rose. I fell from his back, defeated, my shoulder hurting too much to even stand.

"I'm sorry I had to do that, America, but you're coming with me no matter what."

He lifted me from the ground and took all my weight with one arm while he dug into his pocket. A second later I heard the double beep of a key remote and the click of a door. He huffed. "This isn't my truck. Do you know why?"

I didn't answer. Instead I imagined Garran's deep green tunic patterned with gold thread.

"Because," he continued, "the cops have mine. It was taken as evidence. We need to clear up what happened to you. Right now. You have no idea what bullshit Kevin and I have been put through over the last weeks."

"But you don't understand," I slurred as everything spun, the truck, the pine trees, the leather seat Logan sat me upon, and the milky dome light above as the door slammed shut.

"You can't tell anybody what you're about to hear," I said, a little louder than I meant to.

"Okay, I promise." He lifted his head, and the boom of his voice made me tremble. "I won't tell. I promise—for now."

But could I hold him to his promise? What if he told the police where the space ship was located in the woods? What if he wanted to use Garran as evidence to further prove that he had nothing to do with my abduction? "For now" had to be good enough.

"Do you remember the ship hovering over us that night?"

"Yeah, I guess," he answered with more composure, each breath long and slow like he was trying to calm down.

"I mean, I don't know. I'm not sure anymore. Everybody keeps telling us we were crazy. That we're lying. That it was just our imagination."

"It wasn't your imagination. That ship took me away to another planet where I was held a prisoner in a research lab. They did things to me like run tests and take samples of my blood. I think. I'm not sure, really. I was unconscious when they conducted most of their so-called research," I admitted, looking down at my hands in my lap.

"Bullshit."

"I am telling you the truth, and I can prove it," I said, remembering the container of tarla in my pocket and eyeing a crushed bottle of water on the floor by my feet. "Hold out your hand."

"What?"

"Hold out your hand, please!"

I dropped a trio of beans in Logan's hand, and he watched as I shook the last bit of water from the crumpled bottle into his palm. He flinched when the seeds sprouted, sending one bean to the floor. By the time I found it and held it up, it had already blossomed, and the pool of water in the center of his palm was stained amber with tarla's essence.

"What the fuck?"

"Tarla beans from Enestia. The planet where I've been held captive this whole time." I plucked each blossomed bean from his hand, dropped them into the empty water bottle, and screwed on the lid. "Now do you believe me?"

"Oh my God! You really were abducted just like Kevin, Atlanta, and I've been saying?" He turned in his seat to face me.

"They were going to keep me there and let me die, but

one alien felt sorry for me. He brought me back to Earth."

"I told the police a space ship took you that night. Kevin and Atlanta told them, too, but no one would believe us. Now we have proof. You have to tell the cops about this." The excitement in his voice made me sick to my stomach.

"But there's, um, someone who needs help. Just take me back, and I'll find him while you get help." That could give me enough time for me to get to the ship and signal Enestia.

"No, fuckin' way. I'm taking you to the hospital first, and then when I call the cops, I'll tell them there's someone else. I am not letting you out of my sight until the cops see that you're alive and know that I had nothing to do with your disappearance." When he motioned to put the car back in drive, I caught his hand abruptly in mine.

"The police can't search the clearing because the ship is still in there, and so is the alien who saved me," I whimpered.

"You've got to be fucking kidding."

"No, I'm not. The ship's hovering above the clearing. It's disguised, but the alien isn't on it. He was going to drop me off and leave, but when I was attacked by the mountain lion"—I took a deep breath—"he saved my life. He killed it, but he was injured. Badly."

"This is fuckin'…" He shook his head. "I don't know what the fuck to say."

"I left him hidden next to the trail," I continued, "but I need to get back to his ship and send a distress signal back to his planet. Someone will come for him. That's why we can't call the police—not yet. Even if we don't tell them about the alien or the ship still being there, they'll go back to that spot, and they'll find Garran."

"You still don't get it, do you? Right now there are a

set of police detectives and a district attorney who think we raped and killed you that night, and that Attie knows but is covering for me. Do you know what they did to us? They hauled Kevin and me to the police station for questioning," he said sarcastically, "and put us in separate interrogation rooms. After drilling me for over an hour, the detective left, came back, and told me I might as well give up the act because Kevin just admitted to the other detective that we raped and then murdered you. And guess what? They did the same thing to him. We were so mentally tortured at that point, that we almost confessed just to get them to stop."

"Stop," I pleaded, but I was too weak to open the door.

"Here," he said, grabbing a sweatshirt from the backseat. He folded it into a square and pressed it against my shoulder. The pain intensified, and I screamed. "Hold it in place. We got to stop the bleeding."

"No," I said as I placed my palm against the makeshift compress. "We…" But my voice failed. I mouthed the words as the engine started and then everything went blank.

Chapter Thirty-Eight

GARRAN

If I moved my arms, the splintered plates pierced my muscles. If I tried to sit up, my internal organs would spill through the openings in my shell, so I lay motionless, listening first to the rain drops penetrating my weave of leaves, and then to the sound of my own breath and heartbeat.

Yes, I heard it—now that it was exposed—no longer muffled by my thick crust of shell. But I was unable to lift my head for an inspection, considering what that beast had done to my neck with its leap against my back and first bite at the base of my head.

But I had no regrets. It was my duty to take America home, and I'd do anything to protect her from a live dissection. Her soft skin, the fullness of her lips— I envisioned them now as I painfully closed my eyes against the harsh spattering of rain, her loveliness and making love to her a crisp memory.

I wish you could see me here on Earth, Father. This is what you wanted to do to America—cut her skin, crack open her ribs, and explore—a sick notion, especially for a king, and now it has happened to me.

If I was found by the humans now, there wouldn't be much left for their research teams to do to me, considering the fact that I was practically already split in two. They'd just need to wait for me to die or kill me outright like my father would do to one of them.

So here I was, unable to move, my thoughts running wildly in my head, with nothing to do but ponder and question the wonders of the Millennius, hoping America found my ship and signaled Enestia. But even if she had, would my father send someone for me?

The alien moon. I could see it just barely between a light, leaf-laden branch, strategically placed by America as camouflage. Enestia had no moons, at least not like this barren, uninhabitable one circling Earth. Our moons were planets, planets with shelled beings genetically identical to Enestians, though shell color and sheen varied among the worlds in our galaxy.

Beyond our galaxy, there were more differences between shells than first appearance. The shells covering the beings in the next universe were thinner than ours, but still quite durable. The plates on the inhabitants in the second universe from Enestia were thinner still and rubbery, rather than rigid. Then came what the humans referred to as the Milky Way, the universe in which the only life-sustaining planet spun and rotated, Earth, which accommodated beings with soft, easily bruised skin instead of a protective shell casing.

And then it all made sense. How odd this all seemed before, and how clear it all suddenly became at this moment. Why didn't I realize this earlier? The farther the planet from Enestia, the thinner the shells of the beings until shells didn't exist at all. How interesting, yet baffling. Was my father right? Did our external covering make us superior over all living creatures? Enestians did have the strongest shells in the Millennius. Did this factor make it not only our duty, but our right to rule every world? To bully other worlds into submission?

No, of course not, but that's what my father thought. I could hear his lecture now through the pulsing of my heartbeat in my ears: "My young prince, we have to explore, not only our universe, but the three alien universes on our border, snatching living samples to study and prove that we, the Enestians, are indeed the most advanced life-forms in existence." But were we or was it only because of our hard exteriors, something that made us superior—but only physically?

Technologically, Enestians were certainly more advanced than the human race, but was it due to a superior intellect or being an older civilization, one that had more time to develop, invent, and progress? In a few thousand years, could Earth become as technologically savvy as my home planet? I believed it could. I was no smarter than America. I could argue that our levels of intelligence matched. The only thing that separated us was our appearance.

I vowed to stop my father's experiments, end his abductions, and remove his crown, but now, with a broken shell, I was fated to die on this foreign planet, and my father's cruelty would continue until his legacy was passed to the next royal in line—my sister.

My only hope was that the memory of America burned a soft spot in Murelle's heart, and unlike my father, she'd find a way to maintain Enestia's domination over the universe without threatening the weaker-shelled beings into compliance. That she would dissolve the Alien Abduction Program and replace it with one meant to explore and exchange technologies with other worlds, not to disable them and prove we're better.

Two suns instead of one— That was another difference between us and the earthlings. Soon the foreign sun of Earth would rise, and still vulnerable under this bed of leaves, I would strain to live under its heat. The air was thick and moist from the rain, a small, simple shower compared to my planet's violent downpours. The drops moistened my cracked lips, and a few made it to my tongue, easing my thirst.

Weak—so weak from my wounds, or was it solely from the loss of blood. I couldn't tell. I only knew one thing for sure. I had no regrets. America was home.

But would she forget about me and leave me here to die, to be eaten by another mountain lion as it searched for its mate that lay dead to my right?

How many hours had passed? I couldn't be sure, but my father's warning pinged in my mind: "You can't remain in that planet's atmosphere for more than one day."

The planet he referred to, Terinan, was in Sector Four, which meant it was geographically almost as far away from Enestia as Earth was. Why couldn't we stay longer than one day? And if that bit of advice held true for that planet, did it mean the same for Earth? Was it dangerous to stay here any longer than a day? Could this Earthly sun be as hazardous to Enestians as our suns are to humans?

He expressed his caution casually, as if there was no real danger, but I knew my father. He didn't say anything without purpose or unnecessarily. There had to be a reason why we weren't supposed to extend our stay on a planet this far away from our own.

America was injured. If she didn't find my ship, if no one came for me, I'd die from my broken shell soon anyway, so I'd never learn the answer.

I could only hope that I'd die before I was found and taken to a lab to be examined like one of my father's captives.

Chapter Thirty-Nine

I awoke in the warmth of a hospital bed. The thin, low-thread-count sheets, stiff mattress, and the distinctive disinfected hospital smell were a luxury compared to the hard floor and heavy air in my cell on Enestia.

My shoulder was bandaged. Long strips of tape wrapped my torso to keep the pads of gauze in place on my shoulder and upper arm. An IV led from the top of my hand to a bag of clear liquid hanging on a pole next to my bed, and when I lifted the sheet, I saw that I'd also been fitted with a catheter.

Garran— He needed my help! What time was it? How long had I been here? I sat up with a jerk that sent my IV bag into a swing and a sharp pain through my upper body. No money. No phone. No car.

"I'll hitchhike if I have to," I whispered to myself. Ignoring my aching shoulder and wincing, I lifted the edge of the white medical tape that held my IV in place. My clothes and shoes had to be somewhere in this room. As for the catheter, it too would be gone with a good yank.

Two knocks hit the door, and I dropped back against the bed. At first I thought it might be Attie or a doctor, but the knocks were too hard and determined, and whoever it was didn't wait for a "come on in." The door opened a slow inch before the face and the body of a man emerged.

"Hello, America," the man said. "I'm Detective Lewis."

Detective Lewis wore a tan suit and brown shoes. His belly was too big, and his blue and gray-striped tie was too short. When he sat down next to me, his brown belt disappeared under his gut, and his shirt un-tucked slightly.

It was obvious he was a man who didn't like to be fooled, a person who enjoyed intimidating others. As his suspicious eyes fixed upon mine and his mustache twitched with each breath, I realized how easily this detective could make Logan and Kevin squirm during their interrogations and practically confess to something they didn't do. Instantly, I didn't like him.

"Hi," I said coldly but politely. I needed to get rid of this guy as soon as possible, so I could get back to Garran in time. *Play it cool, America. Throw him off your scent.*

He didn't offer a handshake. Was he already trying to set things up for playing the bad cop? He pulled a pen and palm-sized notebook from his coat pocket and gave the notebook a few flips, licking his index finger each time, then using it to turn the page.

"Has the doctor been in here, yet? Has anyone explained your injuries to you?"

"No. I just woke up, but sizing up these bandages, I'd say

it wasn't as bad as it looked."

"Fifty-seven stitches and ten staples— Your mother told me, not the doctor. You know, that whole doctor confidentiality thing."

"My mom's here?"

"She was. She sat through the night with you. I just ran into her in the hall. She'll be back soon. She's just going down the street to get some breakfast."

"How long have I been here?" Pushing up on my palms, I sat up in bed as another pulse of panic burst through my chest, but I fell back against the pillow as the pain in my shoulder returned. I swallowed hard, practically catching my heart in my throat it was beating so fast.

"You arrived last night."

"What time is it?" I asked, noting the bright sun through the window in my hospital room.

He glanced at his watch. "Nine twenty-three."

"Fuck, how do I call the nurse?" I mumbled, looking for some kind of button to push. "I want the hell out of here."

"Why the rush?" asked the detective.

"I, um, hate hospitals."

"And I hate not knowing the truth about what happened to you."

"What do you mean not knowing the truth?" Damn Logan for bringing me here instead of giving me time to help Garran. If it had been space-crazy Kevin who found me, maybe I could have told him about Garran, and he might have believed me…helped me get back to the cruiser to call for help.

"Let's do this. Why don't we just start at the beginning? You were camping with"—he flipped through his notepad—

"Atlanta Davis, Logan Gomez, and Kevin Bolts. The four of you started a campfire. Are we on the same page so far?"

"Yeah."

"And then what happened?"

"I don't know. I don't remember anything. I remember being at the lake. A mountain lion attacked me there. I got away, and then Logan found me and brought me here."

"So you were able to get away from that mountain lion all by yourself? No one was there to help you?"

"No, it was just me."

"You're, what, about five-foot-eight and one hundred and twenty or so pounds, and you're trying to tell me that you fought off a hundred and sixty, say, hundred and seventy pound mountain lion?"

"I didn't fight it off. I scared it off. I screamed, and I, um, ran toward it instead of running away from it. It grabbed me, and I remember kicking at it and yelling, and then it let go and took off."

"And you expect me to believe that?"

"Yeah, I do. Because it's the truth." His eyebrows lifted. What a cocky son-of-a-bitch. "You don't believe that I was attacked? Ask the doctors. They'll tell you these wounds are from a mountain lion."

"Yes, they are. The part that I'm having trouble swallowing is that you were alone."

"I was alone. No one else was there until Logan showed up and found me."

The detective looked up at the ceiling and moved his jaw like he was chewing a wad of gum. "Okay, so, for the time being, let's just say that's true. Now let's go back a little. What happened before you were attacked?"

"I don't know. All I remember is being at the campfire, and then the next thing I knew, I was at the lake and a mountain lion attacked me. Then Logan found me and brought me here," I insisted.

"Well, I think you do."

"Then you're an asshole."

"And you're a liar," he huffed.

"And why do you even care? Have I committed a crime?" My face was hot, and my shoulder throbbed.

"Look, two weeks of man hours have gone into your case."

He pointed out the window. The sky was blue, wisped with circles of clouds. Was Garran gazing at the same ones, squinting in the glare of Earth's sun, or was I too late, and he was already dead? "There was a candlelight vigil—your family, friends, people you didn't even know crying over your disappearance. A pretty college girl disappears, and the people who last saw her claimed"—he snickered—"your friends, oh, boy"—he broke into a laugh I knew was fake—"when they were first detained and questioned, they told us you were abducted by a UFO." He slapped the top of his knee. "Can you believe that?" His laugh faltered, and his stomach stopped bouncing. "But who knows, maybe you can believe it," he said, leaning toward my bed.

"I don't know what to believe because I don't remember."

"The media was all over it. We're talking national headlines. Your friends were suspects. They—"

"Yeah, Logan told me what you did to them, and it wasn't right or fair. I'm going to say this one last time, and then I'm not saying anymore." I sat up and brought my face so close to Detective Lewis's that I could see the hair in his nostrils. "I don't know where I've been, but I do know this—Attie, Logan, and Kevin had nothing to do with it, so leave them alone."

"Not only a liar but a selfish one, to sit there all high and mighty with your trap shut when your disappearance effected this entire community."

"Get out of my room," I screamed. "Now! And you're not welcome to return. I'm going to make sure of that." My voice crumpled. My lower lip trembled, and I sucked it into my mouth, tucking it behind my teeth, to hold my tears.

He shoved his notebook back into his pocket. "Your family deserves to know where you were and why you pulled this stunt. Everyone deserves to know."

"Stunt? Go! Leave!" Tears came but I didn't bother to wipe them away.

"Know this, little lady," he said as he walked to the door. "This is not the end of this case. The FBI is already involved. You'll be here for at least another week, so I'll know where to find you."

"A week?"

"Oh, yeah, that. I forgot to tell you. Your wound is also infected with some type of antibiotic-resistant staph, something that could kill you without continued treatment." He tapped my IV bag. "You'd be a fool to leave this hospital." And with that, he gave me a last peek through the crack of the door before he shut it behind him.

But Garran couldn't wait another day, let alone a week or more. And what about me? An infection? Was he talking about MRSA? People died from that all the time. But I had to take the risk. It was worth losing a day's worth of antibiotics or even more. Garran needed my help.

I scanned the room, looking for something — anything — that could help me get out of here: some clothes folded across the back of the chair, a pair of shoes, some kind of duffle bag with toiletries brought by Attie or my mother. But the room looked bare.

Just as I was going to unhook myself and push away from the bed, so I could check the small closet in the corner of my hospital room, there was a double tap at my door, and it opened a crack.

"Am?"

"Attie!"

"U.S.A., U.S.A., U.S.A.," she chanted as she entered and softly closed the door.

"From now on, you can call me U.S.A. anytime you want, and I'll be happy to hear it," I said.

"I thought I'd never see you again." She bent over me and gave me a half-hug, so she wouldn't touch the bandaged side of my body. "I didn't think you were coming back. I thought you were gone forever." Her strawberry smile quivered, and a tear fell to her cheek.

"I'm so sorry you guys went through all that you did. That all of this happened. That — "

"Hey, it's not your fault," she said, sitting down onto the edge of my bed and dropping her voice almost to a whisper. "Logan told me everything that you told him."

"Everything?" I whispered back.

"Yeah, now we all know that we weren't insane. That we really saw what we saw."

My body tensed. "Did he tell anyone else?"

"No, at least that's what he told me."

"Attie, you have to help me. I need to go back there."

"And help the…?" She blinked hard.

"Yes, we have to get to him before the authorities do. I need to get to his ship ASAP!"

"How? You're stuck here. You could die, Am. You know you're septic, right?"

"Septic? That's serious."

"No shit. People with weakened immune systems are usually the only ones who get it, so everyone was surprised when—"

"The radiation. It had to be the radiation," I mumbled.

"What?"

"Nothing, nothing. It doesn't matter. I need to—"

"No! You're not out of the woods yet. There's no way you can—"

"But I have to. He's hurt. He needs me. I can't let him down," I rambled in one breath, my heart thumping up to my throat.

Atlanta crossed her arms. "You're home. You're safe. You need to get well. That's all that matters. What you need to do is forget about the alien."

I broke out of my whisper. "No. I can't, and I won't. He saved me. He risked everything to bring me back to Earth. If it wasn't for him, I'd still be there, and I'd die there."

Attie's eyes widened, and she broke into a smile I could read a mile away. "You…"

"No, I didn't," I fibbed. My cheeks burned.

"Yes, you did, and now you're in love with it."

"Okay, okay, yeah, I did. I care about him a lot. I have to save him."

"And what are you going to do—tighten your hospital gown and just walk out of here? This hospital is flooded with reporters waiting to talk to you and me, Logan, Kevin, your doctors—anyone they can grab a hold of and interview. They even cornered your mom at the hospital entrance, and your uncle had to push them away. On top of that, what about your infection?"

As for being septic, I'd just have to delay my treatment and hope for the best, but I certainly couldn't have any reporters trying to follow me around when I was making my way back to the Laguna Mountains.

"Are they outside the hospital right now?"

"Not exactly, thanks to your uncle. You won't have to worry about that, at least not for a while," she admitted. "He filed a complaint, and now the reporters aren't allowed anywhere near the hospital entrance. Now they're parked across the street, and there's a security guard checking IDs. The only people with permission to be here are family, close friends, and of course, the detectives."

"Good. I'm going to need clothes."

"Are you really going to do this?"

"Yeah, no matter what. I feel fine, really. Whatever they're giving me for the infection is working."

"For now, but if you stop—"

"I don't care about that right now. Please. I'm going to need your help, and maybe Logan's." With my bum arm, there was no way I could climb to the ship, and Attie, she was the epitome of upper body weakness.

"Are you kidding? He knows how sick you are. There's no way Logan will help us. This whole thing has put such a strain on our relationship that we almost broke it off."

"Then Kevin, maybe he would. In fact, I bet he'd do anything to see a real space ship."

"I'm not so sure. Not after what he's been through."

"We'll need one of them. Neither one of us will be able to climb up to his ship, and if we have to move Garran, the two of us wouldn't be able to do that, either."

"Garran?"

"Yeah, his name is Garran."

Garran's face trickled into my mind, his eyes of blue and amber, surrounded by smooth, contoured shell. But the serene image didn't last. My smile faded, and I shook my head as it was replaced with his badly broken body, the plates of his chin and cheeks shattered beyond repair.

"So what does—?"

"Attie, don't you understand? We have to go—now. We're wasting valuable time." I gripped her arm. Hard. "Look, I'll tell you everything later. First we need to figure out how to help him."

Attie's eyes shifted from mine to gaze at the floor, and with her arms still folded, she tapped her fingers against her upper arms, something she always did when she was holding back her words.

"What?" I snapped. "Just tell me."

"Kevin's waiting for me in my car. I didn't want to come by myself in case I got ambushed by reporters, and I didn't want to drive myself and deal with the traffic."

"That's great! Now we can do this for sure. I bet he won't take much convincing to help us. We've got to go now. Please! Before my mom comes back. She could walk in here any minute."

"Okay, okay. Let me think." Attie stood and twirled a piece of her hair around her finger. She opened the closet, checked the bathroom, and returned with a frown. "Nope, nothing here," she reported. "But…" Her eyes blossomed. "My gym bag is in my trunk. I have shorts, a tank top, tennis shoes — "

"That'll work."

We finalized the rest of our plan, and Attie rushed from my room to get her gym bag and returned as promised within minutes. I barely had enough time to shove her clothes under my sheets before a tiny nurse with a tight bun pushed her way into my room and Attie out of it, and lifted my chart from its place at the foot of the bed. After removing my catheter, she changed out the bag of liquid hanging next to me while I huffed impatiently, and before she left, told me the doctor would be in shortly.

After hesitating for a few seconds, I lifted the tape holding my IV in place, grabbed the tube, closed my eyes, and yanked it away. It hurt, but it didn't bleed.

I dressed quickly and was out the door. The hall was clear when I left my room. Attie, I could only assume, was waiting for me at the car. A nurse turned a corner and bustled nearby with a cart of pills, but she was busy studying a chart and didn't bother to look at me when I passed. A security guard was stationed by the elevator, but since I was going instead of coming, he only gave me a quick glance.

In the elevator and down five floors I went, sharing the car with first a family of four and then a pack of doctors in scrubs. They all ignored me as I kept my eyes on the floor and headed into the lobby.

The sky was bluer than it appeared through my hospital window. The breeze caught my hair, putting it into an irritating game of tag as it repeatedly hit against my lips, and I had to keep brushing it away from my eyes.

To the parking structure. In the elevator. So far, so good. Up one, two, three floors. "Almost there," I half whispered. Attie's car was right where she said it would be. Kevin caught my eye in the rearview mirror and started the engine as I approached.

"Thank you so much, Kevin, for doing this for me," I said as I slid in next to Attie and closed the door.

"I've been studying the stars for most of my life. I'm only doing this for one reason. I want to see a fuckin' alien and his ship. I'd risk anything for that, even going to jail, but I'm not sure I want to risk your life."

"I'll be fine, really. If something happens to me, it won't be your fault. Now just go!"

Chapter Forty

GARRAN

Just as Enestia's two suns were killing America, this Earthly sun, benign in comparison to the suns on my home planet, might possibly be contributing to my death now. It rose against the blue sky, and its harsh rays penetrated my blanket of leaves, baking the crusted blood that oozed from between the cracks in my shell. My tunic and leggings, clawed into shreds, did little to soak away the blood, so it held me together instead.

It was a strange sensation. First I felt sticky, the smell of blood thick and salty. But as my coagulated life fluid shrank and dried, sucking pieces of shell together and locking them into place, I almost felt whole again, solid and complete. But the sensation was a farce. One move from my extremities crumbled the caked blood, and I cringed as the sharp, jagged pieces of shell jabbed into my exposed muscle and organs.

And I was weak, so weak. My thoughts were jumbled but my senses keen, or were they playing tricks on me? How much blood I had lost at this point, I wasn't sure, and trying to lift my head for an inspection would be futile, further damaging my insides and disturbing the dried foliage whose job it was to keep me from human and animal eyes.

I turned my head instinctively to a tiny noise to my right. A big mistake. My broken casing overlapped oddly, pinching what was underneath, and I imagined bands of red muscles and pulsing veins being poked and scraped.

The offender was a small creature, gray in color with big, black eyes and a long tail bushed with animal hair—fur. It scurried and stopped, scurried and stopped, shuffling along the forest floor and digging through the scattering of leaves until it produced something round and brown in its paws, some sort of seed or nut. It gave the nut a quick nibble, its nose twitching, and after alerting to a sound behind it, pounced away, dropping the nut in the process.

The sound that scared the creature away came from a bird with wings made from something I'd never seen before but only read about. It wasn't hair. It wasn't fur, but it was soft, thin, and malleable none-the-less.

My curiosity wanted it to hop closer for a better inspection, but it fluttered off in the opposite way to peck alongside a fallen log. I thought of Murelle's bird, Bell, and how it sat on her shoulder under her hood to keep out of the rain. Murelle. Had she already told her tale of my escape? Were she and Slaine being punished because of me?

Knock, knock, knock came a reiteration of sounds so close together it was impossible for me to count the number of hard taps. But I tried. It kept my mind from the fact that

I was slowly dying.

It came again. *Knock, knock, knock, tap, tap, tap.* But this time a showering of pine needles accompanied the rustic tune. Oh, there it was. Another bird, but very different from the last one that hopped and pecked.

This alien bird was black and white in almost a spotted effect. On the top of its head was a patch of red made of the same soft substance that covered the rest of its body in overlapping layers. Feathers—yes! Now I remembered what they were called.

It continued its drumming after a scan left and right. Was it signaling other creatures of its type? Was it a call of love or a call of warning? Taking a quick breath of damp air from last night's rain and this morning's drizzle, I let out a soft sigh. The odor was fresh, heavy with soil and decaying leaves, but it was still pleasant, soothing in an odd way, though my battered body ached.

The sun cast a glow along the edge of the lion's golden body, its limbs now stiff, its jaw frozen in a grimace of pain and the fear of death.

"I'm sorry I killed you," I whispered. "And here I am, dying on foreign soil without the human girl I care so much about."

I now truly understood how America felt, alone on alien land. This forest was my killer and my cell, as my planet was hers. But I was not sorry that our lives crossed paths. I believed, like she said, things happen for a reason. I only regretted that we couldn't continue to be together.

Chapter Forty-One

"I'm actually going to be inside an alien ship?" asked Kevin.

"Yeah, Garran's body is covered in shell, but it's been damaged. He can't walk, so I need you to climb up to his ship and activate the button that will send a distress signal to Enestia."

"Yee-haw," he said and smacked the steering wheel.

"Shell, and you fucked this thing? How?" Attie made a face and shuddered.

"Shhh." I smacked the top of Attie's thigh.

"He already knows," she said. "I told him when I asked him if he'd help you."

"Enestia," said Kevin. "And it's three galaxies away and has two suns?"

Good subject change. I described the planet's surface, Enestia's atmosphere, and how I became sick under its outpour of radiation. Kevin was so excited that the apples of his cheeks lifted and remained there, his accent becoming more prominent with each question, and I reminded him over and over again that he could never tell anyone about any of this until I was 100 percent sure Garran was back in his galaxy.

Who'd believe Kevin anyway? And even if they did, it wasn't like we had the technology to fly beyond the Milky Way and try to take over the Millennius.

"This is so unbelievable," said Attie. "An alien abduction, a space ship cloaked like a Klingon Vessel from *Star Trek*, a mountain lion attack, and a half-dead alien with a busted shell. Do you know how ridiculously messed up that all sounds?"

"Fucked-up but true. My whole master's thesis will be based on this." Kevin beamed. "My theory that cosmic radiation produced from the supernovae of stars combined with active galactic nuclei exist at intense levels beyond our universe, and that an adaption of skin, something hard and shell-like, a radiation-absorbing casing, could provide enough protection to sustain an advanced population of beings."

"Remember, no pictures. Not with him in the condition he's in. I would never disrespect him like that."

"Okay, okay," he said.

"So when they find out I'm gone, do you think anyone will think we came up here?" The look on my mom's face when she came to visit me after breakfast, I wouldn't want to see that. To disappear, get found, and then disappear again? The ache of guilt hurt worse than the pain in my shoulder and upper arm.

"No. I mean why would they?" said Attie.

"Maybe I should call the hospital and tell them that I checked myself out early, and to tell my mom that I'll contact her soon."

"It couldn't hurt," said Attie.

My message was semi-cryptic. It gave just enough information to let my mom know I was safe but not enough for her to know or guess where I was going. I repeated it to the receptionist twice as she wrote it down. Just as the receptionist said she wanted to connect me to the nurses' station, I hung up.

But it wasn't enough. Guilt continued to stir in my soul, and with my heart thumping in my throat, my hands shaking with nerves, and my whole body feeling sick, I prayed I wouldn't find Garran dead and broken in the mass of leaves. Though he made the choice to bring me back to Earth, I couldn't help but feel responsible for what happened to him, and if he died, that would be my fault, too.

Attie's phone sounded with a rap tune. "It's your mom," she said, glancing at its screen. "See, she got our message." She turned off her phone and shoved it into a pocket on the driver's side door.

We were on the curvy part of the highway now, weaving back and forth up the mountain on a two-lane road lined with pines, and I broke into tears, making hardly a sound, muffling my sniffles with my hand.

"What's wrong, Am?" asked Attie, hugging me at the waist.

"What if we're too late? He snuck me out of the lab, stole a ship, and brought me back to Earth, knowing he'd lose his title as prince and wouldn't be able to return to his planet without being punished for treason. I can't let him die."

"He's a prince, too? Damn, this couldn't get any better," said Kevin.

We drove past the lake, the bait shop, and the general store. *Garran, we are almost there. Hold on.* I sniffled and dabbed my nose with a tissue I found in a crushed tissue box on the floor of the back seat.

Kevin drove into the campsite and parked in the—thankfully—empty dirt lot. Being a weekday and past spring break, it was like a ghost town. "He's down the trail. Come, on. Hurry," I said as we slid from the seat.

I sprinted toward the trail, bracing my arm. The combination of deep breaths and the morphine still in my system made me woozy, and for a moment, the trees began to spin. Controlling each breath to keep myself from fainting, I continued running as Attie and Kevin's footsteps sounded behind me.

"Am, wait up," I heard Attie call, but my legs kept going, as did my heart and faith that Garran would still be alive.

A body lay buried under a bushel of leaves like a corpse dumped into a makeshift grave. "Garran," I said, coming to a stop and walking forward slowly with everything trembling, my arms, my legs, and my bottom lip.

"America?"

"I'm here," I said, dropping to my knees. "I came back, just like I said I would. Don't die. Please, don't die."

Most of the leaves fluttered away with the wave of my hand and a gentle brush, but the dead leaves on his face were stuck to his shell with the glue of dried blood. I picked away what I could but left the ones that would hurt, like it would to peel away a Band-Aid.

"You're well and safe?" he asked.

"Yeah, I'm fine."

"I wasn't sure you'd return." His voice was raspy and I could see why. One big plate of broken shell bit into his neck, slowly suffocating him.

"Of course I would. I could never leave you like this."

"Oh my God!" Attie dropped to the ground next to me; her hand smacked over her mouth. Behind her stood Kevin, his jaw lowered and his eyes full of disbelief.

"Garran, these are my friends, Atlanta and Kevin. They're here to help you, too."

Garran's plates clacked when he tried to smile. "Don't move, and don't talk unless you absolutely have to."

Kevin gave the dead mountain lion a kick with his shoe and mumbled, "Unbelievable."

"Attie, you stay here with Garran. Come on, Kevin."

I grabbed Kevin's arm, and we jogged to the clearing. "See that tree? You need to climb to that limb." I pointed.

"Where's the ship?" His eyes scanned the tree line as he took in a deep breath.

"It's there. Trust me."

He grabbed the first branch and pulled himself up, easily making the climb that took him parallel to what I thought was the location of the opened door.

"I feel it," he said. His palm hit against what looked like open air space, patting up and down and then smoothing against it. "Where's the door?"

"It should be about right there. Hold on."

With my left hand, I awkwardly pelted pebbles at the ship like I had done before. "If one goes farther than the others, it's cleared the door." But each pebble pinged against the side of the ship and ricocheted away. Kevin snapped a long branch from the tree and used it to run the length of the ship's side, but it ran against the ship's metal with an eerie scraping sound, never finding an opening.

He climbed down and scaled the next tree while I tossed pebbles, but his new location took him even farther away from the ship. "I give up," he said and jumped down from the tree. "There's no door. It must have closed."

We found Attie still at Garran's side. She stood up, blinking away a tear, and whispered, "He's beautiful, Am, even like this. I understand now."

"Thank you. Thank you for being here and helping me."

"Always and any time," she said through a sob.

My poor Garran, broken and bloody, sucked in a long breath. "Garran, we couldn't find the door," I cried, as I came down onto my knees next to him.

"I was afraid of that. The sensors. Anything, a bird, a leaf, could have triggered it to seal."

"How do we re-open it?"

"Shell scan. But even if I could get to the ship," he choked, "it couldn't read my fragments of shell."

"I'm not going to let you die."

"Let's take him to the hospital," suggested Attie. "Maybe they can do something for him."

"We can't," I said. "They'd shut the hospital down. Put Garran under quarantine. The military would come and take him to a research facility, and I can't let that happen to him."

"But we can study his culture, his race, his technology," blurted Kevin. "Learn from—"

"We? You mean them. They'd never share this with the public. You and your master's degree wouldn't benefit from any of it."

Garran gave a snort that released a small fragment of shell from his nose plate.

"She's right," said Attie, moving closer. "We have to try and help him here. Maybe we can wrap him in gauze to hold his shell in place until it heals."

"Shells don't heal, remember?" said Garran. "And there's something else, something I didn't realize until your sun hit the center of the sky. As gamma radiation is your enemy, gamma radiation is an Enestian's friend. My father warned me not to stay in this type of atmosphere for more than a day, and now I know why. Gamma rays give Enestians life. As my atmosphere was killing you, your atmosphere is killing me..." His eyes twitched closed, and his lips became limp and parted.

"No, don't die. Please don't die," I cried, wanting so badly to hold his crushed hand but knowing that doing so would only hurt him more. His shell continued to rise and fall. He was just unconscious.

"That piece of shell— It's digging into his throat," said Kevin.

Garran's chest rose with an erratic up and down, and I moved close enough to hear his shallow breathing whistle between broken shell pieces. A moment later, his breathing quickened, and I watched his shattered neck and chest plate and readied myself to grimace as his internal organs poked through.

"We've got to pull that piece of shell from his neck. It's affecting his breathing," said Kevin. "He's slowly suffocating."

"We can't. Garran told me there was nothing under their shells except their insides. He said their shells held them together."

"No, I see something else," said Kevin, leaning forward, and I joined him, squinting to get a glimpse between two separated plates.

"Oh my God. So do I."

Chapter Forty-Two

My eyes — I was too weak to open them, too weak to move. But a strange sensation rippled through my body, beginning at my neck. There was a tug. My shell. Something or someone was touching it. No, doing more. Lifting it away.

Stop! Don't!

The cool rush of wind. Or was it the flow of blood? A lightness I'd never felt before. Another yank at my broken shell released the warmth beneath it. My internal organs were exposed. And I imagined them now, spilling to the forest floor to mix with dirt and dry leaves.

Why are you doing this to me? Stop!

But why did it matter? With a shattered shell, I was already dead.

Another jerk on my body. Cold. So cold. Warm hands. Human hands upon my innards. But still so cold. Fingertips running under the edge of my shell. Prying. Wiping. Wiping what? Blood? Scooping the organs from my body?

Was this it? What it felt like to be dissected alive?

Little pain. My body numb.

Floating. Weightless. Drifting upon a cool breeze.

Was this a dream or was this what death felt like?

Chapter Forty-Three

I reached for a small fragment of shell half covered by his ripped tunic. But did I dare? The plate lifted easily in one section, and what was underneath was not what I expected.

"It looks like skin!" I announced. Attie jerked up onto her feet and backed away.

"That is skin," said Kevin.

"The mountain lion didn't do this," I said, pointing to an exposed patch of pale skin. "His shell did this. It cut into him when it broke. Most of his injuries are probably from his shell and not from the mountain lion."

Holding my hurt arm in place and using my other hand, I lifted the edge of an adjacent fragment of shell and ran my fingers underneath it. The inside surface was slick and kind of slimy, and I held up my fingers to examine the clear, odorless gel it left behind. "The shell must produce some kind of lubricant, something to buffer the shell against the skin."

"So the skin's not attached to the shell?" asked Attie, cringing as I slid my fingers back under another section of it.

"No, it isn't," I said as I pried a Frisbee-sized piece free.

"Are you sure you're not hurting him?"

Something told me I wasn't. Deep inside my body, something gave me a gentle push to continue removing his shell. An unexplained thought made me believe pulling his shell away was the right thing to do.

I peered down at Garran and remembered how I felt when he held me in his arms. I settled my head against his chest and knew why I had to do this.

"It can't make him any worse than he already is. His shell can't be repaired, and he can't move with it like this. The shell would dig and rip into his skin. And look at his knees," I added, pointing to his tattered leggings. "He can't walk with broken knee plates."

His fair, tender skin glistened in the sun, knowing its direct heat for the first time.

Attie took a few steps forward and dropped back onto her knees next to me. "So you want to…?"

"Yes, let's take off as many as we can."

"I agree," said Kevin, his fingers already wedged under a shard of shell.

Attie hesitated, eyeing the goo on my fingers, but after Kevin and I removed three additional shell plates that revealed soft, human-like skin, she picked up a small chip by its corner and lifted it away. Garran didn't stir, but his breathing remained steady while we continued our work, beginning with his neck and chest and moving to his arms as a neatly stacked pile of shell grew behind us.

His biceps and forearms were defined by thick muscle that flexed when we lowered his naked arms to his sides. The shell plates encasing the fingers gave easily, and the thick leather shell attached to it peeled away, unveiling manly hands and fingers topped by nails that grew just to the tip where its growth must have been stopped and stunted by shell.

There were a few fang marks from the mountain lion up and down his arms, but nothing debilitating or life-threatening, indicating he had only survived the mountain lion attack due to the protection of his outer casing. Most of the blood came from small nicks and cuts when jagged shell pieces pierced the skin beneath it.

"There's a lot of blood on his chest. Kevin, help me unhinge the plates," I urged, feeling a renewed sense of energy and determination.

To do the job, it took both of us giving a hard yank on the count of three, but just like his bare arms, his chest and abdomen were that of any athletic, extremely fit twenty-one-year-old guy. The body beneath the six-pack of shell matched its counterpart with bulging, lean muscle. Carrying all that shell around must have been like lifting weights.

Like the rest of his skin so far, his torso was marked with cuts, some deep enough for stitches, but the bleeding had stopped. Even a jagged tear that looked more like it was from a mountain lion's grip rather than a sharp-edged shell fragment had stopped bleeding and didn't need immediate attention.

Garran remained unconscious, but his breath was less shallow now that his throat was no longer squeezed tightly by crushed shell.

"There's one puncture mark at the back of his neck, but it doesn't look deep. It just bled a lot. I don't think there's any major damage," I said.

Garran's leggings were torn at both knees with rips that ended at the top of his boots. From the knees up, his leggings were intact, and with the lack of blood and smooth contours to his waist, it was obvious that the shell beneath there hadn't been damaged.

Attie pulled a plate free from Garran's calf and stacked it with the rest. Like me, she was beyond being grossed out by the thick, broken armor of an alien, its gel-like lubricant, and the sucking noise made when shell was pried away.

"There are only a few more pieces that are broken and detached from his thigh plates," Kevin announced.

We worked our way up to one of Garran's knees and then the other, and by the time we were done, Garran was free of shell with the exception of his feet, face, and his thighs up to his waist.

"That's all we can do," I stated and stood to evaluate our work, "except for his face." The plate at his jaw was askew, with one point of it poking deep into the exposed flesh of a cheek. "We need to remove that plate on his chin. It's hurting him," I said.

His face— That's what I was the most anxious to see. Would it mirror its hard exterior with a delicate nose and prominent jaw, or would it also be like that of a human?

At this point, the throbbing in my shoulder had worked its way down my arm and into my hand and fingers. But I didn't care, and the more I concentrated on helping Garran, the more the pain became a burning tingle that was easy to ignore.

I set my good hand upon the middle of his shell-free chest. His heartbeat was slow but strong. At his chin, I brushed away the loose piece of shell that cupped it. It landed on its end and rocked like the half shell of a chicken egg.

"Go ahead, Am. Keep going," said Attie.

Holding my breath, I twisted two larger pieces away, uncovering one cheek and then the other. Attie helped me pick away tiny fragments on the side of his face, and Kevin removed the biggest part of shell from the top of his head, lifting it away like a bicycle helmet. The head underneath was bald and glossy with gel. So far he was free from any hair, but everything else about him was like a human's.

Was the lack of hair due to the systematic rubbing of shell against skin when he spoke or smiled, or was its growth being inhibited by shell? Or maybe Enestian's were simply hairless?

"He still looks human," said Attie.

The last part of his face-covering rode over his nose, mouth, and each eye. I eased my fingers underneath the thick, leathery plates and rolled it upward until it lost its suction and popped away.

"Oh my gosh," Attie cried.

Except for the lack of eyelashes and eyebrows, everything about Garran's face was human with its defined nose, cheekbones, and lips of soft flesh.

Garran lay almost naked, striped of his shell and tunic, from the top of his neck to the waistband of his leggings. And it was there that we stopped to look at our progress.

"He looks like one of us," said Attie, wiping her sticky hands on the butt of her jeans.

"Yeah, he does," I agreed. He was the absolute perfect

specimen of a human guy.

"So is he a human?" asked Kevin, wiping the gel from his hands onto his pant legs.

"I don't think so. He can't be. All of the beings on his planet are encased in shell."

Garran's breathing was slower now and erratic. Each time he exhaled, I thought it was his last, and then he'd suddenly suck in a thin stream of air, and it would start all over again.

"Removing his shell hasn't helped. He's dying," said Kevin. "You heard what he said. He needs gamma radiation to live. There isn't enough on Earth, even without his shell blocking it."

"I-I know," I stuttered. "I failed."

My body became numb, and everything seemed to stop, the pain in my shoulder, even the beating of my own heart. I choked out a small cry, and as if my body contained no bone, I fell forward limply, barely catching myself with my hands.

"But you tried," said Attie.

"And it wasn't enough," I sobbed. Garran's next breath was labored, making his whole body shudder. "I'm not leaving him. I'm going to stay here with him until the end." I picked up Garran's hand. His skin was soft, baby soft, and warm. My tears came. There was no way to hold them.

"You did everything you could for him," said Attie as she blotted her wet cheeks with the back of her hand.

"He's dying for me. I get to live while he dies. It's not fair. He sacrificed everything for me, and now that sacrifice includes his life." I rubbed my palm along his forearm and then back to his hand where I gave it a squeeze. "I love you," I whispered into what was now a very human-like ear. "I will never forget you."

"I'm here for you, Am. I'll stay with you," said Attie.

"Me, too," said Kevin, "and then I'll help you, you know."

"Bury him," I said.

"Actually, I was going to say take you back to the hospital, and then deal with the authorities for you once we turn over the body. We can't bury him. We've been all over the news. If one of us goes into a hardware store and buys a shovel, it would look suspicious. The cops already don't believe your fake amnesia. We'd be questioned, and—"

"And we are not going to tell anyone else about this. We can't. He's going to rest in peace, not in pieces in a lab. You can sneak a shovel from the bait shop. They've got to have one. We'll bury him and hope he's never discovered."

Kevin's athlete eyes were full of fire, and his nostrils reddened with anger. "We'd never be able to get away with that. Besides, if we—"

Garran gasped, and with a deep inhale, his eyes fluttered open. Blinking against the sunlight, he took another deep breath and gripped my hand, lightly at first and then harder as the skin above his brow wrinkled.

"Garran!" I gasped, sucking in a deep breath that made my chest flutter.

"My shell. What happened?" he asked and lifted the hand that held mine. "I'm not dead, and it wasn't a dream." He clamped his soft lips together and gave them a lick with the tip of his tongue.

"You said your shell couldn't be repaired," I said gently. "And your shell was blocking the gamma rays you need to survive. You were dying, so we, we removed most of your shell."

He gasped again, sitting up and grabbing his abdomen like he needed to cradle his innards and hold himself together, then pulled his hands away to inspect his newly found casing of flesh.

"It's okay. See, you have skin underneath, and with part of your shell gone, you can move again. Your injuries are minor, just some cuts and scratches. Your shell saved you from the lion attack, and now being shell-less might save you from Earth's weak radiation."

"I, I…" He shook, drawing in a deep breath, and using all ten fingers, inspected his torso, pressing lightly at first and then deeper, watching his skin move under the pressure of his fingertips. When he reached his waist, he ran his hand down his hip to his thigh, closing his eyes as it slipped across the remaining pieces of legging and shell.

"Like I said, we didn't remove all of them. Only the pieces that were separated from the middle of your body, the pieces that would jab into your skin if you moved."

He bent both knees, drawing his legs toward his body, and reached down to slide his hands along his calves and to the tops of his boots where shell remained, leading down to his feet. And then, as if in a panic, his right hand shot up to his face to meet his cheeks.

"I feel human," he said and looked at me with knight's eyes that penetrated my soul, taking me back to the small, dark cell on Enestia, back to the first time I realized I cared so much for him.

"You look human."

"I do? How is that possible?" He shivered as his fingertips rode the curves of his own face, pressing and pushing against a now malleable nose.

"I have a mirror," said Attie, holding a compact of blush. "If you want to see yourself."

"Yes, let's look together," he said to me. He swallowed hard, touched his throat, and when his Adam's apple moved, he flinched.

"It's okay. It's supposed to do that."

Attie handed me the compact, and I opened it and held it out to Garran. His touch was too light and then too hard as he adjusted his hold, manipulating it with his new lighter fingers and their greater sensitivity.

The mirror captured both our faces. The gel covering his skin had dried and flaked away. There were a few smears of blood across his forehead and chin, and several nicks on his cheeks and neck like he had battled it out with a razor while shaving that morning, but the small flaws weren't a distraction from his loveliness.

He touched first his own soft, pink lips, his hands shaking, and then mine, his own cheekbones, and then mine. The contour of his jaw came next.

"You're beautiful, Garran," I whispered into his ear. "I hope you're okay with what we did."

"I am. I understand it had to be done." He looked down at his body. A small shell fragment I missed was stuck to his forearm, and he lifted it and flicked it away. "I can't leave this planet."

"No, but you'll be with me. I'll help you. I'll be there for you, and you can—"

A deep reverberation penetrated my body, making my skin tingle, and Attie shouted, "What's that?" as she jumped to her feet.

Kevin grabbed my shoulder. "We know that sound."

And we did. It was the hum we had heard before, the roar of a dual propulsion cruiser, a sound I now knew as well as the sputter of an Earthly gasoline engine.

"Is it your cruiser?" I asked Garran.

"No, it couldn't be. Not unless someone was inside, but that would be impossible."

"Whatever it is, we need to find out." After taking Garran by the arm and lifting him up with me, we stepped away from the discarded shell pieces. "Can you walk?"

"Yes, it feels strange, weightless and restricted at the same time, but I can do it."

The muscles in his arms twitched when I took his hand in mine, and what started as a fast walk became a slow jog as the humming grew louder. We came closer to the clearing and discovered the unexpected.

Garran's cruiser was not only visible, but it had landed on top of the ash and charcoaled branches from the campfire Kevin and Logan made on the night that I was abducted.

"How did it get over there?" I asked Garran.

"It didn't. That's not my cruiser," he said. "I thought you weren't able to send a signal?"

"I wasn't. I didn't. Then who could it be?" I asked as he limped forward, restrained by his remaining shell.

The door of the unexplained ship opened, and a shelled head and face appeared from around the doorframe.

"It's Lestra," whispered Garran. "She won't recognize me."

"But she'll recognize me, and she'll know your voice."

"Lestra," I said to her, taking several steps forward. She hesitated and then came to the top of a small, protruding ramp that led to the forest floor.

She said something in Enestian, a string of clicks and odd consonant sounds, "Garran" being the only word I understood.

"*Lis hjnil kmbrt*," said Garran.

Chapter Forty-Four

GARRAN

"I am him. I am Garran," I said.

Lestra sucked in a hard breath, put her hand over her chest, and lost her balance, catching the doorframe to steady herself before she fell.

"I am changed. My shell. Most of it has been removed. It was damaged, and with it I couldn't survive in Earth's atmosphere. Underneath our shells there is an inner casing — skin like that of a human. The truth has been kept from our people. Why? I do not know."

While I spoke, Lestra shook her head, her mouth agape, the panels of her chest expanding rapidly with each breath.

"No. You can't be Garran. We can't look like that under our shells."

"Yes, we do, and yes, it is me. Shell-less and covered in skin, except for what's left."

I lifted my shirt, exposing the length of shell sticking up from the waistband of my leggings. A small breeze caught the shreds of my tunic, and when my heritage band caught the light, it twinkled in colors of red and green. "See?" I said, holding the badge steady with my human-like hand.

When I let go, I noticed the tops of my fingertips were like America's, covered by thin, transparent shells the size of yarp nuts. How odd it all felt—the wind upon me, the saliva against my lips when I touched them with my tongue, the scouring of tunic fabric against my under covering.

"Why?" she cried, crumpling on the ramp, then drawing her knees into her chest.

"It had to be done. I was attacked by one of Earth's creatures. It destroyed my shell. I'd be dead if—"

"You left the ship? Why? You were supposed to leave, go to Verla Three, and I, I was going to…"

"Going to what?" I asked.

"I was going to meet you there, to help you, to be with you."

No wonder why she wasn't overly upset to see me leave. She planned to join me all along.

"But then your sister…"

I moved close and reached for her hand, but she jerked hers away. "No, don't touch me," she sobbed, with her feet pushed back from me. "I hate you," she screamed.

"What about my sister?"

"You ruined everything. Now you can never come back."

"No, I can't. And I can't leave this galaxy, ever, not without a shell to protect me from the radiation beyond this planet."

"I loved you," she whimpered into her hands.

And then I felt a strange sensation, something odd yet

familiar running against my face. I jerked my hand to my cheek, and when I drew my fingers away, they glistened with water droplets. I'd cried more in the last few days than I had in my one-and-twenty years of life.

"I'm sorry. I'm so sorry. I didn't mean for this to happen, but even if it hadn't and I went to Verla, you and me, it would have never...damn, Lestra. You shouldn't have done this. The ship is visible. What if someone sees it?"

Her crying became erratic. Clicks and wet whistles, the dominating sound as she pressed her forearm against her eyes.

"And now *you* can't go back, either. When my father finds out, he will..."

I sank down next to the ramp, and when I put my arms around Lestra, she didn't move but continued to cry against her knees. "But how did you even get here? You don't know how to fly. Unless... Did my sister have anything to do with this?"

Slaine emerged from the opened door, his stance wide, his arms crossed. "Yes, my royal. Princess Murelle ordered me to find you, force-tether your ship, and bring you back to Enestia.

She didn't want you to go to Verla Three. She wanted you to come home, and Lestra insisted on coming with me."

"And your sister was already in the process of coming up with a lie your father would believe, so you wouldn't be punished," added Lestra. "But now..."

But why would my sister try to protect me? It didn't make sense. She wanted me gone so she could take over my ambassadorship and eventually become queen. "Then you and Slaine, with my sister's protection, you're safe to return to Enestia without consequence."

"Yes." Lestra sniffled and lowered her head. "So now what?" she asked and recoiled when I adjusted my hug and my inner casing touched her bare shell. Her shell was powered, a light dusting of purple that reflected pink in the glow from the door light.

"Now I stay here. America will help me adapt, help me fit in."

"Help you be human," she said, and looked up at me.

I glanced over my shoulder, and after giving America a nod, she approached, and Lestra and I stood.

"We need to go, Lestra," said Slaine. "I took a reading just before we landed. These are the only humans in the immediate area, but that can change."

"And my cruiser?" I asked.

"We will take it with us."

"Thank you."

Slaine hesitated, but he took my hand when I offered it. His grip was a bit too firm, and I winced before he let go.

My last hug with Lestra was long, her fingers gliding along the side of my face, and peering at me through squinted eyes as she inspected my inner body. "You're bumpy and squishy," she said with a half-laugh that turned into a sob.

"I know, but I'll get used to it. I have to."

Lestra turned to America. "Please, take care of him. Protect him. Help him," she said, and as I translated their conversation, America took Lestra's hands in hers and promised Lestra she would.

"Thank you, Lestra. Thank you, Slaine," America told them. Her eyes became watery, and when they re-entered the cruiser, Lestra choking through a sob, America's eyes brimmed and spilled tears.

The door of the cruiser closed behind my Enestian friends. The cruiser rose, steadied itself above my ship, and after becoming invisible and engaging the electric tether, the ships lifted into the sky, stirring the forest debris below and bringing the scent of dry dust to our noses.

A light pressure continued to fill my nostrils and settle behind my eyes. Blinking produced more warm tears, and this time I couldn't help but smile from the strange sensation of water upon skin. No longer an Enestian, the life I'd known was gone, but unfortunately this left no one to stop my father.

"Are you okay?" America asked me as I looked up at the sky. She wiped away her tears and then blotted my tender cheeks with the back of her hand, while keeping her bandaged arm and shoulder tight against her waist.

"Yeah, I'll be okay, as long as I'm with you."

"And as long as I'm with you." She leaned toward me and set her lips against mine, giving me a sweet sensation of softness I never felt before.

"I'm going to have to get used to that," I said.

"Don't worry. You will." She smiled. But then her expression changed, and she dropped to her knees.

"America," I said, while pulling her to her feet.

"She has an infection, something resistant to antibiotics. She needs to go back to the hospital," said Attie.

"And I will, but not right now," said America. "Not yet. I'm okay. I just got a little lightheaded for a minute."

She lovingly brushed her fingertips down the side of my face. "Everything is going to be just fine."

Chapter Forty-Five

"So, I know what I'm looking forward to," I teased. I was still a little swoony, but most of my energy had returned.

"What?"

"Taking you back to my apartment and helping you get rid of those last few pieces of shell. I think I have a hammer that will do the job," I said, reaching around his waist and drawing him against me while protecting my injured arm.

"I bet you do." He smiled. "And then you're going back to the hospital. Promise?"

"Promise," I said, and gave him a spunky kiss. "I love you, Garran."

"I love you, too," he said and caught my bottom lip with his soft, plump one.

"Hey, you two," said Attie. "What are we going to do with all that shell? We can't just leave it there."

"I know what to do with it," said Garran.

And we watched Garran's shell, which we'd neatly stacked in the campfire, go up into flames and turn into a fine ash.

Kevin held up a coin-sized piece of shell he'd kept and said, "I'm saving this piece for my master's thesis."